ABOUT TH

Borrowing Burns, a semi-fictional or "factually dubious" account of the making of his series of Tam O' Shanter murals in Torphichen, West Lothian; and three cartoon compendiums. He has also published a weekly comic strip since 2012, sometimes within the pages of *The National*, Scotland's newest daily newspaper.

A fine art graduate of Duncan of Jordanstone College of Art, an exhibition of his paintings, *Poetic Licence*, was staged at the Scottish Poetry Library in 2022 featuring revised depictions of well-known Caledonian writers.

This is his second novel. His first, *Six Degrees of Stupidity*, was published in 2021 and he is currently working on a third, *Stupid Animals*.

Since he tried to sell a fleet of Trident nuclear submarines on Ebay in 2013, his readers and viewers have become familiar with his ways.

To Michel,
All the best!
Gary

Published by Greg Moodie
Copyright © Greg Moodie 2024

A catalogue record for this peach is available from the
National Library of Scotland and the British Library.

ISBN 978-1-9993627-5-1

Design, layout, cover and illustrations by Greg Moodie.
Author photograph by Arran Mcmillan.
Printed in Scotland by Bell & Bain Ltd.

www.gregmoodie.com

VOTE YES

THE UNBEARABLE STUPIDITY OF BEING

Greg Moodie

CONTENTS

TONY BOAKS

LAFLAMME

ALOYSIUS SPORE

THE ADMIRAL

SIR FRANK GODALMING

BRENDAN MATLOCK

ALLEN STANTHORPE

GEORGE LYTTLETON

JUNIOR

CHAS TARANTELLA

Editor's Note:

The following journal was found amongst Tony Boaks' possessions and is being published here with only minor corrections. Lots of them. His spelling was terrible.

Boaks was a graphic designer, although his design work was largely underused due to his mediocrity in the field and his unwillingness to work. He was also clearly technophobic, a distinct disadvantage for someone in his line of business, although I suspect this was more to do with his general disdain for modern life rather than a singling out of any one objectionable aspect of it.

The journal is being published for the sheer depth of its author's haplessness in the face of the world he was recording. I can hardly believe he was able to locate a journal, let alone write one.

(PS I have chapterised it in order to spare the reader any unwanted sense of whining interminability.)

1.
JUST THE FAX

This morning I received a fax from The Admiral. It was unusual because I don't have a fax machine. There was nothing unusual about its content, at least not coming from The Admiral; it looked like he'd been trying out pens to find one that worked. Anyway, I'd long since given up on any notions of surprise regarding his experiments with vintage hardware, as he's well known for being the Dr Moreau of gadgetry.

One time I suggested we try podcasting, thinking it might involve him soldering a few circuit boards together or writing a piece of software to allow us to record our respective roles from separate locations, thereby taxing his massive cranium for a while and ensuring his sedation.

The Admiral was enthusiastic about recording his mellifluous tones, but was appalled at the idea of faking our encounter in such a remote manner, suggesting it would be similar to 'a retrospective duet with Bing Crosby'. I wasn't sure which of us would be Bing in this situation, but thought I had better take up golf in case it was me.

As a consequence, much of the recording took place on the Brunts-field Links, and the baggy pants I wore throughout the session can be heard flapping around in the actual mix. So the challenge for The Admiral was not virtual recording, but adapting a 2-track reel to reel and sound desk for live field work and then keeping up with a baggy-panted man who has taken up golf in case he has to pretend to be Bing Crosby.

Sadly, by the time we were approaching the ninth hole, The Admiral succumbed to the combined weight of the adapted recording studio strapped to his back, and suffered a slipped disc. But all was well – by then the recording was complete.

I digress. After cursing the fact I'd woken so early (it wasn't yet noon), I made my way over to his office a couple of streets away, aware that the rogue communication might be a summons or at least a cry for attention.

It was a damp morning and I was pleased I'd managed to avoid so much of it. I hate seeing people going about their everyday business; driving, cycling, jogging, being productive. It always made me think about my life choices, which never included any of these. I raised the collar of my jacket and tried to pretend it wasn't really happening; that I was actually still in bed. The five-minute walk seemed an eternity.

The Admiral's office, in common with my own, was the kitchen of his already too small flat and was littered with the tools of our trade: discarded pieces of computer hardware, manuals, cuttings from magazines saved in the interests of providing much needed inspiration. Today there was a dismantled fax machine in the corner. Unlike my own office I could see no empty bottles, but I attributed this to The Admiral's fastidiousness. (I was all too aware of his fondness for industrial strength ale, as befits a man who wears a cardigan.)

I found him in typical pose, hunched over some miniscule device, poking and prodding, his milk bottle glasses thicker than ever. I made coffee and pulled up a chair at the ex-boardroom table. Only then could I see that this wasn't another piece of electronic circuitry. He was texting, and the miniscule device was in fact a phone, devoid of casing and with a screen that had clearly once belonged to a larger device. It was difficult to see how its keypad could be utilised by anyone outside Lilliput and this gave rise to my theory that either phones were shrinking or my hands were expanding.

I wondered how a form of typing could ever have become so popular. If texting were taught in schools, it would surely have become a minority pursuit, like algebra. The fact it's not taught in schools probably helps ensure its continued popularity. I feel sorry for anyone who has taken the trouble to learn to type properly, only to see the practice made obsolete by the sprightly motion of twin thumbs. It's bound to be the evolutionary legacy of our generation – lightning digits. It seemed a shame in The Admiral's case because he could type with all ten fingers and possibly write several documents at once.

"I'm not typing," he said. "I'm tweeting." Even though he was using an adapted phone rather than a keyboard, I still felt he was essentially typing, but he took issue with this, insisting he was neither typing nor texting.

"Tweeting?" I said. "Not typing?"

"Mm."

"Not texting?"

"That's right. It's when you describe in 140 characters or less what you are doing."

"I know what tweeting is."

"It's actually called X now, but nobody pays any attention to that. Let me give you an example." He began thumbing the device. "Going to meet my colleague, the eminent psychologist Lydia Pine-Coffin." He looked pleased with this.

"You're still typing."

"Well yes, but you're missing the point. It's really social networking. Microblogging."

"It's typing." I took the device and punched in the following letters: 'hav just stuffd my armdillo and now thinkng tacos for brekfst'. I showed him this marvellous piece of prose. "Typing."

"You're being childish now," he scolded. "Deliberately obtuse."

"Bum bum bum," I retaliated, deciding to stick with childish rather than have to look up obtuse. "You don't need 140 characters to describe what you're doing. Just write 'typing.'"

But it seems The Admiral is far from alone. Most people's list of pastimes would be headed with 'typing' if they dared admit it. Maybe it was like going to the bathroom – you might enjoy your rest breaks but you wouldn't necessarily class them as a hobby.

"Did you want me for something?" I asked.

(Note: Remember to tell The Admiral this very old Scottish joke:

'What's the difference between Bing Crosby and Walt Disney? Bing sings and Walt disnae.' He will hate that.)

———————————————

I felt a deep sense of dread when the doorbell rang, which was normal; my default response to doorbells. Today it was doubly normal as I knew who was outside ringing it.

Band managers don't usually show up in the same place twice due to the likelihood of them having done something embarrassing there the previous time. But Lyttleton was different. Not that he was guiltless when it came to being embarrassing; he just had no shame. He could show up anywhere and recently he'd taken to showing up at my flat, generally choosing to sit by the window. There wasn't a chair there but he would perch on the sill, and in his slightly too tight lime suit he looked like an overstuffed parrot.

A relic from a bygone era – the 1970s – Lyttleton was a man who had built a music industry career around doing nothing remotely musical. Short, stocky and wildly overconfident, he was never going to allow his lack of interest in music stop him from being a success in the industry. It wasn't that he actively disliked music; he just didn't understand it. Lyttleton actually considered himself the talent.

"Anybody can be in a band," he once told me. "The real skill is in management."

When he called earlier, I knew immediately it was him as I'd given him a special funeral march ringtone. He was calling to change the time of our meeting, so I asked how many hours of life I had left.

He said he wanted to push the boundaries of visual communication for a new album project and that we should 'think inside a box' for ideas. He'd spoken to other managers and they agreed this was the best method for achieving creative breakthroughs.

The trouble began when he arrived carrying the box in question. Even in its collapsed state it was enormous; too big to fit under his elfish arm, so he clutched it before him with both hands slightly above head height. When I answered the door, I faced a wall of cardboard and two sets of disembodied fingers. After the initial confusion, he shuffled in sideways, perspiring heavily and bursting out of his suit.

4

"I've never seen so much cardboard in one place before," I said. "Have you been feeding it?"

"New deep freezer," he replied, catching his breath. "Top of the line. It traps moisture and transfers it outside so you get a lot less frost." I thought frost would be a good thing in a freezer but Lyttleton thought otherwise.

"Forty pounds of seafood in the old one and I couldn't get near it for frost. Needed an icepick. It was like an Arctic expedition every time I wanted to eat."

"Couldn't you just defrost it?"

"I did," he replied. "Do you want some fish?"

Lyttleton shuffled uneasily by his window perch and loosened his collar. I imagined he would welcome frost at this particular juncture.

"The point is," he said, "I've got a new one now and it arrived in a big box."

He rose and began assembling the box in such a manner that he would be inside it when it was complete. There was a certain Lyttleton logic to this as it would spare him the indignity of having to raise his little legs over the steep sides to get in.

Fully assembled and bound up with parcel tape, the box gave the kitchen table a run for its money in the cumbersome stakes and left very little standing room outside of it. Lyttleton sat within, his eyes just visible over the side wall. He implored me to join him but I was reluctant. It may have been a colossus amongst cardboard boxes but with two grown men inside, I thought I might find it small enough.

After much pleading I agreed, knowing that the client, though moronic, would nevertheless be funding my next night out.

We sat at opposite ends of our corrugated thinktank and I surveyed the surroundings. Lyttleton's corner was already damp but luckily the cardboard had a distinctive smell that was strong enough to distract from the less agreeable smell of festering lime-suited band manager.

"Where do you want to start?" said Lyttleton finally.

I sat back against my cardboard gable end and sighed. If either of us died at this point, the other would have some serious explaining to do. What if this were my final resting place? What if my legs gave out and from hereon in, food had to be served to me in my box? The district nurse would bring me scampi and chips and say, 'How ironic'. I would curse creatively and throw pieces of the breaded seafood back at her for attention. It didn't bear thinking about. I resigned to playing Lyttleton's game instead.

"Who's the singer?" I asked.

"It's not important."

"Just out of interest."

"A songwriter by the name of Campbell."

"Glen by any chance?"

"That's right," he said. "Campbell Glen." I made a mental note never to make jokes with Lyttleton as he had no recognisable sense of humour.

"Do we have a name for the album?" I asked.

"Not yet," he replied. "Any suggestions?"

"How about *Zanussi*?" I said.

"I think," said Lyttleton, "the follow-up to his debut album has to be an even bolder visual statement, as the material is much stronger."

"You've heard it?"

"No."

If Lyttleton was saying the material was stronger it was because someone else had told him, as Lyttleton had no ear for music. Whilst a deep freezer salesman might be expected to know something about deep freezers, it was generally accepted that the same did not apply to band managers. Lyttleton knew more about freezers than he did about music.

"How about *Campbell Glen Buys A Fridge*?" I said.

This was ignored and after thirty minutes of thinking inside a box, I realised I had suggested only fridge-related titles and white goods visual motifs for the album, and when I pushed myself to change tack, all I could think of was seafood. However, this led me to suggest *Mock Lobster*, which was met with approval. Lyttleton was delighted his brainstorming experiment was working and decided to put the title to Campbell Glen.

"I knew this was a good idea," he said from his now distinctly soggy end of the box. "And I didn't even have to use this." He produced a harmonica from his inside pocket and began playing it in a childlike fashion, albeit with a convincingly insistent blues rhythm.

"What's that for?" I said, but he couldn't hear me above the noise, compressed as it was in a deep freezer-sized space. I stared at the wheezing little man opposite. It only took me a minute to link the harmonica to 'blues guy thinking'.

2.
THE CIRCLE OF LIFE

I hate starting a new project. I'll do anything to avoid it. If there's a box of wires that need untangling, I'll do that first. I reckon with all the time I've spent procrastinating, I could easily have taught myself violin to a level worthy of Menuhin.

The problem is blank canvas syndrome. You might have heard of it. It's a widely recognised psychological condition, at least widely recognised in my house where I first discovered, diagnosed and named it. Blank canvas syndrome is a debilitating aversion to the void that stretches out before creative types on a new task, even if, in my case, 'creative' might be pushing it. Until the void is filled with something – anything – you'd be better off doing one of The Admiral's 10,000-piece Dungeons & Dragons jigsaws and asking a trained chimpanzee to have a crack.

The name comes from my spell at art college. Because the colour white is daunting, a tutor suggested we prime canvases with a midtone grey. I usually went with bright red just to be extra sure, but it still didn't help.

The Admiral says blank canvas syndrome is a myth and that it's simply laziness. In fact he calls me 'lethargo' as he tells me this. But the truth is I'm an industrious individual who is beset by a debilitating condition that inspires idleness.

I went to fire up the computer, now so old that it virtually involves rubbing sticks together, but reaching for the power switch I found both it and the box it would normally activate absent. In their place was this cryptic, handwritten note:

"I have taken the beast. LF."

Unwilling to draw and lacking a computer, my life as a graphic designer just got a whole lot harder. I was torn between bursting into action and continuing to stare at the void, but I had no idea what form the action might take, and anyway I'm more naturally inclined towards staring. I probably could have remained in this state until somebody poked my atrophied carcass with a stick, but the kitchen door swung open and a distraction and a half walked in (she was never one for knocking).

Raven-haired but otherwise scarlet, LaFlamme had led me astray on many an occasion and I feared, and secretly hoped, today would be no different.

"I wanted to brush up on my typing," said five foot six of badness.

"So you stole my computer?"

"Borrowed," she said.

"Pawned?" I asked.

"No, no. It's in the 'Part Exchange' shop," she replied.

"Pawned," I said. LaFlamme shrugged her shoulders and I had to agree that the entirety of my design back catalogue decaying in some seedy pawn shop was probably no great loss, and actually quite apt. But it did leave a hole in my life as regards making money.

She leaned against the bookcase, casually running a painted fingernail along a shelf and ignoring the dust. "What were you working on?"

"Something brilliant," I said.

"It'll still be brilliant when we get it back," she said.

"What if somebody buys it?" I asked.

"They're buying your brilliance," she replied. "You should be proud." She sat on the desk, spotting the note she had left with the signature 'LF'. She added an extra 'F' then several more. When she reached the edge of the paper, she continued on the desk.

"They might not think it's so brilliant," I said.

"They might write and tell you where you went wrong," she replied.

9

"Maybe they could tell me where my life went wrong," I said, making a feeble attempt to hide the embarrassingly large collection of self-help titles on my bookshelf. *Don't Sweat The Small Stuff. Don't Worry, Be Happy. Don't Be Such A Twat.* There must have been thirty of them. How can someone with so much self-help be so hopeless? Unfortunately, this ruse had the effect of drawing her attention to them, so I quickly abandoned it.

"Misery guts," she said. "What particular strand of gloom are you focusing on today?"

I told her about blank canvas syndrome, my sense of foreboding and my concern that I was doomed to work with nutjobs and psychos and be part of their delusional schemes for the rest of my life.

"You need inspiration," she said, in a tone that almost sounded caring, which was most unlike her. "A sense of purpose. A sense of connection with the past." I wasn't sure where this was going, but I don't normally question LaFlamme as it usually ends in my being stranded down some rabbit hole with nothing but dead ends and no sign of the way back.

"I know just the solution," she said. "Follow me."

We adjourned to an unfamiliar bar with a gaudy purple and jaundice interior and downbeat clientele. A harsh light filtered through the window as if to remind drinkers that they shouldn't be there so early in the day.

"Listen, Boaks," she said over her bourbon and coke (plenty of ice). "We're all going to die soon. You, me, the inbreds in the corner. There's no fun to be had when you're dead. It's all paperwork."

"Paperwork?"

"You know. You're stuck sorting out everybody else's life, like in the movies. You have to have as much fun as you can before you cark it, because everything beyond is just civil service. You think it's tough having to work with delusionals? Big deal. Imagine if you were stuck in an office with the straights day after day." She had a point. Once I had to wear a suit to an interview. It felt like wearing a coffin.

LaFlamme still had the pen she used for her memo and set about defacing a beermat.

"See, most people look at life like it's a straight line." She drew a line from corner to corner. "You're born here, you die here. Okay, these two points I can understand," she said, adding crosses to the beginning and end of the line. "But what happens on this bit in the middle? I'll tell you what – nothing."

She took another beermat. "Then there's those who think about it like an arc." She drew a semicircle like an upside-down smile. "They think life's one huge struggle up to this midpoint when they're happy just for a minute. Then it's all downhill."

She defaced several more beermats in this way with increasingly abstract shapes and equally abstract explanations. When she got to the double tetrahedron I was starting to lose the thread.

"I guess my life's more like a circle then," I said. "Going endlessly round and round, repeating myself and getting nowhere."

"I was coming to that," said LaFlamme. By now she had run out of beermats, so she took the back of my hand and drew a perfect circle on it. "You see, that's exactly where you're going wrong. You have to break that circle and shake the loser in you free." She drew another circle on my other hand then another on the end of my nose. "It's as plain as the nose on your face," she said.

LaFlamme continued her pep talk, drawing a broken circle with a door shape leading outwards on the inside of my left hand. "There's your escape route," she explained.

Running low on flesh real estate and clearly in need of an expansive stretch for her next illustration, she rolled up my sleeve and began drawing a spiral on my outer forearm. It began tightly and opened out to a loose wandering line. "This is how you should look at life."

"Ever decreasing circles?"

"Increasing, Boaks, increasing. Life's a big adventure and every turn leads to new territory, new horizons and in your case moles.

"Think about it like jazz," she continued, "without the beards and the terrible racket, obviously. It doesn't matter what shape your life starts out, you have to improvise, mix it up a bit. You're a designer, right? You take shapes and work them into something pretty. That's just like life. It doesn't have to mean anything. Nothing does. Life is meaningless."

"That was quite a leap," I said. "We started with a straight line and ended with the meaning of life." It wasn't really a serious point, but then

I wasn't likely to be taken seriously anyway because I had a ballpoint circle on the end of my nose.

LaFlamme pointed to the upturned bottle of bourbon amongst the optics behind the bar and drew my attention to the label, a classic black and white collage of shapes, mostly comprising diverse fonts in various sizes.

"Here's a case in point. There's a hundred different typefaces on that label, thousands of intricate shapes twisting and turning, playing together, making a little world for themselves. Like jazz."

"What if you don't like jazz?"

"Who does? That's not the point. Life isn't a rigid affair, it's a big sprawling Mardi Gras. There are no rules."

I was beginning to understand. And I agreed with her about the label. It's hard to make so many typefaces look so good in one design. It broke every rule going. In fact, the more I looked at it the more I felt my spirits soar. Maybe this was the inspiration I needed.

"Feeling better?" she asked.

"Yes, oddly."

"Good. Medicine time." LaFlamme knocked back her drink. "Oh, I nearly forgot."

She reached into an inside pocket of her jacket and from a leopard skin purse produced a dog-eared A4 page that had been folded down to the size of a credit card. "I have an appointment." LaFlamme travelled light at all times. This was probably her diary.

"You have to go?" I asked.

"Dentist."

"Dentist? Now?"

"Mm. Irish girl. Tiny little fingers."

"Tiny fingers, what more could you want in a dentist?"

She rose from the table. "My work here is done. Meet me in the bar on the corner in an hour."

"The karaoke bar?"

"Yes. Ta-ta."

LaFlamme came and went like this all the time. I wished I was higher on her list of priorities but at least it was a dentist she was seeing and not a real person. For example, a real person like Justin Streatham, who always seemed to be somewhere in the background. I'd tried to push him further into the background – a few hundred miles would have done – but to no avail. If I could only find the romantic equivalent of a shovel, I'd bury him under the weight of my vastly more numerous positive attributes.

Their relationship was unfathomable. Streatham was a good ten years older than both of us and seemed to have little in common with LaFlamme. She didn't even seem that interested in him (all men are expendable to LaFlamme). I guess they had some kind of history, and I was never very good at history.

He would show up at the most inopportune moments, like late at night when I was inches from winning LaFlamme over and having her in my arms. Every time he appeared, my heart sank. He was like a reminder of an appointment with an insurance adviser.

Was I jealous? Of course. But there was something galling about his presence that made my jealousy forgivable. We didn't care for each other and he seemed to delight in tormenting me about my obvious desire for the woman I felt he didn't deserve.

"Looking after my girl?" he asked me one night, a question I found objectionable on many levels. A) It was proprietorial; the idea being that I was somehow keeping her warm while he was absent. B) LaFlamme didn't need anybody to look after her and anyone who tried was likely to end up exhausted or sore. C) Nobody besides her father should be calling her 'my girl'. D) I just didn't like him. I wished he'd give up his position on the margin of her page rather than continually show up like a nasty ink blot to irk me.

"How's that web design thing going?" he said once.

"Graphic design," I said. "Excellent. It's really the ideal job. Love it."

"Well, I suppose somebody has to work," he replied. Streatham didn't – family money, I guess. He couldn't have been wealthy through his own efforts because he never seemed to do anything. It was doubly infuriating because on paper it looked like such a cliché – younger woman falls for wealthy older man. But LaFlamme had little interest in money; she certainly wasn't impressed by it. If she was, she wouldn't be hanging out with somebody like me.

"You look tired," he said. "You must be working too hard."

"No," I replied. "At my age you don't tire so easily. You probably don't remember."

Was I attracted to LaFlamme because she was unavailable? Maybe. Human beings are a deeply flawed species and all the flaws are generally exaggerated in me. Here, take this straightforward, available girl who likes you, has a good job and wants to settle down? No thanks, I'll hold out for the difficult one I can't have, who lives hand to mouth and doesn't care whether I live or die. To be honest I don't suppose availability matters because LaFlamme projects unavailability whether attached or not.

Weeks would go by without a sign of Streatham. Every time LaFlamme called and we arranged to meet, I'd think she was going to announce that finally she'd broken up with him. But it never materialised. Despite my repeated efforts to woo her, this was still a painfully platonic relationship.

From time to time, I'd try to force the issue in as subtle a manner as possible.

"He is such a dick," I said, in one such approach. "What do you see in him?"

"He's convenient," said LaFlamme.

"What kind of convenient?" I asked. "I could be convenient. Where could I learn to be convenient? What do I have to do to be convenient?"

"Stick around," she said. I didn't know what it meant but I wasn't going anywhere anyway.

The karaoke bar was half empty when I joined LaFlamme ('half full', she said), and the patrons appeared to be predominantly pierced and tattooed types who might have looked more at home in a heavy metal club. It remained relatively quiet throughout the night, which was a blessing given the events that were to unfold.

LaFlamme browsed the song catalogue and returned selections to the DJ before launching into her next exposition. I would have been quite happy to continue the discussion we left off, but she had moved on, and once LaFlamme moves on there's no returning.

"You know how everybody works five days a week and then they take two days off?" she began. "Whose idea was that?"

"I really can't imagine."

"Well, think about it. Wherever you go in the world, this is what the straights do. Year in, year out, five days on, two days off."

"Two weeks in the summer."

"Who thought that was a good idea?"

"Surely must have been a collective decision."

"You think a bunch of stiffs had the imagination to sit down together and work this into a plan?"

"That's what the stiffs are good at," I chirped. "Making up stupid rules that the rest of us have to follow."

"But why didn't they say, 'Okay, we'll work every day from ten till one, then we'll have the rest of the day off'? Forget about weekends."

"Maybe they liked bowling on Saturdays," I said. "How should I know?"

"I suppose without a Saturday, Friday nights wouldn't be the same," mused LaFlamme. "But they can't have invented the system just because they liked Friday nights."

"I like Friday nights," I said. "I think they were on to something."

"Then why didn't they work for five months and party for two? That would have made it worthwhile."

"Maybe they didn't like a seven-month year. Anyway." I paused for effect. "I'm sure the church had something to do with it."

"Hmm. But why are they still doing it, now that they've proved there's no god?"

"I don't remember them actually proving there's no god," I said.

"I can prove there's no god," she countered. "You know that guy on TV? Buzz cut? No discernible talent?"

"Simon Cowell?"

"He's famous. There's no god."

Her reasoning was flawless. Maybe this wasn't such a change of subject after all. Maybe the real reason people stick to a system of five and two is that in a godless universe they can still rely on the structure of their stupid working week to see them through difficult times. Take that away and the whole fabric of society might collapse.

"The whole system is lopsided," LaFlamme continued.

"How so?"

"Well, I wouldn't mind working two days a week if I had five days off." Mid-sentence, LaFlamme had overheard the DJ announcing her song and stood up to head towards the stage. I myself didn't hear this, which reminded me that although she always had one hundred per cent of my attention, I could never be sure of hers. Nobody could. LaFlamme's attention didn't belong to anyone or anything.

I heard the familiar opening bars of 'These Boots Are Made For Walking', and as LaFlamme stepped on to the stage and took hold of the microphone there was a notable change in the atmosphere, as if the entire bar woke up.

She cut a striking figure up there, her milk-white skin offset by the jet-black ensemble of tangled hair, wraparound shades, PVC jacket, skintight skirt and Doctor Marten boots. She was confidence personified and with good reason, relaying the song as if it was her life and not once referring to the lyrics on the monitor.

The karaoke bar erupted when she sang *one of these days these boots are gonna walk all over you*, and I can't deny that at that point my body had no idea what this peculiar cocktail of exhilaration and fear was all about.

She left the stage to rapturous applause. There was no doubt about it. For everyone in that bar, the night had just begun.

"More drink," she said on her return, and it wasn't put in the form of a question.

An hour may have passed before LaFlamme spotted the DJ again and said, "Okay kid, I think you're up."

"I'm up?"

"It's your song."

"Me? I can't sing."

"Since when did that matter? It's karaoke."

"What song?"

"'All My Life's A Circle.'"

"What?" I said. "If you wanted a circle theme, couldn't you at least have chosen something cool like 'Ring Of Fire'?" This crowd might not appreciate a drippy song from the early '70s, and hearing it sung by a man with ballpoint on the end of his nose and up and down his arms might tip them over the edge.

The DJ was pointing directly to me as I sat frozen in my seat.

16

"Yes you, the lucky gentleman with the French chanteuse. Come on up, Charles Aznavour!"

The audience howled. There was no way I was getting out of this. "What are you waiting for?" said LaFlamme coolly. I made my way up to the stage as the introduction to the soft country ballad began, figuring I wouldn't be able to see anything much for the strong stage lights. Sadly I could see every face, and as I began singing I could see the expressions change from enthusiastic welcome to open-mouthed awe.

I croaked my way sheepishly through the first verse. It was the only time I've ever seen a karaoke crowd genuinely confused. By the time I reached the second verse some were singing along. It may have been a horribly wet, cheesy song being mauled by an idiot covered in biro, but at that time of night karaoke bars can get sentimental. And what really feeds sentimentality is a nice tune. Couples sat arm in arm, gently swaying along to the rhythm and by the final chorus most of the bar was singing. One misguided soul wiped away a tear.

"*The seasons coming round again, the world keeps rolling by.*"

I had reached the final line and not only had they decided I could live, some wanted more. I wisely decided to quit while I was ahead and left the stage to a respectable ovation.

"Nice ink," said a Harley fan with extensive artwork of his own.

There was more to the night. There must have been. At one point I remember taking a call from George Lyttleton, but I managed to blot that out.

By closing time, LaFlamme had a table of bikers convinced she was the reincarnation of Marie Antoinette, the inventor of bicycle clips and a Michelin-starred pastry chef from Boulogne. I'd had roughly the same amount to drink and could barely remember my name.

3.
SELF-HELP FOR IDIOTS

I awoke in unfamiliar surroundings. It wasn't the first time, and experience had taught me not to try moving. This wasn't so much a hangover as a bourbon-induced breakdown.

I was aware of a thunderous clattering on the other side of the room and figured it was a stampede that might trample me to death and put me out of my misery. Hopefully. Instead it was LaFlamme thumping away at a typewriter – not the polite tip-tappying of a computer keyboard, but the brute force hammering of a ribbon-wound Underwood. A stack of pages lay testament to her all-night effort.

"Room service," I croaked.

"Help yourself," she replied, and continued typing at a frantic pace. "Writing."

"Writing? Writing what?"

"Self-help."

I rose from the sofa, hastily pulled on my jeans and stumbled across to the desk, LaFlamme stopping just long enough to show me a title page. Her unique take on the self-help genre was to be called *Help Yourself to Drink*.

A tidal wave of nausea threatened to sweep me up and carry me out to sea, and frankly at this point I'd have welcomed my watery fate. Had

Streatham been present, my dry boak might have turned to something more substantial, and if it was substantially over him that would at least have made it all worthwhile.

"I think I need to be somewhere," I said, careering unsteadily towards the front door.

LaFlamme turned and paused briefly.

"Somewhere in time? Somewhere only we know? Somewhere over the rainbow?"

"Somewhere that doesn't have typewriters."

"Big baby," she said. The hammering resumed.

Despite the pain, time spent with LaFlamme usually has a way of raising my spirits, and last night's pep talk certainly inspired me to try pushing beyond the crippling mental torment of blank canvas syndrome.

Sadly, when I tried to recall any specifics of the conversation, my mind clouded over. (Admittedly my mind exists in a state of perma-fog, the arrival of clouds just meaning a slight deterioration in visibility. What I really need is one of those machines Kate Bush invented.) I hoped something might click into place on the way home.

Outside, the low winter sun was harsh. It was difficult not to take its blinding brilliance as a personal attack, as if it knew I was suffering and wanted to rub it in. But I persevered and noticed how my thoughts turned from self-pity to self-loathing, which I considered progress; now I wasn't so much regretting my plight as despising it.

The cold winter air was making me panicky. I know, warm summer air makes me panicky too. And the air in between. Look, I have issues, okay?

Panic is not a new thing in my life. To be honest, it's so familiar I'd feel weird without it. One time I went to see a clinical psychologist in the hope of becoming somebody who isn't a total mess.

"What do you have to panic about?" he said. I resented the question. As if I didn't deserve anxiety unless I was being chased by a mammoth. What is there not to panic about?

"Well," I replied, "what if I go to the supermarket, I'm looking at yogurts, I can't decide which to buy. I start sweating, that makes me breathe heavily, that makes my heart race. I sit down on the supermarket floor. What if it's a heart attack? Nobody wants to die in Tesco. Lidl, maybe. Aldi at a push.

"Then what if it's not a heart attack? What if it's sudden, inexplicable incontinence? What if I lose control of my bladder and relieve myself there in the dairy aisle?

"What if it's Tourettes? What if I develop a whole range of tics and involuntarily call a random shopper a felchbag? What if it's all three? I'm sitting staring at cheeses, having a cardiac arrest, soiling myself and abusing shoppers with random obscenities and dog impressions?"

"That's an awful lot of what if," he replied.

"Then there's the indisputable fact that the world is teetering on the brink of collapse through any one of a number of possible scenarios. Putin, Netanyahu, Trump, Simon Cowell. You must admit, none of it's good."

"I agree Cowell is out of control. But if the world is going to collapse, then there's nothing very much Tony Boaks can do about it. You might as well relax."

Needless to say, I'm still a total mess.

Some people have to go skydiving or bungee jumping to get the adrenalin they need to awaken their sluggish systems. Only by engaging in something potentially life-threatening can they experience the fear I get just going to the shops. I guess if your stupid parachute doesn't open, you'll feel the ultimate thrill of knowing you're about to die in ten seconds, and then your happiness will be complete. *You're* the one who needs therapy.

The galling thing is that after years of being told I'm unimaginative, I found out you need a fertile imagination to have panic attacks. Really? I have enough imagination to be afraid but not enough to be creative? Well, make up your mind, quacks.

At least I discovered blank canvas syndrome – I have enough imagination to know being me sucks.

I unlocked the stair door and climbed to the third floor. As I was approaching the landing, I became aware of another presence, a chilly one, and sure enough, standing outside my front door was a gangly gentleman of around six foot five, immaculately dressed in black, including cape, vaguely reptilian, and distinctly albino. He looked like a pint of Guinness.

He said he was interested in engaging my services and introduced himself as Aloysius Spore. I wondered if he might be an undertaker or mortician. It turned out he was a venture capitalist, which was far worse.

I invited him in and he slithered down the hall into the sitting room, his presence immediately cooling the air. He reminded me of somebody. I think it was Uriah Heep.

Placing a silk-covered package on the coffee table, he proceeded to unfold it with great delicacy, revealing an ancient leather-bound book.

"Harry Potter first edition?" I asked.

"It's not so much the book that concerns us – *Religious Symbology*, in this case – as a certain insignia contained within its pages."

He opened the volume at a bookmarked page and withdrew a single loose leaf, which was adorned with a monogram of quite stunning awfulness. It was the worst logo I've ever seen.

"Oh, my," I said, unsure where to begin.

I've seen design atrocities over the years and have, in fact, been responsible for many. But this was something else. I handled the page and studied its contents – a simple crest with the word 'AS' laid out in a relative of Gill Sans. I wished it had been a more distant relative.

Below the letters was a series of decorative vertical and horizontal lines. I use the word 'decorative' loosely as the combination made me feel nauseous, something you wouldn't normally associate with decoration.

"As what?" I asked.

"As I said, I require the services of one well-versed in symbols and their interpretation."

"I don't see why you'd want to change it," I said. "It's perfect as it is." His brow furrowed and I felt a certain frostiness in its wake.

"As a fellow historian," he said, "I imagine you're aware of its significance, and indeed the fact that it's been attracting rather a lot of unwanted attention." I hadn't noticed. And just because I work in graphics doesn't mean I know anything about symbols.

What I had noticed was that Spore was tailored to perfection, which suggested he may be filthy rich. I am conspicuously not, and that requires a certain tolerance when it comes to clients. I depend on such characters to keep me afloat, even if they are shady, so I had little choice other than to entertain his nonsense.

"What did you have in mind?" I asked. Spore advanced slightly and I recoiled in equal measure.

"An exercise in rebranding is what's required," he replied. "Can you make it less prominent, less recognisable? Lower the tone of it?"

I said I'd always been good at lowering the tone in any situation, but I wondered why anyone would want their branding to attract less attention. It would fly in the face of every design and marketing principle I'd ever learned, had I ever learned any.

"Well, Mr Spore," I began.

"Call me Aloysius."

"Do I have to?"

"How about Al? It was my mother's name."

"How do you propose we go about it?" He thought for a moment.

"We could rearrange the letters."

"There isn't an awful lot of scope for that here."

"How about changing them altogether?" he said, a tone of desperation creeping into his voice. "Instead of 'AS', perhaps it could be 'BS', or 'CS'. If it was 'PS' we could be relegated to a footnote."

"Wouldn't that confuse the target demographic?"

"Exactly."

"That would be one approach," I said. "A crazy person's approach. Isn't it just your initials?"

"Coincidentally, yes. But I could change my name. To Pignacious Spore, for example. Friends could call me Piggy."

"You'd be prepared to have your friends call you Piggy?"

"The 'P' could be silent."

"Iggy Spore. Why not just 'IS' then?"

"I don't think I'm prepared to go quite that far."

I sighed. It didn't make any sense. Brand recognition is crucial in business. Consumers navigate towards logos they recognise and trust. Here was a guy who wanted to destroy that recognition and was willing to change his name in the process. What was he trying to hide?

Spore walked the line between odious and certifiable and it was difficult to predict which way he might fall. In the odious camp he'd simply join most of my other lowlife clients, but in the certifiable he'd be amongst a more rarefied group of three or four.

"I really don't know much about symbology," I said, in a last attempt to dissuade him. "Religious or otherwise."

"I think you know more than you care to admit," he replied, unfolding his arachnoid limbs and reconvening by the window.

"Let's just say that I need an individual with certain specialist skills and I'm willing to make it worth their while." He fixed me with steely blue eyes.

"Please, Mr Boaks. Work your magic."

I reluctantly accepted the challenge to modify his branding, despite having no understanding of his motive, and proposed a wildly inflated budget in order to compensate for the intense chill I felt standing next to him. Clearly my heating bills were set to escalate.

The Admiral's explanation of Twitter (I refuse to call it X) had been typically opaque, to the extent that I asked him for a diagram. It didn't help. Later, fighting my force ten apathy towards social media, I began to explore for myself, thinking there had to be a reason for its popularity.

I arrived at the conclusion that the world was in the grip of some typing-induced delirium, because after an hour amongst the random keyboard spawn, I was unable to find any actual writing. Where was the attraction in following the nonsensical ramblings of total strangers? I could barely follow my own.

But just when I was about to give up on the site altogether, I stumbled upon a correspondent by the familiar name '@Spore', who was about to change my opinion.

I browsed through the postings on his profile. Momentarily there was an update.

'Found suitable lackey to assist with the project. All satisfactory. Meeting Stephen Fry later.'

At this stage there was nothing to suggest I was the lackey in question, although 'Lackey' is my middle name. The message was followed shortly by another.

'Discussing fiscal arrangements. Spoke to Fry and have decided he's a knob.'

This confirmed what I've always thought about Twitter – it's like walking into a roomful of strangers in mid-conversation; most of them talking to themselves, some talking to others, some talking to others in some other room. And every room has Stephen Fry in it.

'Taking the necessary steps towards setting up the lackey. Fry has taken the huff because I unfollowed him. Knob and a half.'

Setting up the lackey? That could mean one of two things; either setting him up in business or framing him.

The information overload was overwhelming. I felt a panic attack of seismic proportions take hold and had the urge to start removing clothes. (I only resisted because Spore's profile and Fry's omnipresence made it seem innapropriate.)

I calmed myself with thoughts of giving up computers and living in an electricity-free state. Soon I was breathing normally. Until this:

'Fait Accompli.'

The panic became full scale alarm. Whatever this loon-supreme was up to, I sure as hell didn't want it accompli-ed, with or without Stephen Fry.

I stepped out into the night, knowing that cold air can be a highly effective antidote to the sort of manic hysteria I'm prone to. Unless it makes it worse.

I needed something – reassurance or inspiration, something that might ground me in the balanced world. I remembered a modest break in the gloom yesterday when I studied the bourbon label design, possibly enhanced by the effects of its contents. It wasn't exactly a revelation (the only revelation last night was that LaFlamme could drink with both hands), but a low watt bulb clicked on in my head and for a moment there was a clarity unlike anything I've ever experienced. Unfortunately, it clicked off again shortly after.

Stumbling into an off-licence, I scanned the well-stacked shelves that showcased an extensive selection of wines and spirits, and navigated towards the more vigorous proofs. There amongst the bourbons was the distinctive white on black design with its conglomerate of typefaces.

Having located the object for study, which faced me at eye level, I then became aware of a slight flaw in my plan. Due to the previous evening's drain on my finances, I would be limited to study only, which I did from a distance of around three inches. This was inevitably met with consternation from the shopkeeper and I don't imagine it helped that I was probably still sweating out the spirit I was inspecting so intently. His composure hardened and I felt a wave of disapproval cross the room.

"I wonder if... if... I could borrow this," I finally blurted out. It proved to be a moment of synchronicity as we both decided simultaneously that I should leave.

I was no further forward. But I was no further back either. It's amazing what can pass for progress in my world.

4.
NO CLAMS BONUS

If Lyttleton had any real skill, it was in projecting the idea that his time was invaluable. Anyone granted an audience with this little weirdo and his epic delusions was supposed to feel humbled because he once got lucky back in the day by signing a girl group who went on to have a massive hit. It was definitely luck because he wouldn't know the difference between a girl group and the girl guides.

Now he was out on his own and, despite being a small-time operator, insisted on discussing his agency in the most bombastic manner, announcing the addition of certain 'associate directors', who were other no-talent suits he had picked up along the way.

"I'm about to go public with the formation of a new arm of the business," he began. "It's an executive production company called 'Overhead Communications.'"

"Why 'Overhead'?" I asked.

"It's an umbrella group," he replied. I groaned. "A holding company for the other divisions."

"How many divisions do you have there?" I asked, immediately regretting this question too as he rattled off a list of probably fictitious company names, making frequent use of words like 'limited', 'incorporated' and 'consolidated'.

"But on to today's agenda," he said. "I've brought photographs."

He opened a cardboard-backed envelope which contained a selection of pictures of himself in various holiday locations.

"Wouldn't it have been better to bring photographs of the singer?" I asked.

"Well, I didn't want to prejudice your design. It's important to me that you employ whatever type of image you see fit. I have no clams about it."

"You have no clams?"

"That's right," he said. "I'm not concerned." Lyttleton may have been as confused as I was, but even I wouldn't mistake misgivings for shellfish.

"I've also written a piece for the gatefold." This was another hangover from his background in the industry. By no stretch of the imagination could a CD sleeve ever be described as a gatefold, and anyway how would this be useful in today's world of downloading? I took the handwritten note and gazed at it blankly.

"I think a written piece adds weight to the release, don't you?" he continued. "We want it to have impact. It can't just go off like a damp squid."

By now I was starting to wonder if I'd been hearing these words wrong all along and simply missing all the seafood figures of speech in everyday language. I was even being drawn into his world and finding the image of a detonated wet cephalopod sufficiently daunting.

Luckily at this point LaFlamme made a surprise appearance, arriving just in time to spare me having to read the piece. Lyttleton rose from his perch.

"LaFlamme," he said, bowing his head slightly. This was unnecessary as she was already a head taller.

"I'm usually very good with names," said LaFlamme, "but I've deliberately forgotten yours." Lyttleton shifted uneasily.

"Well, I think we're pretty much done here," he said. There had been no mention of budget and that's the way Lyttleton liked it. Wasn't it enough to have the privilege of working with one of the greats and being a moth around a magnificent flame?

"We can discuss costs later," I suggested.

"Costs," he said, vaguely unfamiliar with the term. "Of course."

He left to continue building his ridiculous fictional empire elsewhere.

LaFlamme meanwhile was flicking through Lyttleton's pictures, and had opened the window in order to casually release each in turn out into the wild. Eventually she reached a shot of a tall, lean young man wearing a pork pie hat and carrying a guitar case. I assumed this was Campbell Glen.

"Not bad," said LaFlamme. With the exception of young Elvis and herself, I had never heard her describe anyone in complimentary terms. I felt a pang of jealousy but decided to play it cool.

"Total loser," I said.

"Can we hear him?" she asked.

"There might be a CD," I said, "but if it was blank, Lyttleton wouldn't notice. A Lyttleton production is just that – product."

LaFlamme had found some photocopied press clippings within the package, providing a range of reviews and opinions on our subject. Most suggested Campbell Glen was a little troubled and unusual, and actually, having skipped through a few, I began to feel some sympathy with him. He sounded lost.

'Does the world need Campbell Glen? I don't know. Part jazzer, part hobo, part interior decorator, West Lothian-born Glen never seems to know which part is expected of him. He often confuses fans by turning up at their doors asking to read their meters. A die-hard outsider, he shuns the spotlight and can only be heard via cans attached to string. This is no barrier for his admirers who flock to their cans, often just to hear his semi-coherent ramblings about the work of the mole people. In recent months he has become convinced he is a sous chef and this confusion, whilst diverting, may ultimately lead to his undoing. His latest recordings sound remarkably like recipes.'

Other reviews were more positive.

'Whether you like desserts or not, flake-par-excellence Glen can cater to all tastes.' – The Post
'I generally prefer a starter, but 'Marinated Pears With Red Wine' really hits the spot.' – The Star

'Loon-supreme Glen has a recipe for success.' – The Chronicle
'He kind of lost me with the mole material, but 'Your New Flock Wallpaper' is a great track.' – The Times
'If I hadn't given up pole dancing to become a journalist, I'd have taken up singing to be like Campbell Glen.' – The Herald

Interesting guy. I looked at the picture a little closer. His shoelaces were untied.

By this time LaFlamme had lost interest in the subject and was drawing on the table again. I got the feeling if I ever turned my back on her she'd be drawing there too.

At that point, I decided if I wanted to get anywhere in graphic design, which was a big if, I might have to get my computer out of hock, and that would require cash. There was no point asking Lyttleton for an advance; he would need the concept explained to him. But I figured I might be able to hit Spore, so I set out towards his urban villa on the south side.

It was an area that bordered a thriving, upmarket part of town whose cafés and bars I knew well. But after turning off the main thoroughfare, I realised I hardly knew its back streets at all. It was clearly an area of affluence with large stone-built Georgian houses, some three stories high. Each was fronted by forbidding gates that shielded secluded grounds within. When the sun dipped behind clouds, the area took on a menacing, gothic appearance and I almost expected thunder. It looked like the Munsters might live here.

Spore's gate was adorned with a brass plate bearing his trademark symbol. I pressed the intercom buzzer and the gate swung open. As I made my way up the blue slate path, Spore became visible in the doorway, wearing what appeared to be a one-piece suit of heavy thermal underwear. On his chest was stitched a familiar insignia – a five-point star in a circle. I tried not to let the possibility of his Church of Satan membership deter me, as I was after all here on a mission.

"Come in, dear boy!" he effused. "What a pleasant surprise."

The house was swelteringly hot, easily forty degrees, and even at this coldest point in the year, it felt oppressive and unwelcome. Spore must have been in training for hellfire. I was reminded of how reptiles like to bake in the sun because they have no means of producing body heat of their own.

"Are you auditioning for *The Exorcist*?" I said, nodding towards the symbol on his chest.

"You jest, of course," he replied. "I'm sure you're well aware that the pentagram is no more evil in origin than the so-called swastika. Both are ancient emblems which were misappropriated to serve more dubious causes."

Evidently he still took me for a scholar of religious symbology, and I might have taken this remonstration more seriously had he not been wearing long johns.

"What they call the pentacle or pentalpha in fact stands for quite the reverse of what you suggest; it signifies power over evil. And the Third Reich may have embraced the equilateral cross but of course it was originally used to depict the sun; the return of a new dawn."

"I didn't really rate the remake," I said, finding the history lesson unnecessary. A drawing lesson would have been more useful.

"What I find most fascinating about symbols is that they are generally artistically unsophisticated patterns and yet, over time, they can assume great cultural significance. If you think about it, simple shapes are capable of carrying meaning far beyond anything which more complex expressions cannot.

"For example, in our own culture one can draw two parallel lines together without them necessarily meaning anything in particular. But draw them curved together to form the shape of a heart and you have a symbol of love."

"I suppose if the Nazis had hijacked the heart symbol instead of the swastika, Valentine's Day could be quite alarming."

"Exactly. Were I to take six lines and tattoo a hexagon on my forehead – and don't think I haven't considered it – people might think me odd. But were I to take the same six lines and tattoo the symbol of the new dawn in the same space, my appearance would more likely cause distress." His appearance was causing distress anyway. I wished he'd put some clothes on.

But the more I thought about his point, the more I realised there were other implications.

"What if you're not very good at drawing and you accidentally cause distress?" I asked, suddenly concerned. "I could have been trying to create an instructional diagram and just through artistic incompetence frightened somebody."

"You wouldn't be tattooing an instructional diagram on your head though, would you?" he said. I conceded the point.

The combination of this mini-guilt complex and the intense heat was beginning to make me feel panicky, so I thought I should probably cut this short.

"Look Iggy," I said, "I'll come to the point."

I explained about the misappropriation of my computer and how I'd been led astray by a raven-haired karaoke queen who may or may not have been sent by the devil, two events not entirely unrelated.

"So I wonder if you could give me an advance."

"You disappoint me, Mr Boaks," he replied, his fingers making a revolting waxy sound in connection with his ear. "I thought you were bringing me good news. Nevertheless, I may be in a position to assist."

I left Mockingbird Lane with a modest advance and a laptop – probably the smallest laptop in the world. I think it was divine retribution for my comments on the subject of portable devices that I should be forced to create my epic works of design genius on a comically small computer.

Now I had run out of excuses. I was going to have to work.

5.
NOT A DIARY

For all Spore's talk of symbols, he had neglected to explain the signif-icance of the one he commissioned me to rework. In fact, he assumed I already knew. I really should have told him that what I don't know could fill an ocean.

What was so important that he would be willing to change his name in order to transform his logo beyond recognition? I sensed a golden opportunity for procrastination and excused the diversion as 'online research'.

It was only a matter of seconds before I recognised the folly of conducting an online search for 'AS'. Whatever Spore was trying to hide, he'd already played a blinder by naming his organisation after one of the most common words in the entire English language. There was less chance of finding it than finding the Lost City of Atlantis or the positive case for the UK.

I never find what I'm looking for anyway because what I'm looking for has to compete with the vast vault of gibberish produced in the name of blogging. Despite possible genius The Admiral doing his technical best to explain the concept to me, even showing me examples, I still found blogging impossibly silly. Millions of pages clogging up the net with twaddle. The Admiral said they were 'good for search engines', although how being awash in a sea of drivel could be good for any kind of engine is beyond me.

But as I sat there pondering my next move, The Admiral's explanation, coupled with my acute blogophobia, combined to inspire a truly brilliant idea – couldn't we split the internet?

The limitations of a single internet are clear. Billions of websites covering millions of topics, all jammed together in one channel, making filtering nigh on impossible. If each topic had its own internet, I might be able to find the thing I was looking for.

You wouldn't expect to switch on the TV, pick a news channel, then have to wade through game shows, movies and ten seasons of *Celebrity Trepanning Challenge* to find news. Maybe soon I wouldn't have to contend with bloggers when I went searching for religious symbology because I'd be on the channel devoted entirely to crackpots.

I called The Admiral and ran my obviously Nobel-worthy idea past him.

"Your asininity may have reached its apotheosis," he said.

"Right?" I could tell he was impressed.

He may not have fully grasped the magnitude of the concept, however, because then he sighed heavily and said something about life not being short enough.

But after a moment I sensed his great brain whirring into motion and making a mental connection between the germ of an idea and the potential for great wealth, a very typical Admiral response.

"There is a filtering of sorts already in place, of course," he mused. "Or at least that was the original intention behind the top level domain extensions, dot com, dot org etcetera."

"Don't forget dot crap for blogs," I said.

"Indeed," he replied. "But stricter delineation for each level would facilitate greater search satisfaction. So for example someone shopping for a fridge would not end up being directed to the Chicago Bears, who have a *player* called The Fridge."

"How can we be sure?" I asked.

"Because they'd be connected to the shopping internet and not the fridge-shaped athletes internet."

"What if they were shopping for a fridge-shaped athlete?" I said.

"Well," he replied, "we'll cross that fridge when we come to it." I groaned, which was a very typical me response.

"Tony," he continued, "you know I'm quite discriminating when it comes to taking on a project…"

"What about your baldness cure?"

"Now that's unfair. Technically it worked, just not where we expected."

"That poor man has to shave his back every day."

"Nevertheless, it was worth pursuing. As is this. Despite the logistical ramifications, I think your idea may have legs."

"It has a whole body. It's borderline brilliant. The Nobel people will be falling over each other to get here."

"It would be most unusual for a graphic designer to win the Nobel Prize," he pointed out. But I was already thinking about my acceptance speech.

I'd tell the Swedish audience how I'd risen up from appalling squalor and that at the time of my brilliant idea, I had a hole in my shoe which I'd been trying to fix for some time. And in fact, that's what caused the hole – I was trying to nail the sole back on.

How I Won the Nobel Prize would be the name of my best-selling memoir. It didn't matter to me that it would be The Admiral's efforts that would bring the idea to fruition. I was the one who came up with it. He wouldn't mind that I got all the attention. I would mention him in the book.

I left him to take the initial steps, which presumably involved vast feats of calculus between the computer and the kettle. The Admiral's enthusiasm for new projects was irrepressible, at least until the new project was replaced by a newer one. As a consequence, many of them remained unfinished.

For example, there was his organic fuel creation – a gasoline substitute made from urine, vinegar and molasses. Had it been a success, this would certainly have had a major impact on global events, given that it offered potential solutions to the problems of both fuel scarcity and waste product transformation, as well as giving me a use for the half empty tin of molasses that sat at the back of my cupboard for five years. But unless he was going to see it through to a conclusion, it was always just going to be urine, vinegar and molasses.

Despite initial success when it was tested on his mother's Vespa, the project faltered after The Admiral's chemical analyses suggested it required another half tin of molasses, and neither of us was willing to house the remaining half for another five years. I suggested making double the quantity in order to use up a full tin and avoid the whole molasses issue, but by then he and the Vespa were far away.

It was always possible that The Admiral would return to a project at a later date, as he was usually unwilling to close the door fully on any of them. If he'd been able to close the door on his organic fuel product, the house might not smell of urine, vinegar and five-year-old molasses.

After taking in the entire first season of *Celebrity Trepanning Challenge*, it was hard to avoid Spore's leather volume and the loose-leaf page with its 'AS' insignia by my side. I'd been delighted to have avoided work for another day, but now the world's smallest laptop was open before me. I bit the bullet and searched for 'religious symbology'.

After rigorous filtering I found exactly what I expected – nothing helpful. I did however discover that there are far more deranged conspiracy theorists in the world than I imagined. Site after site threw up revelations of secret societies and obscure religious orders – real cloak and dagger stuff. Spore would be in good company in cyberspace. (I'm sure he has a dedicated cloak wardrobe and at least one dagger drawer, probably next to his socks.)

After an hour of this piffle, I felt that I knew less than when I began. I was falling into the cyberspace vortex, a black hole of browsing typified by ever expanding results and possibilities that, far from narrowing a search, increases it to a point that makes grown men want to weep.

I logged onto Twitter to check up on Spore. His latest tweets were more perplexing than ever. If I thought he was unhinged before, then tonight he was surpassing all expectations.

'Aerosol backwash pitfalls.'

Typical social media nonsense. Any random delve into the realm tends to leave me thinking either everyone's an imbecile (except me), or everyone's a genius (except me). It's like being an uninvited guest at either a Mensa gathering or a Village Idiots convention, but not knowing which.

'And he's the virulent swindler.'
'Amuses sheer tonnes.'

There were lots of these obscurities, each as baffling as the next. I wrote the first three down, fully aware that it would take some kind of miracle for any meaning to attach itself to them.

When I returned to the worst logo in the world, I found myself staring at it with a helpless rage. I stared until I could only see it as a shape, a shape devoid of meaning. It stopped being the word 'AS', or even letters. It was just a series of marks.

The intensity of my concentration was such that eventually I felt the shape taking on a mystical form – in that moment it seemed like an expression of oneness. Was the unthinkable happening? Was I experiencing enlightenment?

Maybe this was the religious symbology Spore was referring to. Maybe it wasn't the worst logo in the world; maybe it was brilliant. Maybe it was like French Connection's 'FCUK' logo – so appalling it had to be genius.

This quasi-religious epiphany was short-lived. It soon retreated into playful curiosity, back further to the original revulsion and was finally replaced by nausea.

"I believe your logo may be haunted," I said to Spore when I finally tore myself away from the design and picked up the phone. My client sensed a man in emotional distress.

"It's 4.00am, you dolt," he said.

I could already hear the clattering of the ribbon-wound Underwood as I climbed the tenement stairs. Nudging the front door, which was slightly ajar, I saw LaFlamme in exactly the same position as I left her several days before. The typing was deafening. I could feel the vibrations rattling through the floor.

"Have you had any sleep?" I asked.

"I'll sleep when I'm dead," she replied.

I figured she was immortal anyway and would need a stake through the heart to derail her. I'm constantly amazed that somebody who apparently never needs to eat or sleep can look so good. She's a miracle of nature.

LaFlamme ripped a page from the machine and added it to the top of a sizeable stack, whilst simultaneously thrusting a separate page my way. "Piece of cake," she said.

"What's this?" I asked, slightly fearful.

"Publishing interest," she replied, grabbing two glasses and filling them with what looked like sherry, but could have been anything.

"It's my duty to relate the sum of knowledge I've gained so far. People need to wake up and realise there is a better way to live."

I gazed at the letter in disbelief. LaFlamme's self-help book had been accepted by a leading agent and was now under review by several publishers. It didn't even look like she was finished. My hopes of winning the Nobel Prize seemed hollow in the light of this. I felt an exasperation that I'd previously reserved for extraordinary pique.

"Notice anything unusual about the design?" she asked, nodding in the direction of the letter.

I hadn't. Years of graphics torture had left me immune to the charms of my own trade, to the extent that I now mentally blank out anything that isn't 10-point Times. I took a second look at the document, topped with the company name, 'Vague, Vague and Steadfast'.

"At the bottom," she said, pointing.

And there it was – 'AS', the world's worst logo. Now there were two of them in my life.

"Spore gets around," said Laflamme.

"I feel like I've already had a lifetime of despair, but it may be that the real thing is just beginning. Can I keep it?"

LaFlamme shrugged her shoulders, so I folded the letter and filed it within the pages of this book. Unfortunately, that drew her attention to the book, which I knew was a mistake.

"Are you keeping a diary?" she asked.

"More of a journal," I replied.

"Isn't that just a diary?"

"It's a journal."

"Diaries are dull. And yours is likely to be even worse."

"It's not a diary."

"Let me see." She grabbed hold of the book and began flicking through the pages.

"Blah blah blah. Busy little scribe, aren't you?"

Editor's Note: The following entry was evidently not written by the author. Although the handwriting is askew and apparently written in haste, the spelling is impeccable. We can only assume Ms LaFlamme was responsible, which is not something often said of her.

DIARY OF T BOAKS, AGED 10 AND A HALF. TUESDAY. Suddenly the front door burst open and the reptilian client Spore stumbled in, collapsing onto the hardwood floor with a crumpled slip of paper in his outstretched hand.

"Dramatic," I said, "Is it from *The Maltese Falcon*?"

"The what?"

"Detective fiction. Is that what you're writing now?"

"Better than a diary."

"Journal. And the whole point is to record your actual experiences, not make up new ones that never happened."

"Why would anybody do that?"

"Because that's what you're meant to do in a diary."

"Journal," said LaFlamme. "Well, if I were you, I'd fictionalise. It's like being offered two lives and choosing the same one twice. Don't you want your second life to be different?"

"I'd very much like a different second life, but instead I've chosen to record the utter futility of the first one." LaFlamme had probably used up two lives already and wasn't yet thirty.

I handed her the page of Spore's tweets, which she took and read aloud.

"Aerosol backwash pitfalls. And he's the virulent swindler." She raised her eyebrows.

"James Joyce?"

"Too brief," I replied.

"Well, I might have missed all the other anagrams in this story, but I'm not about to miss this."

"What?"

"In the name of science," she continued, "I did a little research. It seems there's a secret society of desperate weirdos who like nothing better than to huddle together on Saturday nights and solve anagrams. Probably in tanktops."

"Right. Because tanktops help you solve puzzles."

"They're called 'The Anagrammatics'. It's all in here." She handed me a well-thumbed book by Dan Brown. "Not really, but sort of."

I hadn't even noticed my copy of *The Da Vinci Code* was missing. I'd begun it some time ago but didn't get far – it seemed like an awfully long way round for a car chase. If I have to endure a 300-page tome, it better explain the meaning of life, or at least have some kind of falcon in it.

I remember there was something about anagrams in the movie version but it must have washed over me. The whole movie did. If anagrams are crucial to the plot, you're going to lose me. I could have told Ron Howard this in advance.

I've always thought puzzles, jigsaws, crosswords and the like were for people who were simply out of touch with their true sloth. Why would I want to waste precious loafing hours trying to fix something that was deliberately broken just to keep these unbelievably bored people and their overactive frontal lobes happy?

"Okay, let's start with the shortest," she said. "Amuses sheer tonnes."

I tried my best, which was far from great. After thirty minutes putting pen to paper, LaFlamme took pity.

"It's just as well you're pretty," she said, using her knuckles to make a hollow knocking sound against the top of my head. "Better leave the thinking to me." I happily relinquished the task as I feared any further brain strain would lead to a hernia of the head.

"Perhaps we need a drop of liquid inspiration," she suggested, causing me to visibly wince. When LaFlamme administers this type of inspiration it can have devastating results.

"I'm not sure I can handle being inspired right now," I protested feebly.

"Nonsense," said LaFlamme, pouring two massive belters of who knows what. It turned out to be bourbon. Why she didn't just get a funnel and inspire me to death was beyond me.

Suddenly LaFlamme stirred. "I'm a genius," she declared.

"You are?"

"Yes."

"And?"

"Tennessee sour mash?"

"I've had enough, thanks," I said.

"No, Dumbo. Amuses sheer tonnes. It's an anagram of Tennessee sour mash."

"It's *Mister* Dumbo if you don't mind."

"You can be *Emperor* Dumbo if you like," she replied. "Don't you see? It's been staring us in the face. Literally."

She hovered the bottle before me, as if practising hypnosis, and slowly it began to sink in. But LaFlamme needed no practise. I'd been hypnotised for years.

Despite being awash with the stuff, it had taken an hour for us to realise Tennessee sour mash bourbon was the solution to the puzzle. But why would anyone set such a puzzle? Did Spore know it was a regular thing in my life? And if so, how?

By the time the question arose, LaFlamme's 'liquid inspiration' had left us very heavily inspired and I was unable to walk in a straight line, let alone find an answer.

"We might need help," said LaFlamme. "Professional help".

"Agreed," I responded. "I think a professor of religious symbology could get to the bottom of this."

"I was thinking AA. But your idea's good too."

6.
A FRANK EXCHANGE

I was now juggling two design commissions at once, which was two more than normal. Any more and I might start considering myself successful, even 'in demand', and I wasn't sure what impact this might have on my strictly slacker ethos.

As I sat darning my socks by candlelight, in itself an act that could be considered diligent, I wondered if I should try showing some ambition by promoting this striving new instance of myself. Perhaps I could use this journal to write a little about the trials of being a graphic designer in an effort to bring in new business.

I mean, by now you're probably wondering what all this has to do with graphic design. But what does anything have to do with anything nowadays? I bought that Dan Brown book thinking it had something to do with literature and look where that got me.

It was in the early hours of the morning that these musings were interrupted by the arrival of a slim-built stranger wearing an obvious disguise. (The glasses and moustache might have fooled me, but the plastic nose was a giveaway.)

"I need some branded elements for a small business startup," he offered hesitantly, in a soft, posh-Edinburgh brogue. "Money is no object."

41

"At 2.00am? Can't it wait till daylight at least?"

"My apologies. I'm on Malta time."

"It's about 3.00am there," I said. He told me he needed a new watch.

I invited the stranger in and he peered round the room shiftily before entering.

"You come highly recommended," he said. I'm sure I do. I have excellent word of mouth amongst the local business lowlife.

"Thank you, Mister...," I replied.

"Smith."

"Mr Smith. What kind of business are you starting?" I was reasonably casual about this introduction as so many of my clients had fallen by the wayside after revealing themselves as complete twonks.

"It's a bank," he said.

"A bank? You're starting a bank?"

"Yes," he stated frankly. "It's really not that difficult." I was about to show the goon the door when he got his chequebook out. He was an old-school goon. Well, there was no point in being hasty.

"I can give you an advance as a retainer and cover your daily expenses for, shall we say, two weeks?" He was already writing the cheque so it would have been impolite of me to decline.

"We shall," I said. He thrust the folded note my way then retracted it slightly.

"My one condition is absolute discretion. I must insist that this arrangement remain strictly entre nous."

"I don't speak Maltese," I replied. "But we could just keep it between ourselves. Perhaps you could tell me a little about the project."

"Of course. My background is in finance, investment banking mostly. Unfortunately, I met with some, well, call it bad luck in my previous endeavours and it is my intention to put things to rights by settling some old scores."

"I know all about bad luck," I said. "It's the only luck I know."

"Then I'm sure you'll understand. You see, there are those who say I went too far, that somewhere along the way I crossed a line. But I believe that on the contrary, the problem was I didn't go far *enough*; that if anything, I was too accommodating, too reasonable. With my comeback, I plan to take up where I left off and see the task through by whatever means necessary. They can drive me out of banking but all that does is force me to operate underground. And this time I won't be stopped."

It was late and it may have been that I misinterpreted Mr Smith's plans as a bid to hold the world to ransom through his determination to become banking's first criminal mastermind. But I don't think so. I had to ask myself why was it so difficult to find upstanding, respectable clients with no murky past and a continuous supply of worthwhile, challenging assignments. Is it really so much to ask?

"Do we have a name for this new organisation?" I asked.

"Yes," he said. "We're going to call it Bear Stearns."

"Bear Stearns?" I replied. "Isn't that name already taken?"

"That's the beauty of it. Nobody expects Bear Stearns to play nice. When I saw the name was set for the scrapheap, I knew it could only be an opportunity."

Though baffling to me, I had to admire his ingenuity. Clearly this type of thinking was what had propelled him to the top of his profession, even if it had propelled him straight back down again.

He rose to leave. "You will be contacted by telephone on the stroke of midnight each night this week. In this method you will receive instructions for the assignment. Please avail yourself."

"You could have contacted me at the stroke of midnight tonight instead of waiting till 2.00am when I was nearly asleep," I ventured.

"Apologies. It took me hours to find my cuddly." He removed a piece of bobbly, pastel blue cotton from his jacket pocket and waved it in my direction.

The stranger bowed his head at the doorway and as he did so, the disguise slipped momentarily from his face. I had a brief glimpse of the features beneath and they seemed vaguely familiar.

"Adieu," he said, making his way hastily out the door.

A swift scrutiny of the name on the cheque confirmed my suspicion. This was no Mr Smith; it was Sir Frank Godalming.

Godalming had been chief executive officer of the AUA, the Allied Uber Alles, one of the largest banking operations in the world until its spectacular collapse. Despite its name, the AUA did not originate in Germany, but did appear to be inspired by its early 20th century expansionist philosophy. When the bank imploded under his watch, Godalming chose not to join other high-ranking officials fleeing to Argentina and instead skipped off to the south of France, having first ensured he was obscenely rich from the operation.

He was a despised figure in his native Scotland, where bankers are publicly flogged and made to wear floral headdresses to distinguish them from normal people, and notorious throughout the rest of the Western world.

This notoriety would go some way towards explaining his unsociable hours. But I also couldn't help noticing that he cast no shadow and had no reflection in the mirror.

When I dropped in on LaFlamme the following day, she was standing at a shredder, feeding pages individually through its cutting mechanism and delighting at the lines of confetti being spewed out at the other end.

"I see the writing's going well," I said.

"These are bills," she replied. "Apart from this one."

"What's that one?"

"Final notice."

"You should probably keep that." It was too late. Now it was wedding fodder.

Then came a page I recognised.

"Hang on, those are Spore's anagrams." I could tell she was in a shred-happy state and that it was taking real willpower to withhold the page from the hungry machine. "That's what I wanted to talk to you about."

She relinquished the sheet along with another in her own unmistakable scrawl, then grabbed a stapler and punched the two together.

"You solved the anagrams?" I asked.

"Yes," she replied. "I had to pretend I was somebody incredibly tedious in order to do it."

'Aerosol backwash pitfalls.' Solution: 'Spore calls Boaks a halfwit.'

'And he's the virulent swindler.' Solution: 'He will never understand this.'

44

"It's hard not to feel slighted by this," I said. "Why would anyone want to spend their time being insulting in code?"

"Sheer dedication to the art," she replied. "This is just exercise for The Anagrammatics. We could reply in similar fashion but they'd love that. Probably get them all steamed up."

"What's this?" I asked, spotting a letter from her agent, Vague, Vague & Steadfast, which had so far managed to avoid the shredder.

"No big deal," she replied.

Apparently there is now a bidding war between publishers for LaFlamme's self-help folly, *Help Yourself to Drink*. Had I not spent more than half the day sleeping, I might have felt more begrudging of her success.

"This could make you rich," I suggested.

"Publishing make you rich? Have you lost it, Boaks? I guarantee right now they're all breaking open their piggy banks and finding nothing but buttons." She was probably right. Publishers are notoriously hopeless with cash.

"Here's how it works," she continued. "For every book like mine, there are five turkeys. Publishers can't tell the difference, so they hedge their bets on a bunch of titles. The good stuff cancels out the turkeys, and the publishers break even in the end."

"What if the turkeys win prizes?" I asked.

"Sometimes they do. Doesn't mean anybody reads them. *Life Of Pi*. Turkey. Lots of prizes."

"It sold a million copies."

"People bought it," she declared. "But they didn't read it. Every so often, readers get guilt pangs about the garbage that heads up their 'next' pile and go all self-improving. So they buy one of these life-shorteners and it sits by the bed for a year untouched. Did you read *Life Of Pi*?"

"Of course not."

"Did you read the stuff in your bookcase?"

"Maybe." LaFlamme shot me a glance that said 'I rest my case' and fell into the sofa.

"Anyway," she continued, "they asked me to think about a sequel."

"Already?"

"Yes. I suggested *Help Yourself 2: Drink*." She wrote this down in a huge scrawl so I could see the distinction between the sequel and its predecessor.

"But first I'm writing a guide for office drones. It's called *365 Days Of Mediocrity*." She shuffled some pages on her desk and handed one to me. "It's to help the plebs through their humdrum lives."

The book appeared to be a collection of 'inspirational' life coaching tips from someone who didn't care if their advice is helpful or not. I attach a sample week:

March – Week One

Monday: Live up to everyone's expectations by reminding yourself how incredibly low they've fallen.

Tuesday: When your boss suggests taking a small idea and making it bigger, try extending your lunch break to five hours.

Wednesday: In today's world, career goals are increasingly important. Try asking a friend what the phrase means.

Thursday: You have all the skills necessary for success. Try not to let them be outweighed by your phenomenal talent for failure.

Friday: If your boss encourages you to be more spontaneous at work, demonstrate your willingness by going straight to the pub.

Saturday: Success often depends upon one's ability to use a tool skilfully. Show your colleagues how proficient you are with a corkscrew.

Sunday: Today you may encounter alien beings scouring the earth for signs of intelligent life. They shouldn't bother you.

It seemed that publishers had taken to LaFlamme in a big way. She could be onto something as long as her typewriter ribbon holds up.

"Do you want to play with the shredder?" she asked.

"I don't have time right now," I said, checking my watch. "I have to get back by midnight."

"Is it a pumpkin thing?" she asked.

"It's a work thing," I replied. "You wouldn't understand."

'Mr Smith' turned out to be a demanding client. After a week of working nights, I was starting to feel like a real graphic designer.

During my initial midnight instruction, he outlined the nature of the work I would be undertaking each night between the hours of 12.00am and 6.00am until the task was complete. He was most insistent that there should be 'no deviation' from this timetable and that I am to work by candlelight alone – electric light is forbidden. I'm unsure of the point of this, as I'm working on a laptop that gives off quite a glow.

Godalming was cagey about what information he provided throughout the week, but each night he let his guard down a little further. On the first night, he suggested I call him Frank and on the second he admitted Smith wasn't his real name. When, on the third night, he said his real name was Montezuma, I reminded him he signed his name Godalming. He told me that was a stage name. On the fourth night he said he'd changed his stage name to Carlos 'the Jackal' Santini and later that he'd retired from the stage. But by the fifth he'd given up all pretence of not being Sir Frank Godalming, which was a relief as I was ready to start calling him Mr Twat.

During the penultimate consultation, his design requirements being close to fulfilment, he outlined the next phase of the plan for his underground banking venture.

"Soon you will be contacted by my associate, who is sadly detained at this moment in time. Contact will be made by letter. It normally takes five to seven working days." It was typical that even an underground bank took five to seven days to send a letter.

"My colleague is one of the shrewdest and most unscrupulous financial practitioners in the world," Godalming continued, "and that is why he was chosen as a collaborator. You see, in the past I put up with the so-called fair working practices of well-intentioned, level-headed types at the expense of building a truly evil empire. I told my former colleagues we could one day conquer the world but they pooh-poohed me. My ambitions were stunted by acquiescing to their reasonable notions of decency."

I should have known this was part of Godalming's plan, as I'd been working on their branding for a week and spotted some familiar names creeping up in their corporate literature: Brendan Matlock, Allen Stanthorpe, Nick Liamson and Jerome Kerevan. For an evil underground organisation, their credentials were impeccable.

"How will I know your associate?" I asked.

"He is likely to try and fleece you," he replied. "After all, he is Brendan 'Matty' Matlock."

I was impressed. I knew Matlock as the man who had run the biggest investment scam in history until the bubble burst a few years back. It was incredible how he'd managed to cling onto that balloon for so long and only surrendered himself to the authorities when they discovered that in fact, he was the balloon in question.

I still wasn't sure what an evil underground bank did though, and hesitated to bring it up in case the answer made me want to slap Godalming about his stupid face.

"I'm glad you ask," said Sir Frank. "Essentially, we buy government debt in the form of gilt-edged bonds. The government pays billions in interest on these bonds. Because we're a bank we can borrow from them at 0.5% interest, buy bonds and earn 3.5% interest back from them."

"Wow," I said. "You borrow from the government to buy government debt then charge the government interest? That's fairly evil."

"That's not the evil part," he replied. "We already did that at the AUA. Back then it was even better. The government had bailed out the bank, so we were buying the bonds with government money. That meant we didn't have to borrow at all. We just took the money, bought bonds, and took the money again in interest. Ah, those were the days. But now we're more sophisticated. We've upped the evil quotient."

"How?"

"Now we don't tell anybody."

"But couldn't anybody do that? Me, for instance?"

"Are you a bank?" he replied.

"No."

"Well then," he said. "Unless you're a bank, you won't be able to borrow from any state reserve." I knew I'd end up wanting to slap him.

"I hope that answers your question. Now, there is one remaining item on my agenda. A small insignia. You'll find it in a brown envelope in your top drawer." I opened the drawer and saw the unmarked sealed envelope sitting on top of a random assortment of office paraphernalia.

"This is a trade association with which we have an affiliation. It's most important that this is displayed prominently but discreetly. I suggest you include it in the footer of our stationery."

It's hard to describe the chilling mixture of shock, confusion and despair I felt when I opened the envelope and unfolded the single sheet within. There it was. The worst logo in the world, Spore's 'AS' monogram.

Now there were three of them in my life.

I had warmed to Godalming over the course of the week's calls. He may have been intent on taking over the world with an evil underground bank, but otherwise he seemed like an okay guy. And unusually punctual, calling at exactly the twelfth stroke of midnight each night. But tonight was different.

On the twelfth stroke, nothing happened. On the thirteenth stroke, nothing happened. Another couple of dozen strokes went by before eventually there was a ring. Not the telephone, but the doorbell. Thinking it would be my client, I carried a candle through the hallway and unlocked the front door. There in the flickering candlelight stood a tall moustachioed man with wild blue eyes and an insane grin. I figured either he was on something or it was Texas billionaire Allen Stanthorpe. Unfortunately it appeared to be both.

"I'm here for the interview," he declared excitedly, that crazy grin growing by the second.

"Interview?"

"Sure," he said, thrusting a large manilla envelope my way. "Sir Frank tells me you're the guy to know round here!" I took the envelope and reluctantly invited the grinning fool in.

The envelope contained my instructions for the final night's labours. The contents were several pages long and included various hand-drawn diagrams of stickmen, along with measurements and detailed descriptions of materials and methods. It looked like he was ordering a suit.

'Hello Tony,' the cover letter began. 'Please excuse the rather impersonal nature of my greeting this evening. I have been detained in New Orleans. There was a fire and, well, it's a long story. As my co-conspirators in this venture are also detained, albeit in correctional facilities rather than angry mob-related incidents, I suggest it falls to you as default second in command to make a small human resources decision.'

Godalming went on to explain that he had been so pleased with my design work, he had assigned me an executive role in the new venture and I was now, unfathomably, in a position of some authority. Clearly the loss of his previous bank had shattered his tiny mind. If you think the bankers made a mess of things, wait till you see what the designers can do.

'The gentleman before you is eager to obtain gainful employment. I've explained that he's already on the board of directors and therefore need only be a drain on our employees. But he's an enthusiastic chap, as you can see.' Stanthorpe was just about doubled up with excitement at this point. 'Can you give him something to do?'

Interviewing a Texas billionaire for an unnecessary position in a new underground bank was certainly one of the more unusual tasks I've been assigned as a graphic designer. But Godalming, for whatever reason, seemed to trust me, and the grinning buffoon was standing in my kitchen, so I decided to make the best of it.

I began by asking for his CV and he duly obliged with a wide-eyed eagerness rarely seen in adults. As it turned out, the semi-literate hand-written note he jabbed me with was also remarkably childlike. I decided to quiz him directly rather than attempt a deciphering.

"What experience do you think you could bring to this role, Allen?" It was the first and undoubtedly last time I'd ever utter these words.

"Gee," he replied. "Well, I guess I built my own bank in the Caribbean."

"Hmm."

"It done went from strength to strength."

"That's not particularly deviant or wicked though, is it?" I asked. "You are aware this is an underground organisation?"

"Yeah, but then I got loaded and blew all the money in Vegas!"

"Aha!" This was more like what Sir Frank was looking for in his team. In fact, Stanthorpe was the perfect candidate. Not only was he childish, greedy and remorseless, he was also a hopeless gambler.

"I think you're just the man we're looking for," I said. "You're hired."

7.
A DEFINING MOMENT

It had been a rough week. I wasn't used to working more than two days in a row and this was more like five. I believe there are some who do such things regularly. How? I'm calling it a one-off. At least now I can keep the wolf from the door. I don't even lock the door anymore because the wolf and I became friends.

I like money as much as anyone else, but if you think about it, the concept of printed cash is pretty weird; odd little slips of paper that have a specific value if they carry a certain design. They're not even paper anymore – polymer.

'I promise to pay the bearer,' it says. I promise to pay the bearer what? Chickens? Tankards of mead? It's all so abstract; an IOU with a logo. The unknown graphic designer sweated over it on the orders of some drone banker, and if he tried making his own copies he'd go to jail. I bet he was paid buttons too. Hardly ever saw his own creations.

Imagine being a designer at The Royal Mint. The possibilities for subversion would be irresistible. I could create something that looked just like a bank note, beautifully crosshatched and engraved with the head of some old duffer, then in the tiniest possible point size I'd add, 'I promise to pay Tony Boaks', along with a copyright symbol.

Other kinds of money are no less weird. A strip of plastic wires your bank and tells them to subtract a sum from the pile they're meant to be holding for you. But they're not holding it at all. They spent it on unfathomably convoluted investment schemes and now nobody knows where it is. When the banks crashed, even *I* had more money than them. I hadn't done too well, but at least I didn't lose a hundred billion quid of somebody else's cash.

This is what was going through my head as I stepped into Spar, a grocery store that thinks it's a supermarket but is more of a kiosk. They always cram too many aisles into too small a space, then make the mistake of offering shopping baskets. Three of these in an aisle and you're talking major congestion.

I only wanted coffee and bread but I picked up a basket and so did everybody else. I was lucky this time as everybody else appeared to be much shorter and looking for goods on lower shelves, whilst the bread and coffee were both higher up. The result was like a two-tiered bridge as shorter people made their way under my basket. None of us really noticed each other.

When I reached the till, the assistant rang up the items and I handed him a five pound note. He held it quizzically up to the light.

"Draw this one yourself, did you?" he asked.

"Pardon?"

"It's pretty good, I'll give you that."

"Thank you," I said. "I like it." He couldn't possibly be admiring the design, though he did everything but get out a magnifying glass.

"Do you have another one?" he said, handing it back. Being conditioned to accept notes whatever the circumstances, I took it.

"Are you saying this is a forgery?" I asked him.

"Feel the paper," he replied. Obviously I wasn't as accustomed to handling money as he was; no designer would be. I caressed the note between my fingers but could feel nothing unusual about it.

"It feels like money," I said, but it was clear he had no interest in a debate. "What am I meant to do with it then?"

"Take it to the bank," he replied.

I crossed the street and tried to remember where the dubious note came from. I suppose having the head of an underground banking organisation for a client would be an obvious starting point – but

Godalming paid by cheque. It's possible that, unimpressed with the quality of available forgeries, he planned to have me design new ones, but that wouldn't explain where this one originated. (In future, if the banks are ever trying to identify forgeries by yours truly, they'll know to look for the words 'Godalming is an arse' somewhere in the margin.)

Am I the only one who gets nervous in banks? As far back as I can remember, I've always felt somebody somewhere is watching my every move on a wall of grainy, black and white monitors, waiting to see what I do next. I'm pretty sure if I start discussing forgery with their tellers, a red flashing 'grifter' alarm is going to bring down steel security doors and everyone will point at the guy with the dodgy fiver.

"Where did you get it?" asked the teller.

"I didn't forge it," I blurted defensively. She switched on an ultraviolet light below the counter and scrutinised the note.

"I'm afraid I'll have to confiscate it." I hadn't heard the word 'confiscate' since primary school and it reinforced my acute banking anxiety. I felt like I'd just stolen a Curly Wurly from the tuck shop.

"You're confiscating it? Do I get a replacement?"

"I'm afraid not. There are only so many notes in circulation."

"There are billions of notes in circulation. Why do you have to take mine?"

"I'm sorry."

"What about 'I promise to pay the bearer' and all that?"

"Look," she said, taking a pay in slip from a drawer. "Your piece of paper is worth exactly the same as this one." She wrote 'I promise to pay the bearer the sum of five pounds' on the back and handed it to me.

"If it helps, you can have this piece in exchange for yours." She smiled.

I had no idea bank tellers could do sarcasm.

Between bills, repayments and the odd forgery, most of my new-found wealth vanished as swiftly as it appeared. This always seems to be the case. It's like being chair lifted out of a well, then climbing straight down again. (I believe there are people who actually do this sort of thing for kicks.)

There was a certain comfort in knowing I wasn't alone at the bottom of the well. The Admiral's possible genius status didn't prevent him being completely hopeless with money, though I recall a defining moment when he made the mental connection between using it sensibly and having no electricity.

There had been a Vigorous Dark Ale Festival in the beer garden of a bar I mostly associated with beardy types. Unlike the social refinement you might encounter at a wine tasting, Vigorous Dark Ale Festivals tend to be boisterous outdoor affairs frequented by rugby players, as well as pale, interesting types like The Admiral and I.

On this occasion, a group of the former had discovered that the trays being used to carry pints around were made of a particularly light and malleable metal; so malleable that any knock they received left a distinct impression. Under the bewildering spell cast by Vigorous Dark Ale, they decided to see who could deliver the greatest cranial tray imprint when taking turns bashing each other's heads. This started a competition amongst the men, who it's likely had very little to lose in the way of brain cells even before the ale set in.

As each new crack of a tray led to greater and greater impressions, we could only marvel at how much a grown man's head could shape a serving platter. I winced as the current recipient encouraged his friends to hit him harder and reminded myself to redefine my understanding of the word 'stupid', as this spectacle had made all previous definitions redundant.

"Shall we give it a go?" asked The Admiral.

"No thanks," I replied. "I won't need a metal tray to have a sore head tomorrow."

"What if there was a wager? What if we put a hat down and asked for tips?"

My ears perked up.

"You know, like buskers." This got my interest. But there was no way I was going to test his theory by hitting him repeatedly with beer trays to prove I could get a better impression of his head than he could of mine.

It was several hours before The Admiral conceded defeat and the rugby players crowned me king of beer trays. There were many demolished examples and even more empty glasses, all testament to this clash of the stupid Titans. The Admiral wasn't too unhappy about being runner-up because his theory had been proven correct – as buskers and as gamblers, we made a killing. After paying for a new supply of outdoor trays, there was still enough money for several more rounds.

The event lasted all weekend and The Admiral would have remained beyond its conclusion had I not been there to remind him that he had a life outside of beer. Even with the reminder, he felt inclined to remain, in fact with a renewed enthusiasm, as he said he did not want to live without his beer. But eventually the guest ales were sent home and so were we.

Not to be deterred, he assured me his newest batch of homebrew was 'ready enough' and insisted we adjourn there for a sampling. At 1.00am we stumbled through his front door. It probably would have been an idea to try opening it first.

"It's very dark," I said, from the comfort of what I took to be an armchair.

"Is it?" he said. The Admiral had no interest in lightbulbs beyond their science and generally lived by the light of a monitor, but even this appeared to be dim. The only illumination came from the orange glow of streetlights shining in through the window. At least we didn't have to worry about our eyes adjusting to anything brighter, which could have been traumatic.

"Homebrew's over here somewhere," he said, tripping over something large enough for him to fall into and remain. The room became quiet. Very quiet.

"Admiral," I said.

"Yes?"

"I think I've gone blind."

"Hmm," he mused. "I did think that last pint was rather suspect."

The silence was comprehensive. I know a power cut when I hear one.

"Admiral," I said.

"Yes?"

"I think the electricity's off."

"That does appear to be the case, yes," he said.

"Why is that?"

"I'm not sure."

"Did you forget to pay the electric bill?"

"No."

"Good."

"I lost it."

"I see. What are we going to do?"

"I think," he said, pondering the question, "it's the perfect opportunity."

"For what?"

"A blind tasting."

He climbed out of whatever he had fallen into and his silhouette hovered uncertainly by the window as he fumbled his way to the cupboards. Various unknown kitchen implements crashed to the floor before he located a cabinet containing glassware. There were a number of casualties before he found two pint glasses and made for the dispenser on the counter top.

Eventually the tank produced a gurgling sound and I was satisfied that beer was being poured. It was a while before I heard it pouring into a glass however, and I imagined much of the room would be awash by dawn.

"What am I sitting on?" I said, sensing an arrangement of unusual plastic shapes beneath me.

"Might be clothes pegs," The Admiral called back. "I was interested in whether they could be adapted to produce mousetraps."

"And?"

"Negative."

"Well, it's good to know that your mice are still running free."

I began playing with these oddly pleasing objects, snapping them open and closed and attaching them to the sleeves of my jacket. In situations like this, peculiar things can be pleasing.

The Admiral handed me an overflowing glass and together we toasted the new brew.

"God bless her and all who sail in her," he said.

"Success to temperance," I replied.

It's fair to say that after a weekend of sampling bizarre and experimental ales, our tastebuds were far from their sharpest. But I could tell immediately this was no ordinary brew.

"Tangy," said The Admiral. "Spicy undercurrents."

"It's brutal," I said.

"Rich, all right. Might be the best batch yet."

"Is it meant to be this sweet?"

"Patience," he replied. "It needs a little time to breathe."

He then proceeded to tell me everything I could ever need to know about the art of brewing, and quite a lot more besides. It was a thorough lesson and after several minutes I could feel my life force start to drain away.

By the time he was through, the unusual combination of flavours had begun to grow on me and I was reminded of something my father told me before I was old enough to understand the appeal of such a vile drink. "Beer is an acquired taste," he said, powering his way through several. He clearly had no trouble acquiring it, and neither had I, but I have to say The Admiral's potion was challenging.

"You know what we should do?" I said, and I wasn't sure if it was the beer talking, or the beer trays for that matter. "We should bottle this stuff and sell it."

"That's an intriguing proposal," he replied.

"We could open our own microbrewery."

"Well, it would have to be a mini-microbrewery because we don't have much room."

"You take my point. We never have any money and people like beer."

"Ah, beer."

"And people who like beer will like this."

"*People...*" The Admiral began singing. "*People who like people... are the people-est people... in the world.*"

"Silly man," I said, before joining in on the chorus.

We continued to quaff the heady mixture into the small hours, and I dreamt of making some kind of success that didn't rely on lowlife clients, only heavy drinkers. There in the darkness, surrounded by mice and awash with 'ready enough' Vigorous Dark Ale, I was inspired. A mini-microbrewery may have been one of my more off the wall ideas, and who knows if it would stand up to scrutiny. I suppose we would find out when faced with the cold light of day.

The cold light of day came soon enough and sadly there was no shortage of it. The dim orange glow had become a coarse, brilliant white glare. I cursed The Admiral for his lack of blackout curtains.

I appeared to have an old sock in my mouth, or something similar, and the kitchen too smelled of stale feet. Next to me was a beer tray that bore a remarkable resemblance to The Admiral.

Something stirred in the hallway. At first glance it appeared to be an animal of some sort; a large dog or Shetland pony. At second glance it looked more like The Admiral, crawling on all fours, his bed covers strapped across his back like a cape. He was trying to tell me something. It sounded like 'war'.

"Water," he finally uttered.

"Where?" I asked. My need was at least as great as his.

"At the tap," he said slowly, pointing vaguely towards the sink.

"That's miles away," I said, remaining motionless on the sofa.

It proved to be a tap too far for The Admiral, whose limbs gave way beneath him, leaving him slumped face down on the floor. I would have to make the monumental sacrifice of fetching us both water.

He slowly managed to bring himself to a seated position on the floor, his back against the wall. Once I handed him a glass of the best water either of us had ever tasted, he appeared to notice me afresh.

"Did you know you're covered in clothes pegs?" he said. I went to the bathroom to check my reflection in the mirror. Clumps of my hair had been pinned in bunches and both my jacket sleeves were adorned from shoulder to wrist.

"It's something I'm trying," I said, propping myself beside him on the floor.

From here, our immediate view was the sink and counter area, on which sat two semi-translucent plastic tanks, each capable of holding around twenty gallons. Each had a label sellotaped loosely to the front and was inscribed with a heavy marker pen. The full tank on the left contained a light brown liquid and was labelled 'AB55'. The half empty tank on the right contained a darker liquid and was marked 'XY33'.

"What's the AB55?" I asked.

"That's the homebrew," he replied.

"But it's full," I said. There was a befuddled pause as I struggled to form a follow-up question. "What's the XY33?"

"That's the organic fuel." A somewhat more anxious pause ensued.

We stared at the tanks. We stared at each other. We stared at the tanks again.

"I could have made a mistake with the labels," he offered finally.

We rose to our feet and studied the labels intently. On the back of each was printed matter that suggested they might be two halves of the same page.

"Ah!" said The Admiral, piecing the two halves together. "Good."

"You made a mistake?"

"No, there's no mistake," he replied. "But I've found the electricity bill."

8.
THE ART OF BOREDOM

Lyttleton called, asking how the Campbell Glen sleeve was coming on. I told him it was marvellous, then went to make a start on it. I shuffled through the material he'd left me, as well as my notes from the meeting, which were hardly inspirational.

> *delusional*
> *singer*
> *rhinestone cowboy*
> *why me*
> *anagram*

It was interesting that the only relevant piece of information here was 'singer', which made me think I should give up taking notes and indeed give up writing altogether, a suggestion you may heartily agree with. Interesting too was the inclusion of the word 'anagram'. Was it simply that my mind had wandered back to Spore's cryptic messages, or was it something Lyttleton said that I thought might have been scrambled?

I tried to remind myself of anything noteworthy in our exchanges, but looking for 'noteworthy' in a Lyttleton conversation was always futile. 'Not worthy' came up frequently as it was something he tried to instil in his minions. Everybody was a minion to Lyttleton.

"Is Campbell Glen an anagram?" I asked LaFlamme.

"Rather than a real person?" she asked.

"He might be a real person too."

"He could be a figment of your imagination."

"My imagination isn't all that great."

"Have you ever seen him?"

"No."

"So at this moment he only exists in your imagination."

"I guess so," I said. "And in the hearts and minds of music fans everywhere."

"What if he's an anagram of somebody else?" said LaFlamme.

"He's certainly an anagram of Glen Campbell."

"That's not an anagram," said LaFlamme. "That's more like a roll call. Boaks, Tony. Glen, Campbell. A dedicated Anagrammatic would come up with something better than that." I always thought being in a relationship with LaFlamme would be awesome, but in reality it may well just be exhausting.

She said we needed a distraction and suggested a trip to an art gallery. It had been a greyish kind of morning and I was probably going to do something pointless anyway, so I thought why not. Crucial to this decision was the fact that it was free, a point that was not lost on LaFlamme, who was also chronically short of cash.

As a gifted copywriter, LaFlamme certainly had the means of making good money when needed but it seemed she was too opinionated for mainstream journalism and too honest for advertising. At least that was the judgement of her former employers, despite LaFlamme's protestations.

"I can be dishonest," she said to the advertising agency. "I can write like a pleb if you want," she said to the magazine editor.

But it was clear that the issue was consistency. LaFlamme had the skill to write in whatever style was required, but on a day in, day out level the boredom factor would creep in and her irrepressible personality would take over.

One memorable piece for *Home & Garden* began innocuously enough as a review of a middle-aged celebrity couple's overblown abode:

Charles and Georgina DeMille describe the effect that their home has on guests. "One particular guest compared it to a Hermes handbag," said Georgina. I nodded in a knowing way, although I had no idea what she was talking about. Why would the guide of the underworld be designing handbags rather than protecting the way of travellers? I suppose he might have designed the odd bag in a moment of extreme tedium. In fact, I've worked out a particularly fine design in my head as I continue to trudge around this dreary abode.

The house is the epitome of neoclassical style, ideal for the particular drones currently inhabiting it because a neoclassical home removes the need for any personal sense of style or taste and replaces it with an overwhelming sense of smugness in its owners. "I like to keep it simple," says Georgina, and she ought to know, as she's a walking vacuum.

Husband Charles is an ideal match for hoover woman, and I ask him how it feels to be unburdened by complexity. "I'm an American," he says. "We don't really do substance."

As we enter the dining room, Georgina tells me it was the classic proportions of the space which first drew her and her divot partner to the home they now share with their obnoxious offspring, Charles Junior, aged nine, and Wolfgang Amadeus, six. Together they truly are a gift for advocates of sterilisation and I end my interminable visit by warning the family they should probably be confined indoors at all times.

Unfortunately this article was actually published, as no one in the editorial department ever read the ingratiating puff pieces written as side accompaniments to the main attraction, the glossy photographs. It was only after receiving a letter from the DeMilles that the editor became aware of its existence.

To: Edward Wonderful (Editor)

Dear Mr Wonderful,
We the DeMilles would like to thank you for your excellent fea-

ture in this month's H&G. It's marvellous to see your publication
continue to use such quality paper despite these difficult times.

Your reporter was most unorthodox in her methods but was a
regular Rosalind Russell in the field. Her jokes about sterilisation
may not have been to everyone's taste, but being members of the
Conservative party, we found them most amusing.

We have since replaced the broken items and replenished the
drinks cabinet.
Yours,
DeMille x 2

This was sufficiently unusual to compel Mr Wonderful to reread
the original article and LaFlamme's career as a freelancer diversified
from that point.

But it wasn't just the monotony of the nine to five world that drove
LaFlamme to these measures. There were 'office procedures' that were
a dependable way of ensuring intelligent people with imagination
would not fit in.

"What's this?" she asked, having once been handed a sheaf of papers
marked with lined tables.

"These are your time record sheets," said her supervisor. "You need
to write down how much time you spend on everything you do during
the course of a day, along with the start and end times of each task."

LaFlamme studied the pages and looked dumbfounded. "Does
everyone have to do it?" she said. "Or have you singled me out for this
particular torture?"

"It's important that we get a feel for how much time employees are
spending on individual chores. It will help us to make efficiency savings."

"It's not a particularly efficient use of paper," said LaFlamme.

"Could you just do them, please?"

"You want me to write down the time I spend on everything?"

"Yes."

"Everything?"

"Yes."

"You want me to write down the time I spend filling in the time
record sheets?"

"Well I suppose so, yes."

"That's going to cause problems."

"Why?"

"Feedback."

"What?"

"You know, like when you're at karaoke and you point the mike at the speaker, you get feedback."

"I wouldn't know about that."

"Yeah, you don't strike me as the karaoke type. If you point a microphone at a speaker, you'll get feedback. If you hook up a video camera to a TV and point it at the TV, you'll get feedback. If you have to time record your time recording, you'll get feedback because then you'll have to time record the time you spent time recording the time recording. Do you want that kind of noise in your life?"

"I'm not sure."

"What about the time we're spending having this conversation?"

"You should probably include that."

"Good. I'll write 'spent half the morning wasting my breath'." LaFlamme knew it was pointless arguing, but kept haranguing the supervisor, probably just for sport, as he made his way down the corridor.

"What about the time I spend calling you an idiot? What about the time I spend looking for better jobs?"

Similar circumstances may have been the launchpad for many a freelance career and it was no surprise that LaFlamme and I gravitated towards each other and towards vast loafing areas like the Scottish National Gallery of Modern Art. The gallery has huge sprawling grounds perfect for those of an idle disposition and consequently I had spent many fine hours there, drifting in and out of daydreams.

I think it's important that a place like this should be maintained in the centre of the city to remind people that work is futile – a total waste of time only tolerated out of necessity by the powerless. I was surprised that LaFlamme had any interest in art but she too seemed to have grasped this idea intuitively. Today it was cold so we ventured inside.

The hallway was lined with a selection of framed pieces by controversial conceptual artist-magpie Damien Hirst, and to me they cemented his status as somebody whose work I'd rather not see. The artist was better known for suspending dead animals in formaldehyde and recently surprised nobody but himself when he picked up a paintbrush and discovered that painting was more difficult. This inspired one of LaFlamme's finest headlines: 'Formaldehyde boy tries painting – gets in a pickle.'

I didn't mind too much that he was exhibiting here but it tended to mean there was less room for people who weren't complete asshats.

I caught up with LaFlamme as she stood before a large and imposing abstract expressionist work on paper (I guessed maybe Pollock or somebody else who'd given up trying – I can never be bothered looking at the labels). The painting was a monochromatic, typically messy affair, and the black and white stripes of LaFlamme's top blended so well that it was a surprise to suddenly see them move. I enjoyed the effect but had to admit there was very little point in only liking an image when LaFlamme was standing in front of it.

"Sometimes I find the title can help give me a way in to understanding a painting," I said. "What's this one called?"

"*Untitled*," said LaFlamme. We moved on.

There were a lot of abstract expressionists in the vast space, which certainly helped fill it; one Barnett Newman alone and you wouldn't have room for much else. It occurred to me that this might be budget strategy on behalf of the curators. You could put four Magrittes in that space but one of these big boys would do for a quarter of the price.

Just when the sheer scale of these walls of colour was starting to make me feel nauseous, I was relieved to find a room of smaller, less overwhelming works by Picasso. They were from a period I might have said was Cubism if I knew anything about art.

"He must have been really bored," said LaFlamme.

"Why do you say that?" I asked.

"By the time Picasso was twenty, he was already one of the greatest painters alive. He would get up in the morning, throw off a couple of sketches and people were in awe. He'd done everything he could do within the limits of traditional figurative painting, and now it was all too easy. He was bored. So then he thought, 'What would happen if I broke this image down into little squares of its constituent parts and rearranged them into something else?'"

"Like an anagram," I said.

"It's a silly idea, but that's the sort of thing people do when they're bored. Cubism was his way of staving off boredom. Most new things start with boredom."

"The last time I was bored, I don't remember revolutionising modern art."

"Well, you're better looking than him," she said, causing me to blush.

"Americans were still painting cowboys at this point, and they weren't bored enough yet to do anything about it. Even when there were no cowboys left, they were still painting them because they had no history, nothing remotely like what we had in Europe. Just cowboys. What else were they going to paint?"

"I may actually be learning something here. You should probably stop."

"Then one day splatter-boy comes along."

"Pollock?" I asked.

"Him. He sees Picasso in a book and says, 'Where are the cowboys?' He's confused. Next time he goes back to his easel, he tells his cowboy model to take five because he's realised a great truth."

"What?" I asked.

"He's bored," she replied.

LaFlamme was never short of a theory and this one seemed credible, at least to me. I liked the idea that someone could be so sure of what they were doing when they got up in the morning, so confident of their abilities, that boredom could set in. When I get up, all I wonder is what fresh hell awaits. Every day is different and the only constants are general bewilderment and the uncertainty of paying rent. I never have the chance to get bored. I suppose that's why I'll never create anything resembling a masterpiece. That and having no talent.

The truth is I ended up in my line of work by default. I came out of art college with just enough ability to secure a temporary placement with an agency, a job that lasted two years. When it was over, I was too traumatised by the world of work to consider finding another, but I'd made enough contacts and gathered enough technical ability to eke out a living doing the same thing without being tied to one employer. I don't feel like I chose this job; I fell into it.

Some people say they stick with their line of work because it's the only thing they know how to do. It sounds candid and you might sympathise with the plight of someone who maybe doesn't have too many practical skills. But usually, you find out they could build an entire house from scratch with their bare hands if they wanted to and that there's nothing they don't know about carpentry, electrical wiring, plumbing, plastering, roofing and gardening. They're usually great cooks too, which just adds insult to injury.

I, on the other hand, definitely don't have a lot of practical skills. That doesn't stop me from having a go at whatever DIY task is necessary around the house, but anything I fix only stays fixed for a short time. I replaced a light switch once. Minutes later it fused and I had to call a plumber. I know plumbers don't normally fix light switches, but I'd burst a pipe above it.

We took the stairs down to the basement coffee shop, avoiding the actual coffee due to its prohibitively expensive and essentially crap nature, and stepped out into the gallery grounds. The garden at the back is a secluded stretch of well-maintained greenery enclosed by hedges and bordered with a fine collection of sculptures; Hepworth, Caro, Paolozzi, and I thought I spotted Henry Moore (he didn't see me).

Exiting through a gate at the foot of the green, we followed a path through a line of mature sycamore and oak that winds round to the more open and expansive front garden. The bulk of this area is landscaped with a striking environmental sculpture built around three twisting ponds and rising over several levels, its turfed spiral forms reminiscent of a series of relaxed apostrophes. Unusually for a work of art, visitors are permitted to walk on it, and this made me wish galleries were more open to the idea of public trampling of their exhibits. I'd love to be allowed to walk over Damien Hirst's work.

We followed the curve of the rising apostrophe until we stood at the sculpture's highest point and turned back to face the neoclassical building, constructed in the Greek Revival style popular in the early 19th century. Mounted to the top of a series of six Doric columns is a neon sculpture illuminating the words, 'EVERYTHING IS GOING TO BE ALRIGHT'. Even in broad daylight the piece is impressive.

"Do you think this guy got up one morning and said, 'I know exactly what I'm doing today. I'm going to build a big bastard neon sign'?"

"What, you think artists have all the answers?" she replied.

"It looks like he might know a thing or two."

"It's a bluff," she said. "Everything *is* going to be alright, but not because some artist said so."

"What do you mean?"

"Think about it like this. The straights have a certain way of dealing with the world. For them, there's an order to things and they have all kinds of constructs in place to reassure themselves of it. They have a set working week. They get holidays at fixed intervals. They get told that if they buy the right car, they'll be a success. And just in case that's not enough and they start to question any of it, they have God to tell them it's all okay."

"What does that have to do with neon?" I asked.

"Along come the artists and they don't have any of that stuff. That's why they get called 'tortured'. You'd be tortured too if you didn't know when the weekend was. But what they do have is the knowledge that neither they nor anyone else has any idea what's going on."

"That's good?"

"It's liberating," she replied. "The minute you admit you don't know what's going on is the minute you start out on the road to wisdom."

"I ought to be a sage by now," I said.

The bold forms of the spiral landscape twisted and unfurled beneath us. Children scrambled up the multiple levels of the landform and tumbled down the other side. The sound of the cool breeze through the great oaks lining the walkway was calming. I was with LaFlamme. I wished the moment would never end.

Sadly it did. Later I think the plan was for me to rustle up a bite to eat back at the flat, but we had no sooner arrived when my phone rang and LaFlamme picked it up. Normally I hated when she did this but as I'd been LaFlammed into serenity, I decided to allow it.

"Hello?" she said. "Yes, it is. Yes, we can do that. Yes. Yes, that's a speciality of ours. Well, that depends on the area. Yes, we can be there in half an hour. Okay." She hung up the phone.

"Who was that?" I asked.

"Wrong number," she replied, reaching for her jacket.

"That was an awfully detailed conversation for a wrong number."

"Well, *they* didn't know it was a wrong number. Come on," she said, wrenching me out of my chair.

"Just a minute," I said, my body often being a slave to inertia. "Do you mind telling me what this is about?"

LaFlamme sighed. "They asked if this was 'A1 Ornate Decorators' and I said yes. They asked if we did something called 'rag rolling' and I said yes. They asked about stencils and some other stuff I never heard of and I said that was a speciality. Now can we go? We have to give a demonstration."

"I don't know anything about rag rolling," I said, having my own little demonstration.

"Don't worry about that. I've got an idea."

LaFlamme whisked me downstairs and out towards a tiny vintage automobile, an Austin Mini with a convertible roof.

"Where did you get the car?" I asked.

"Borrowed it." The owner was most likely unaware of this loan agreement, but it would serve a purpose for now.

We clambered into the vehicle and immediately my height conspired against me. Not only was my head touching the soft top roof, it was forcing a me-shaped lump through it, stretching the canvas material upwards by several inches. Unfortunately, it was raining and bitterly cold so I'd have to put up with it.

Even LaFlamme's petite frame was a tight fit. With her back arched, she leaned so far forward in the seat that her chin was practically touching the steering wheel, her eyes barely clearing it. I suppose people were smaller in the 1960s.

LaFlamme's driving can best be described as experimental. Had my head not been so firmly wedged into the rooftop, the g-force as we set off would have propelled me hard into my seat. LaFlamme made every dangerous move possible and others that I firmly believed were not. By the time we reached our first stop, I considered my restricted view of the road a blessing.

She jumped out at the local library, leaving the car motor running. I wanted to explain the concept of parking to her, as did the line of cars behind us, but she was gone. Five minutes later, she reappeared carrying a large format coffee table book, *Advanced Decorating Techniques.*

69

"Here," she said, passing it my way and setting off again at a furious pace. "See if you can find out what rag rolling is."

"This was your great idea?" I said.

"Look," she replied. "We need money. Now. And not that theoretical money we sometimes get." When I stared at her quizzically, I received the following explanation at breakneck pace.

"You know, you work on something then send out a piece of paper with the word 'invoice' on it, the client ignores it for three months then sends you a piece of paper with the word 'cheque' on it, you take this piece of paper much more seriously than the first piece and go to the bank, the bank takes it seriously too, so serious they keep it for a week before they credit you, if they decide they don't like the piece of paper after all, they give it back."

"Right," I said. "Theoretical money."

"We need actual cash in hand and that's how decorators get paid. Without cash there's no booze tonight. Or food."

"Interesting that you put it in that order," I noted.

"Yes, interesting," she said with more than a hint of sarcasm. "Interesting like graphic design is 'interesting'. Do you know anything about rag rolling yet?"

"I know it's on page seventy-six," I said, finding it in the index.

"Good. Because we're nearly there."

"What?" I yelped.

"Relax," she replied. "You've got a couple of minutes."

I've crammed before, but nothing will ever compare to the sheer volume of decorating tips I forced through the funnel of my tiny mind in those couple of minutes, all the while being jettisoned across town with my head firmly ensconced in a canvas soft top.

LaFlamme pulled up at the salubrious address, which was in fact close to the gallery we had visited earlier, and this time she made concessions towards the notion of parking. Having pulled up only a couple of feet from the kerb, she hopped out and rummaged in the trunk of the car, finding an old duster.

"Here," she said. "Throw this across your shoulder, it'll make you look like you know what you're doing. Which will be a first."

I reluctantly left the book on the front seat and we sauntered up the drive as if we were two aesthetes who occasionally like the thrill of slumming it by getting their hands dirty.

"Don't we need paint?" I asked under my breath as we stood at the doorway.

"Of course not. You think decorators provide free paint?"

The door was opened by a tall, slightly-greying woman who immediately struck me as someone who had made a lot of the right life choices and now, for whatever reason, was choosing to have her walls defaced by an idiot with a duster.

"Oh, hello," said LaFlamme in refined tones that I was unfamiliar with. "This is Anthony, my assistant."

"Come in, come in," she said, leading us through the stylish Georgian townhouse into a spacious ballroom with a high ceiling and ornate cornice. The décor was the height of New Town elegance; a ridiculously opulent chandelier, red velvet drapes and a rococo-framed mirror above a marble fireplace.

"This is the room I was hoping to decorate. Would you be able to demonstrate your techniques here?" It took a supreme effort of will not to reply, "Seriously?" I wondered if she was one of those people whose life is so perfect they feel compelled to break something in it. Mercifully the room was sparsely furnished, which would limit the damage a man with paint and no idea what he's doing could inflict.

"The supplies are in the corner," she continued. LaFlamme threw me her best 'told you so' look as I hunched my shoulders and reluctantly headed towards my doom.

The walls were currently an off-white, like natural linen, but the paint colours she had chosen were deeper golden browns, variations on caramel. Had she chosen inoffensive pastels, a nice cream or magnolia, it would have a better chance of not looking like a dirty protest. I consoled myself with the fact there would be just three of us present to witness this interior design car crash; at least my humiliation would be confined.

At this point, a husband, several small children and an elderly couple appeared, and this was also the point I realised my life could not be any more ridiculous. Here I was, nearly thirty, with nothing to show for my life, scraping a living by bluffing well-to-do types out of their cash. If anyone ever had high hopes for me, they would be disappointed to see them being crushed on the rocks of my total hopelessness.

"Raymond," said the woman, "you're just in time."

"Would you like to get started, Anthony?" said LaFlamme helpfully – it was clear she would be directing from the sidelines.

I had two choices. Either I could begin sobbing uncontrollably and confess that my life was a sham, or I could take a leaf out of the LaFlamme playbook and pretend I was the greatest decorator who ever lived and that they were extremely fortunate to be granted even five minutes of my valuable time.

"The beauty of the rag rolling technique," I began, unbuttoning my sleeves and preparing to dazzle, "is that it will disguise any imperfections in the wall surface." I cast a critical eye over the state of their walls. "You could certainly benefit from it."

I poured some 'Cocoa Pecan' emulsion into a tray and took the duster from my shoulder, treating it as if it were a valuable tool by laying it down gently on the protective linen floor covering and folding it into a triangle.

"Typically, a lighter shade is used for the base colour. What you have here is not ideal but it will do for demonstration purposes." This was a classic LaFlamme move – prepare the way for any disaster by blaming the client in advance for not providing the right conditions to begin with.

I doused the rag in paint, squeezed it out into the tray, then twisted it into a length before rolling it onto the wall in what *Advanced Decorating Techniques* assured me would be a pleasing ripple effect.

"Like many advanced techniques," I said, quoting liberally from the book as I defaced their wall, "this is something best left to a professional."

"Ooh, I see," said the woman.

"Very stylish," said the husband.

"He really is quite the artiste," said LaFlamme.

I was too scared to step back and judge the results of my efforts, thinking it was best to concentrate on the application.

"The next stage, of course, would be to allow this initial layer to dry before applying a secondary colour."

My bluff appeared to be working, but bluffing has a way of increasing the heart rate to dangerous levels. This, combined with irregular breathing due to intense concentration, meant that after a few minutes in the hot seat I was in danger of passing out.

"What about stencilling?" asked the woman.

"I'm glad you ask," I said, falling to my knees through lack of oxygen. "I'll need scissors and card." One of the children was sent out to retrieve the items and I continued my masterclass.

"Stencilling is a very effective technique, *in the right hands*," I emphasised. "Done well, it can breathe life into border areas or bring out high ceilings."

I was presented with scissors and a sheet of heavy construction paper. "This would not be my ideal choice of paper, but again it will suffice in the circumstances."

I cut three horizontal rectangles followed by three vertical rectangles, reproducing the building blocks of Spore's logo, then presented it to the wall and took a brush loaded with 'Tuscan Tile' across the card. Shifting the template several inches further right, I applied the technique twice more.

"I like that," said the older woman.

"It reminds me of something," said the husband.

"I imagine you've seen it in a friend's house somewhere," I replied.

As I continued applying the stencil, now with a confidence that was quite unwarranted, LaFlamme took the hostess aside to discuss details of a full quote. She knew exactly what she was doing in situations like this and, by the time we were ready to leave, had charmed the entire household into believing we were a leading design duo courted by Salma Hayek, Britney Spears and Victoria Beckham.

"You were brilliant," she said as we clambered back into the car.

"It was an unholy mess," I said. "Why did they seem so pleased?"

"Rich people like mess. They think it makes them bohemian. Look what everyone else has on their walls. Crisp sharp lines, solid blocks of colour, everything tidy. You won't see any rag rolling there. Know why?"

"I guess they don't have Britney's cash."

"It reminds them of mess. That's the last thing they want because anything messy has to be cleaned up by their own fair hands. Rich people don't have that problem. Something messy in their house, somebody else cleans it up. Not their problem. In fact, they probably like it because it reminds them they're wealthy and can afford staff. Think about it. When have you ever seen rag rolling in the house of someone who wasn't filthy rich?"

LaFlamme may have been onto something here because I think the last time I saw decorative painting was on Spore's walls. (I didn't recognise it as rag rolling at that point, I just thought the paint was melting in the heat.)

"Here's another thing," she continued. "Look what the rich hang on their walls. Big splashy abstracts. Total mess. Won't see that stuff hanging in a pleb house. Know why?"

"I really can't imagine what the plebs' problem with modern art is."

"Because it looks like something else they have to clean up. Anyway, you're missing the whole point of this exercise."

"You'll have to remind me of that. All the blood drained from my head some time ago." LaFlamme pulled a handful of notes from her jacket pocket and waved them in my direction.

"They gave you money for what I did to their ballroom?"

"Yep."

"But it was only a demonstration."

"An advance," said LaFlamme. "Tomorrow, we eat. Tonight, we drink."

I had to hand it to LaFlamme. She would never go hungry.

9.
A SINKING FEELING

"I have your box of earth downstairs," said the delivery driver.

"Why would I want a box of earth?" I asked him.

"Shipment from New Orleans," he said. "Can you give me a hand?"

It wasn't that the crate was heavy (Godalming was wafer thin), but I really didn't see why I should have to carry him up three flights of stairs. Next time I'd tell him to take the bus and climb them himself.

We dropped the wooden case unceremoniously in the kitchen and I signed for it, the return address stating 'Wiggly Wrigglers Worm Farm' – Godalming really knew how to travel. There was a ticking sound coming from within, which could only be a clock, as it couldn't possibly be a heartbeat.

Being familiar with his nocturnal routine, I knew it would be a number of hours before Godalming woke up, and it occurred to me that this could explain why I'd been singled out as a 'preferred supplier' – I'm sympathetic to the idea of sleeping during the day.

By the time he was set to rise, I was dozing at my desk in the kitchen watching the old black and white TV (actually a colour TV that was petulant about the current state of broadcasting and refused to display anything made in colour. This suited me fine as I often refuse to watch anything made after 1970 anyway). At this time of night, I usually look

75

for a Universal horror from the '30s and tonight I found *Mark of the Vampire* with Bela Lugosi.

I had just reached a point in the proceedings when the frightfully English non-vampire cast members were discussing the problems they were having with awfully large bats, when I heard a ringing from within the box of earth. Extensive shuffling followed, and then the ring intensified as the lid flew open and Godalming, wearing a nightcap and clutching an alarm clock, sat bolt upright. It was a few seconds before he came to his senses, by which time I too was wide awake.

"Could you switch that off please?" I said. He complied, and seeing that the room was filled with a monochromatic glow and that he had reached a safe haven, he burst into song.

"*Night time, is the right time, it's alright time, yes it's the right time for me!*" He yawned extensively.

"Would you like a tomato juice?" I asked him.

"No time, Mr Boaks." He stepped out of the crate and removed his nightcap. "I have many appointments this evening."

I turned my head to the window, where I heard tapping. To my horror, the grinning Texan Stanthorpe was clinging to the drainpipe, peering in. He waved enthusiastically.

"Come in, Stanthorpe," said Godalming, opening the window and allowing Stanthorpe's six-foot frame to clamber in.

"How long have you been there?" I asked.

"Coupla hours," he said cheerily, if a little out of breath.

"We're on the third floor," I said, more out of wonder than anything else.

"I wun't in no hurry," he replied.

"Stanthorpe and I have many duties to attend to," Godalming explained, "including the procurement of new underground offices. You see Mr Boaks, amongst the many reasons you were selected for this assignment was locality."

"I'm only five thousand miles from New Orleans?"

"You are situated by a canal with a little-known labyrinth of inter-connected chambers below – a network of disused mines, in fact. These subterranean borings will both help to avoid scrutiny by the authorities and prohibit entry to the general public – ideal for a bank." His financial instincts were as sharp as ever.

They prepared to be on their way, Stanthorpe assisting him in donning a black bowtie and velvet cape. I opened the window in anticipation of a winged exit but Godalming eyed me quizzically.

"Presumably you still have stairs?" he said.

"Of course," I said, closing the window.

"Come Stanthorpe," he said to the wild-eyed one. "The night is young and so are we."

"You bet," replied Stanthorpe.

"Don't stay out too late," I called after them.

I trusted it had been a successful night for Godalming because by the time I awoke the following morning, his crate was securely fastened and there was a trail of bank notes leading up to it. I – ahem – tidied these away as I didn't think Godalming would miss them. He was probably clutching a sack full close to his chest.

When the post arrived, I was surprised to find a letter marked 'Pentonville State Prison'. I couldn't recall knowing anyone residing in a correctional facility but thought it might be for Sir Frank, who was bound to know quite a few. In fact, it was the letter I'd been promised from fraudster supreme Brendan 'Matty' Matlock.

Good day Mr Boaks,

I am Brendan Matlock (Mr), chief accountant representing the Bear Stearns Organisation. Not that Bear Stearns, the other one. I trust you are well.

After trawling through our records department, I discovered an account opened in 1998 by the late Alexander Rollington, a German national and banker at the Kreuzberg Gold Company. The account, which contains USD $86 billion, has remained inactive since his untimely death in a curling tong incident in 2005. As Mr Rollington had no named beneficiary, it falls to me to distribute this fund however I see fit. (Don't ask why, it's technical.)

Unless you have any objection, I have stipulated that you become the initial recipient – the reason being that the transfer requires an account held by a genuine foreigner and you are the only person I can find who fits this description.

Once the transfer process is initiated, I will be sprung from my current lodgings and can join you in your country, whence we can partition the sum accordingly. Please send me the details of your nominated bank account with haste and I will proceed.

Perhaps at this point you could consider how you might like to put your good fortune to use. A new bicycle perhaps, or train set. Roller skates are nice. Maybe a fish pole.

I strongly believe that our association will derive a huge mutual success thereafter and count on your confidentiality in the matter, as it may be considered in poor taste should it be known that we plan to squander old Rolly's cash.
Yours truly,
Matty X

Godalming had assured me this letter would begin the second stage of his business proposal but it was difficult to see how Brendan 'Matty' Matlock cleaning out my bank account in a blatant Nigerian-style spam fraud would be in my interest. Had Matlock really sunk this low? He should never have tampered with his epic Ponzi arrangement which, in its brazen simplicity, had proved so successful. Until he was rumbled.

I mean, a fraudster with such an impeccable track record would surely know his mark and target someone who owned something – not a graphic designer. But what if this offer was genuine, and just a benefit of my association with Godalming?

Unusually, given his circumstances, there was an email address included. This was convenient in that a dialogue by post could take time – not only because Matlock's letters took five to seven working days to arrive, but because it would take me forever to find a stamp.

Knowing I had already cleaned out my bank account and had nothing to lose, I sat down to compose a reply.

Dear Mr Matlock,
Many thanks for your invitation to assist in the squandering of a

dead stranger's wealth. Please consider me a willing dupe for this latest inspired wheeze.

Thanks also for the suggestions as to how best to fritter away this ill-gotten loot. As I already have a train set and am about to turn thirty, I shall be spending the money on strong liquor. I feel this has served me well in the past and given me strength in times of need.

I'm sure this venture will lead to us being able to spend a great deal of time together in Pentonville State. I look forward to your arrival in my country, where perhaps we could go fish poling together. Bank account details below.
Yours,
Boaks, Tony

After just a few minutes I received this succinct reply.

Tony,
Many thanks for this. The money should be in your account shortly. Please don't spend it until I arrive, in approximately five to seven working days.
Kisses,
Matty x

It was certainly the easiest $86 billion I'd ever made.

Concerned about the low light levels at this time of year, and eager to avoid scurvy, I took the radical step of going out during daylight hours. On opening the stair door which led into the street, I was greeted by a random assortment of cast-off furniture. This, for some reason, is a regular occurrence here. Tables, chairs, sofas, whatever you can think of, I guarantee it's been left here at some point.

I'm not sure why anyone would leave a sofa in the street. It's not like it would just go in the back of the truck with the regular trash. But it doesn't matter, because long before any special uplift arrangement can take place, somebody else always comes along and carts it off. It's a very efficient system – leave your garbage outside my door and watch it disappear in an hour. There's really no need for a cleansing department.

Today there was a pristine office swivel chair in royal blue, the type with levers to control the seat height and angle of the back support. I could really use one of these as I am generally parked in an uncomfortably-upholstered wooden dining chair, bent double over the desk. I never work hard enough to get repetitive strain injury, but if I did, I think one of these slick little numbers might help.

I tried it out, there in the street, swivelling around, adjusting the levers and propelling myself back and forwards on its wheels. It appeared to function perfectly, and with all these features it was difficult to see how you would get any work done. Maybe that's why its previous owner abandoned it – too distracting.

I thought it would make an excellent addition to my growing collection of cast-off furniture and carried it upstairs, thereby proving my own theory that all it takes to get people to recycle is to leave your stuff outside my flat.

By the time Godalming and Stanthorpe had risen and scaled respectively, ready to resume their duties, the chair was in place, giving the room a new professionalism only let down by my presence. I was trying to watch *The Wolfman* with Lon Chaney Jr (I only ever watch it for the bit where he changes into a werewolf, as the rest of the story seems implausible), but it was hard to follow the story with the sound of bozos in the background.

"Take a letter, Stanthorpe," Godalming had begun. The Texan took a seat in the new chair and prepared to type at the mini laptop.

"Don't you have offices now?" I asked. It wasn't that I minded them working in my kitchen, but I thought a third-party business might conflict with the terms of my household insurance policy, had I ever bothered to get one.

"Indeed," said Godalming. "However, they are in a state of unreadiness at this precise point."

"They're gettin' painted," said Stanthorpe, his excitement at the prospect clearly visible. "Blue!"

"Brendan, comma," continued Godalming, as Stanthorpe did his best with one finger typing. Unfortunately the office chair, which had coped just fine during my lightweight street trial, was coping rather less well under Stanthorpe's more robust frame, and was sinking slightly lower to the ground with each hammering of a key. He continued undaunted; either he didn't notice, or didn't mind.

"We have received the necessary papers and will now proceed with phase two of the operation, full stop. Arrangements are in place with your captors for your imminent release. I suggest you pack a woolly jumper or two, as the climate here may be a little inclement for your rich blood. The food, too, is a trifle bizarre, so I hope you like trifle.

"Mr Boaks has been extremely co-operative, malleable even, and I think you will agree has been an excellent choice of patsy. I should mention that The Order are very pleased with the latest developments and that at the next gathering I shall be making a full presentation. Possibly even Powerpoint."

By this time the chair had sunk to its lowest position, about eight inches from the floor, but Stanthorpe soldiered on regardless, his arms raised above shoulder level and his neck stretched so he could see above the table top. Now I knew why it had been discarded.

"In conclusion," said Godalming, "we look forward to scheming and conniving with you soon. Till then, yours, Frankie. Sign and print."

"Gotcha," said Stanthorpe.

I suppose I should have felt slighted by some of these comments, but the truth is I've long since given up caring. I'm used to clients taking appalling liberties, making no effort to disguise their contempt and generally hanging around my kitchen annoying me. This was nothing new.

After the boys finished their cocoa, once again Stanthorpe helped Godalming with his bowtie and cape, and the duo prepared to leave.

"Can you bring in some milk?" I asked. "We're running low."

"What flavour do you want?" said Stanthorpe.

10.
UPPER MISMANAGEMENT

I had a restless night. Sleep didn't come easily, even though I'd been reading Dan Brown. When I did manage to nod off, I dreamt feverishly, one half-formed scenario segueing into another without any apparent purpose or flow. A bit like this journal.

I don't remember much, but at one point I dreamt there was a plot of land at the back of my house which opened out onto woods leading down to a stream. The sunlight filtered through the trees creating speckled patterns like leopard skin. I made my way through the dense greenery. There was a deep sense of mystery but I was also aware of the tremendous beauty of the scene.

Out of the lush vegetation came a threatening presence. Some of the speckled patterns rose out of the undergrowth and were followed by the crisp sound of twigs underfoot. I realised I was surrounded by wild animals; hyenas, jackals, wolves, foxes. Probably my imagination wasn't sharp enough to conjure up any one beast and shifted between a bunch of them.

I saw what appeared to be a clearing in the woods and ran for it as fast as I could. The animals pursued and as the clearing led to more and more dense growth, for a brief moment I thought I was going to be savaged. Then I realised I wasn't being pursued; I was running with a pack. The fear was replaced by a tremendous sense of exhilaration as I broke deeper into the forest, bruised, scratched and perspiring heavily.

Eventually I became aware that the pack had splintered off. My pace slackened and I was left with a lone fox at my side. This beautiful feral creature was following a scent and pursuing it intently, first on all fours, then, rising onto its hind legs, it gripped my hand and led the way with determination. Walking upright, the fox only came up to my waist, but it was strong enough to drag me by its paw towards a light in the distance.

The end of the woods opened out onto a scene that was familiar to me, not from any place I know in reality but familiar in my dream, a piece of land that had been cleared in order to build a house. The foundations were in place, the concrete floor was levelled and the timber framework surround was in the early stages of assembly.

Having led me here, the fox returned to all fours and looked up at me, panting. I felt immensely grateful and thanked it, then the creature left.

"Been having funny dreams," I said, when LaFlamme called first thing – she said she was awake and didn't see why I shouldn't be.

"Talk about funny," she said in her finest psychoanalytical manner.

"Well, I don't know. People tell you their dreams and they're always kind of stupid and pointless."

"I'm sure yours will be too," she replied. "Probably more than most."

I hesitated to discuss the details of my fervent dream life in case LaFlamme's resulting theories showed me to be thoroughly twisted. But let's face it, she already knew.

"That doesn't sound so bad," she said. "In Japanese folklore, foxes are mystical creatures. As they get older, they grow in power until they can shapeshift and even possess people. If you were being led by a fox you were being led by someone who knows what they're doing. I'd say it was a good omen."

This was encouraging but then I remembered that these days I was a busy and important man of business and didn't have time for frivolity. We arranged to meet later, by which time no doubt I would have accomplished all manner of things.

I had no sooner hung up when The Admiral called, wondering if I was ready to push the button on splitting the internet. This was surprising – both that he appeared to be close to achieving his goal, and that he was asking me what to do. The latter meant either a) he had decided taking instruction from a graphic designer was wise, or b) that he foresaw implications in the current task should it succeed.

With hindsight, it was clearly b), but at the time I was enjoying the idea of being somebody's boss.

"I guess you could take some time off if you want."

"Thank you," he said dubiously. "And I would, had I not several other pressing tasks lined up."

"Then shouldn't you be getting back to work?"

"It's just the question of what might happen should anything go wrong."

"What do you mean?"

"Splitting the internet may result in overspill. Say for example there is leakage from one sector to another. That could mean trouble. What if a page begins life as a blog but then strays into thoroughly useful territory?"

"Then I suppose someone would have to police it."

"They can't even police one internet, let alone several. Unless you live in China."

"We could move," I said hopefully.

"What I'm getting at here," said The Admiral, "is that it may be the start of unpleasantness. The process of breaking and disseminating could result in hundreds, then thousands, then potentially billions of internets."

"We could be overtaken by drivel?"

"A proper tsunami."

"Couldn't we just press 'undo'?"

"By that time, it would be too late. There's no putting the genie back in the bottle after he's bolted the stable door."

"If you're saying we can't do it, then maybe we should quit while we're ahead."

"I didn't say we couldn't do it, just that there may be repercussions."

"Leave your drums out of this," I said. "Stick to computers."

I was clearly ready for upper management. But then I remembered there was still grunt work to do.

After several hours and several minor hallucinations, I thought I'd made a breakthrough with the Spore rebrand. But it turned out I was just looking at it upside down. Between the concentration-induced altered states and my talent for sloth, I couldn't seem to get beyond tinkering at the logo's edges.

Just as I was considering calling Spore to tell him of my difficulties (not something clients generally like to hear), my phone buzzed into life and a chill came over me.

"Boaks."

"I have good news, Mr Spore." I was trying to think quickly, as any good manager would, putting my concern in such a way that would assure him his money is being well spent. Managing his expectations, so to speak. You know, stalling him.

"Call me Pian," he said, pronouncing it 'Pie-ann' with the emphasis on 'pie'. "I'm rebranding myself as Pian Spore, or 'PS' for short."

"But I'm working with 'AS'."

"It's one stroke less. I'm cutting down your workload!"

"Why Pian?"

"Well, Pignacious seems excessive. Besides, have you read *Life of Pi*?"

"Of course."

"Alas, I have not. But I plan to."

"Well, if you start now, it will fill the few weeks it's going to take me to finish."

I followed this up with some hollow reassurance about it all going swimmingly, and the admonition that genius mustn't be rushed. Then I suggested thinking about an overall brand relaunch.

"Canapés and grenadine! I was thinking of the Royal Yacht Brittania. Did you know I once took tea with Princess Anne? Marvellous woman. Still a bit horsey."

I did not know. And I did not care. I wondered why Spore didn't show an interest in seeing any work in progress. In fact, I got the feeling that any new design would do, as long as it wasn't his.

What do I care. Relaunching an individual would be a novelty. And as silly as it sounded, I had to admit it wasn't any sillier than most of the other rebrands I'd seen over the years. I still haven't forgiven them for 'Snickers'.

At this point I noticed a stack of promotional flyers had been dumped through my letterbox, a clear sign that there was an election looming, and I was hugely irritated but only mildly surprised to see the 'AS' logo on many of them. The greatest mystery of all time was beginning to bore the pants off me.

This time the logo was embellished with a tagline, a different variation on each. 'Firmly committed to the principles of AS,' said one. 'Guilt-free selfishness for all,' said another. 'Self-serving since 1980,' said a third. This suggested that the AS was some kind of self-preservation society, and it therefore wasn't a huge shock to find that a lot of politicians were members.

I'll be honest, I have no interest in politics, especially local politics, which seems to be the exclusive preserve of lawyers. I don't want a lawyer telling me what to do unless I'm in prison.

I studied the leaflet of one such shyster, Charles Monteith: 'A firm believer in free market principles and in favour of light touch regulation of the banking system. Pro-life and a committed Christian. Tough on immigration and crime. Small state.' He was standing for the Labour Party. Politics has really changed.

Then the doorbell of doom rang, which was the final nail in the coffin of my upper management fantasy. I'd already taken several phone calls. I don't think making decisions and dealing with people is for me.

"Collection from Boaks," said the courier, the same one who had delivered Godalming.

"Collection?" I said. "You're picking something up?"

"That's right." He made a beeline for Godalming's crate which, being midday, was sealed shut. "Can you give me a hand?"

"Not again," I said, realising that I was still serving the bankers even as they slept.

At least tonight I could watch TV in peace.

11.
MOST LIKE A STOOGE

Other artists might see a blank canvas as a challenge, a platform on which to flex their muscles. But I need a design to be halfway there before I can get creative. Three quarters, even. Hell, if it was nearly finished, I wouldn't be needed at all and that would suit me best. Cut out the middle man.

Experience had taught me that a rough design, even if it was terrible, could be reworked into something slightly less terrible, then something mediocre, and finally something that scraped acceptable. What I needed was someone who could work up designs to that halfway stage then allow me to step in, be fleetingly brilliant and take all the credit. But where would I find such a person?

I considered a blindfold and even hypnosis to convince myself that I was a gifted but junior designer who loved the initial excitement of the artistic process and simply lost interest after the first burst of creativity. But that was never going to work. Nobody wants to be a junior.

I gazed out the kitchen window and let me mind start to wander. But it was never going to wander far because Stanthorpe's grinning face suddenly came into focus. He nodded enthusiastically and mouthed the words 'It's me!' as he clung to the drainpipe. I groaned.

"Can't you just use the stairs, Stanthorpe?" I asked, opening the window.

"Aw, I'm sorry, Mr Boaks. I couldn't find 'em."

"You walked down them the other night with Frank," I said.

"I could find 'em to walk down, but not to walk up." He was an idiot. But not without charm. And come to think of it, he might make an enthusiastic junior.

"Allen," I said. "Do you like finger painting?"

"Do I!" he replied, with an energy that seemed to radiate through his entire body.

This was a long shot. A long, long shot. But a few basic designs in a primitive style might give me a halfway point for a Bob Dylan-type painting on Lyttleton's album cover. Maybe not even as bad as that. There was no point sticking him in front of Photoshop, he was likely to get hurt.

I looked out my Dennis the Menace apron (a birthday gift from The Admiral), a set of poster paints and some sheets of A1 paper – I hoped pages this big might contain some of the mess. Not that I cared about mess. If he came up with anything I could use as a starting point, it would be worth it.

The effort required to find a new and interesting way of avoiding work had left me exhausted. Sometimes my diversion ploys are almost as tiring as work itself. I hit the sofa for a nap and left Stanthorpe to it.

Later I discovered that there is mess and there is mess. I expected a certain level of disarray, but nothing could have prepared me for the visual cacophony that had now overtaken my kitchen. Paint was everywhere; on the walls, the window, in the sink. Had I been able to afford a carpet it would have been ruined.

Stanthorpe was utterly absorbed in his work and had created what appeared to be a dozen or so mini-masterpieces of naive art in the hour I had slept – even Picasso wasn't that good. He was kneeling on the floor with the legs of his suit trousers rolled up to his knees, his back towards me.

"Not bad, Allen," I said. "Not bad at all." It was only when he turned around that the full extent of his body art became apparent. Paint coloured his hair, his face, the front of his clothes, as if he'd slipped and fallen onto one of his creations, which he did again now, this time backwards. The apron had been discarded (he said he didn't want Dennis the Menace to get dirty), and his tie must have been dangling in a pot of paint as it was now a solid, crusty green.

"I done run out of paint," he said, standing up.

"That's probably a good thing," I replied.

Stanthorpe's paintings were colourful, energetic and expressive, with a sense of freedom and experimentation that was oddly pleasing to the eye. They were reminiscent of the French painter Jean Dubuffet, and that's just what I was looking for – rough-hewn designs that, with a bit of tweaking and typography, would make a fine cover, in a Dylanesque, crap kind of way.

Sensing they may not be abstract, with some trepidation I asked what the paintings were about.

"This is Mr Frank when he first met Mr Matty," he said in his childish way.

"Very nice," I said. "Is that green hills in the background?"

"That's a big heap of money!"

"I see. What about this one?"

"That's Mr Frank and Mr Matty at the beach!"

"Aha." There was a large, round multicoloured object in the foreground. "Is that a beachball they're playing with?"

"No, silly," he said. "That's me!" Only then did I notice the moustache.

Another image showed the green hills parted in the middle, creating a valley, with the two figures at opposite sides. When Stanthorpe turned his attention to this one, his demeanour changed.

"This is what it might be like if Mr Frank and Mr Matty go their own ways," he said solemnly.

"Why would they go their own ways?" I asked.

"Creative differences."

It was interesting to imagine that one day these two rapacious profit mongers might fail to see eye to eye with one another's methods of unscrupulous plunder. Stanthorpe was showing all the signs of a true naïf – a certain sensitivity, an exceptional aptitude in one particular field, and otherwise comprehensive idiocy.

"How would you like to see this one on a record sleeve, Allen?" I asked him. He began to hyperventilate.

"Gee Mr Tony, I don't know what to say! Y'all been so good to me, lettin' me paint your house, then makin' a record from it!"

"If you come back next week, I'll get some emulsion and you can paint the whole flat."

"Gosh!"

"You better run on home now though," I said. "Sir Frank will probably have your spaghetti hoops ready."

"My favourite!" he replied, putting his suit jacket on over his well-daubed shirt.

"Shoot, I clean forgot!" He slapped his forehead, adding another layer to the facial paint cake. "Mr Frank wants to see you in his new office."

"Tell Frank he'll have to come and carry me down the stairs first."

"Uh, ok," he said, heading out the door.

"Allen," I called after him.

"Uhuh?"

"Best roll your trouser legs down."

Now that I had a starting point for Lyttleton's artwork, the other elements would hopefully fall into place. But the album title still hadn't been decided. Lyttleton said Campbell Glen quite liked my *Mock Lobster* suggestion, but explained that there was a notable lack of seafood references in his material. I picked up the phone.

"George," I said. "Is this a bad time?"

"Yes," he replied.

"Good. What are we calling this masterpiece?"

"I was thinking *Bridge Over Troubled Water*."

"Are you sure?"

"Anything wrong with that?"

"It's not very original."

"It was good enough for Paul Simon."

"Maybe you could come up with a title that says something about the artist."

"Okay." He thought for a moment. "Let's call it *The Best of Campbell Glen*."

"Isn't this only his second album?"

"It's still his best stuff. What are you, a critic now?"

"Why don't you name it after one of the songs?" I glanced over the track listing. "How about 'Midnight of the Mole People'?"

"Is that original?" he asked.

"I can pretty much guarantee there is no other album called that."

"Then we have a winner."

There was only one problem with 'Midnight of the Mole People'. Scanning Stanthorpe's delightfully bright images, I began to wish Glen had written more songs with titles like, 'The Moles go to the Beach on a Sunny Day', or 'The Moles Drive to the Country in Bright Daylight', as moles are not known for their eyesight, and the fact that it was midnight suggested it was dark even for them.

But then I had an idea, my second this year. Taking one of the beach scenes, I inverted it, like a negative, in Photoshop, and immediately the pale blue of the sky became a deep gold and the dark orange of the sun became a light turquoise moon. The little figures could easily pass for mole people, at least to moles, and with the title slapped across the top, Lyttleton would have his cover.

Turning my attention to the inside sleeve, I remembered Lyttleton had written something for inclusion. Now I might have to read it. It was a typically vain idea for the manager to write an introductory blurb, but at least it would save me having to design much.

I used to play guitar. Seriously. I was the only guy around who could play 'Bridge Over Troubled Water' using just two chords. I bowled them over, for sure. People said I should 'desist', but I was never that keen on protest songs.

When I began managing bands in the 1970s, it was a rich period in pop music history. Managers could have their pick of any number of great groups back then. There was 10cc, Roxy Music, Cockney Rebel, Thin Lizzy. If only I'd picked one of them and not the turkeys I ended up with, I might not be here working with Tony Boaks.

But it's all water under the bridge – troubled water, which brings me to Campbell Glen. I think this kid could be my salvation. And for those of you who read the papers and think you see a pattern emerging in my life – the making of a small fortune followed by

allegations of tax avoision (look it up), bankruptcy, ignominy and
a non-voluntary stay at a correctional facility – let me say this. I
only need Campbell Glen for the first bit. I can do the rest myself

I may not understand his music, but when has that ever both-
ered managers in the past? I know a good thing when I see one, like
the first time I saw Dire Straits. Unfortunately, it was at Wembley
Arena so I was too late to sign them.

And it's not that I don't like Campbell Glen's sound, even though
everybody knows music's gone downhill since the invention of stereo.
I mean, one speaker was good enough for Phil Spector and if it
wasn't broke, why fix it? Spector may have been a major twonk,
but if Erasure had traded their four cloth ears for just one of his
they might have come up with a decent record.

That aside, I think you'll agree that Campbell Glen could do
wonders for my bank balance and help to erase some of the terrible
things that have been said about me in the press. Who knows, he
could even be the next Paul Simon.
– George Lyttleton, Band Manager

I was glad I finally found the courage to read it, but was even gladder
when I reached the end.

Okay, what does that leave? Credits. Copyright. Fine print. Record
label info. I rummaged through Lyttleton's notes and found a handwritten
post-it stuck to one typewritten page. It read: 'Tony, call me when you
get to the record label stuff'.

My heart sank. I'd have to speak to him again.

"George," I said. "Is this a bad time?"

"No."

"Okay, I'll call you later."

An hour later I called back.

"George," I said. "Is this a bad time?"

"Generally? Or just to speak on the phone?"

"You decide."

"Well, I have an enlarged prostate."

"Excellent. Now, what do I need to know about this record label?"

"Ah, yes." But I already knew what he was going to say.

"Before you go any further," I said. "Just tell me… is it a two-letter name?"

"Yes."

"No problem. Your secret's safe with me."

"You're one of us?"

"That's right," I bluffed.

"Did you get the letter?"

"Of course."

Try as I might, I couldn't think of another way of getting more information from him without actually saying, 'It's a secret fraternity with codes of honour and bizarre rituals, isn't it?'

LaFlamme appeared in the middle of *Devil Doll*, which couldn't have been more apt. I was sitting in the dark with only the black and white glow of the TV bouncing off the walls. I wasn't trying to save electricity; I just couldn't face getting up to switch the light on.

"Wakey wakey," she said, clapping her hands loudly. "Everybody up."

"I'm awake," I replied. "Sort of." She stomped across the room.

"Did I miss the air raid siren? I demand to be seen and admired." This finally prompted me to throw some light on the situation, something that wasn't generally expected of me. No wonder it seemed dark to LaFlamme. She was still wearing shades.

"I'm going to need an assistant," she said, sitting on the desk. "Who do you know?"

"Like a PA?" I asked. "Or a secretary?"

"Which one's most like a stooge?"

"I don't know. Both seem quite glamorous to a graphic designer."

"I won't beat them or anything."

"Good," I said, "because I don't think employers generally beat their assistants anymore."

LaFlamme was certainly a stranger to employer/employee relations. The fact is, both of us are pretty much unemployable in the conventional sense, due to our shared lack of any conventional sense. Neither of us ever had the luxury of a minion, with the exception of my recent session with Stanthorpe, who I might have mentioned to her were I not concerned about having to share a flunkey at such an early stage in my power trip. She could find her own.

"Let me think about it," I said. Clearly LaFlamme's new career as a self-help guru was taking shape.

I began rummaging through the flyers on the desk and picked out one with the 'AS' insignia at the base. (I wasn't deliberately retaining it; it was just beyond throwing range of the wastepaper basket.)

"What do you make of this?" I said.

"Interesting," she replied.

"Is it?"

"Not really." She folded it into a paper aeroplane and projected it to the other side of the room, where it bounced off a corner and landed snugly in the wastepaper basket.

"I have something for you too," she said, reaching into a gold lamé polka dot purse and unfolding another A4 page. It was Spore's last Twitter posts, which I'd almost forgotten about since my last attempt at reworking his logo ended in impotent rage.

'Hooey! Trusty roundhead.' Solution: 'Does your head hurt Tony?'
'A warm, nauseating hooky.' Solution: 'I know you hate anagrams.'

"I can't believe he's doing this," I said. "Why would he go to such lengths just to torment me?"

"That's the face of addiction," said LaFlamme.

I took out my phone.

"Let me see if there are more."

"Look," she sighed. "I'm not sure I'm enough of a dweeb for you."

"What?"

"I know you kind of like doing anagrams together, and that's sweet."

"I'm not doing this because I like it," I insisted.

"Exactly," LaFlamme replied. "That's how it works. You don't think The Anagrammatics like doing anagrams, do you?"

"What do you mean?"

"Alcoholics don't like the taste of alcohol. The Anagrammatics are hopeless addicts. And anagrams are just the start. A few here, a few there, then they need more. It's the law of diminishing returns."

"So they turn to..."

"Crosswords."

"Is that so bad?"

"Are you kidding? Once somebody turns to crosswords, there's no turning back without an intervention."

"I just thought crosswords were TV for brainiacs."

"You don't know the full horror. Soon they need a crossword every day just to make it through. And that's when they hit the hard stuff."

"Rubik's Cube?"

"Sudoku. Then you've lost them. They'll have to join Mensa just to get a taste of what they need. But by then it's not enough. It's never enough."

"Well, you needn't worry," I assured her. "I won't be joining Mensa anytime soon."

12.
THE VAULTS

The courier arrived with Stanthorpe at his side. "Delivery for Boaks," he said. "Sign here."

"What am I signing for?" I asked.

"The big fella," he replied. Stanthorpe had a postal sticker on his forehead.

"He sent you recorded delivery?"

"I guess so," said Stanthorpe. "Otherwise, I woon't be here!"

"The window would have been easier."

"Why would Mr Frank send over a window? You already got one!" The courier looked confused but took his signature and left.

"What can I do for you, Allen?" I asked.

"Mr Frank wants to see you, so he sent me to collect." He picked me up and slung me across his shoulders in a fireman's lift.

"This really isn't necessary," I complained, knowing that resistance would be pointless.

"Mr Frank's orders," he replied.

"I'm actually quite used to walking down these stairs myself," I said to the base of his spine.

Exiting the communal stairway into the street, Stanthorpe carted me a hundred yards over the bridge that crossed the canal, unburdened by my weight. We descended the concrete staircase that led to the underside of the bridge, then Stanthorpe forcefully opened the solid wooden door to the vaults below.

Through a series of narrow passageways and damp musty chambers, dimly lit with crude mineshaft fixtures that revealed rough stonework and low ceilings, we gravitated towards the rich majestic tones of a pipe organ, which became increasingly thunderous and alarming as we progressed. The alarming part was that I recognised the music, Bach's 'Toccata and Fugue', a suitable choice for a deranged underground banking operation.

It was only when we reached a vast hall, meticulously carved into the bedrock with high-arched ceilings supported by ornate pillars, that Stanthorpe finally set me down. I had to give it to Godalming – if he was trying to locate a suitable meeting place for the clandestine gatherings of a society with nefarious intent, he had struck gold.

Now he was seated at an impressive pipe organ, the type seen in grand cathedrals and other religious settings, his cape flowing behind him as he moved from Bach to a medley of Elvis Presley songs. It was really quite good until he got to 'Yoga is as Yoga Does'.

Godalming swung round dramatically.

"*Tony Tony bo bony, banana fanna fo fony, fee fie mo mony, Tony!*" he said, by way of greeting.

"Hey," I replied. I wasn't about to try 'The Name Game' with 'Sir Frank'.

"How do you like our little chambers of commerce?"

"Very nice," I said. "Understated."

"I was considering some branding for the main hall." So that's why the nutjob wanted me here. Well, it was only ever going to be that, wasn't it? He wouldn't be inviting me for a dinner party.

"The Bank of BS, just above the fireplace," he continued, "in neon." He pointed towards a mosaic-tiled walk-in fireplace that was easily my height. It would take a lot of logs to feed it, but no one was ever going to be cold once they had.

"It's a bit unusual for a bank to go with neon, isn't it?" I pointed out.

"We're a very unusual bank," he replied.

Stanthorpe had found a jigsaw at the fireplace hearth and was trying to force two ill-fitting pieces together. At least he wouldn't make a mess.

"Walk with me, Tony," said Godalming, "I want to tell you a story."

He led the way across the hall towards a wide ascending staircase lined with statues and artefacts. The walls were ornately decorated with stylised leaves, sea shells, flowers and elements of mythology. He certainly knew his Rococo.

"When I was growing up in a small town on the west of Scotland," he began, "we didn't have much money. My father was a humble chartered accountant, my mother a quantity surveyor." I was going to ask Godalming to define 'much' in this instance, but let him continue.

"They were simpler times, and I was truly happy. But we were torn apart by unfortunate circumstances."

"Professional rivalry?" I asked.

"The west of Scotland was split by an earthquake and they ended up in Florida. At least that's what they told me."

"That *is* unfortunate. And highly unlikely."

"I went to live with my Uncle Bertie, a retail banker by trade. He was a cold and distant man, but he introduced me to the profession that would allow me to amass the priceless collection of objets d'art you see before you." I thought it was a pity his uncle hadn't introduced him to taste, as Rococo is surely the gaudiest of all styles.

"However, despite their undoubted worth, my worldly goods have not brought me happiness."

"They haven't?"

"No. I've had to rely on my money for that."

I admired his honesty. Most billionaires would deny money ever brought them happiness, but that's just something rich people say to distract you from their bulging coffers. Would they be happier in the suburban terraced flat where they grew up, or in the luxury villa with swimming pool in Monte Carlo that is now just one of their many homes? Yeah, right.

"There is, however," he continued, "one item which has always brought me joy throughout the years. A lasting symbol of my childhood innocence."

He led me to the underside of the staircase where he opened a broom closet and unearthed a child's sled. It was an interesting place to keep the one object he truly loved. If it were my house, I'd have put the sled on the wall and the Rococo under the stairs.

The sled was well-worn, the wood splintered and cracked, and in faded decorative text were eight letters forming an arch that echoed the rounded shape of its crest. The letters formed the word 'BUTTHOLE'.

"A gift from my father," said Godalming, wiping away a tear. "It was his pet name for me."

Godalming's sob story sounded vaguely familiar. I had a moment of déjà vu, something I'd experienced many times before, but I wasn't too interested in sob stories.

"Why are you telling me this, Frank?" I asked him. He turned to face me, with a look of surprise.

"Perhaps I credit you with too much intelligence," he said.

"That happens a lot."

"Then let me make myself clear. In the event of my untimely demise, I may utter a somewhat obscure final pronouncement which would lead to press speculation."

"Your last words?"

"Yes."

"You already know what they will be?"

"Certainly. Don't you?"

I thought for a moment.

"'What was all that about?'" I suggested.

"It's important that someone in the organisation be aware of the significance of my words, in order to help put my life into some kind of context. I could have bequeathed this task to Stanthorpe, but as you can see..." Stanthorpe was now hammering pieces of jigsaw together with his fist, "...his talents lie elsewhere."

"So," I surmised, "someone should be able to explain your final pronouncement because it will be the key to unlock an important fact which goes some way to explaining the nature of your life and work?"

"Not really. But it will save everybody a lot of head scratching."

"I suppose that would mean there wouldn't be any need for a biopic that tells the story of your life through a series of brilliant and innovative flashbacks." I was being unusually lucid. I wish I'd had a tape recorder.

"I would still argue the case for a biopic," Godalming insisted. "With Marlon Brando in the lead."

"Brando's an interesting choice," I said, "but I can see several problems there."

"You can?"

"One, he's a much heavier man. Two, he bears no facial resemblance to you. Three, he's notoriously expensive. Four, it's not the type of role he would choose to play. Five, he's been dead for twenty years."

"He may have lost some weight by now," said Godalming.

"Yes," I said. "I imagine he has."

This was as good a time as any to leave – I had my instructions and all this Rococo was starting to make me feel sick.

"Okay, I'll get your neon sorted out. We can talk about the biopic later."

"Very well," said Godalming. "Taxi!" Stanthorpe jumped to attention.

"That's alright, Allen," I said weakly. "I can manage."

"I insist," said Godalming, as the lumbering Texan slung me back over his shoulder.

I must confess it was quite enjoyable being carried by the bankers, because in recent times we'd all become more familiar with the reverse.

13.
CLUB SELFICANA

I've never been one for clubs, probably due to my experience of them as a youth. I always seemed to be the new kid in town, even though we never once moved house, and I was sent to every scout club and little league going. Most of these trials by peer group never lasted more than one session. I'd have a whole week to dread the next one and then I'd conveniently forget about it.

I'm not very good at showing up for things at regular intervals and precise times because I hate having to constantly keep an eye on the clock. It's possible that the less you do in your life the more of an issue this becomes, which would explain why I feel it so acutely. People with busy lives have no problem showing up on time. You'd think it might be the other way round – busy life, poor time-keeping – but it's not. They'll be there. I probably won't.

Maybe there's a club that wouldn't mind if I never showed up, but I suppose that would defeat the purpose. I could pretend I belonged to lots of clubs and not show up for any of them, then I'd be a lot happier and I wouldn't have to stand up and tell the group about myself.

If the AS was some sort of self-serving, back-scratching club, it would only reinforce my opinion. But armed with this new information, I was now in a position to conduct a more refined search online.

I typed 'AS and self-serving' into the search engine. It returned a single result, followed by "the rest of the results might not be what you're looking for", which was certainly helpful, and better than having to narrow it down from a hundred thousand.

I clicked the link and just as I was being taken to a site called 'The Order of the Absolute Self', LaFlamme rang.

"Have you found it yet?" she asked.

"Found what?"

"The Absolute Self."

"How did you know I was searching?"

"I am LaFlamme," she explained patiently. "I know all."

I scanned the page before me.

'Originally a jazz band in 1960s San Francisco, The Absolute Self specialised in a form of bebop that was largely unappreciated by audiences of the time, most of whom were greatly relieved when the band chose to discontinue. They evolved into an order of crusading monks and adopted the ideals and practices of the Knights Templar, but the lack of available crusades in '60s San Francisco became a stumbling block and they soon realised that even jazz was a more worthwhile cause. Luckily for the citizens of San Francisco and indeed the world, the popularity of jazz was on the wane and by the dawn of the 1980s, the order had settled into its current form, the international brotherhood of self-serving, self-promoting, self-righteous seekers of selfdom.'

Well, well, well. It made perfect sense that an exclusive organisation comprising the most selfish individuals on earth should have begun life as a jazz band. But what really interested me was further down the page.

'The symbolism of the 'AS' insignia has been a topic of discussion for decades and has remained shrouded in secrecy. The distinctive three vertical lines followed by three horizontal lines, repeated three times, has been most commonly interpreted as three pillars and three steps, the pillars representing columns of strength and the steps being steps to ultimate selfhood.

It's an unusual building that would have pillars and steps laid out in such a manner, but I'm no architect. I suppose as long as the foundations are laid correctly, it will probably be solid enough – unlike my house, which has subsided so badly it's started making its way down the street. At least the climb back up the hill each day is keeping me fit.

I would suggest the real meaning of the insignia is somewhat simpler. If you consider the columns and pillars as abstractions of the Roman alphabet, three columns would represent the letter M, three steps would represent the letter E. Repeated three times consecutively, the symbol would spell 'ME ME ME', a sentiment fully in keeping with the Order's principles.'

"I can hardly believe it," I said to LaFlamme.

"I know," she replied. "Who'd have thought jazz used to be popular?"

As I made my way over to LaFlamme's, I was stopped by a cherubic young man in black tie and evening dress. He looked as if he'd never done an honest day's work in his life. But then neither had I, so I don't know why I mention it.

"Do you know the way to the Assembly Hall?" he asked.

I hate being asked directions. To me, geographical points only ever exist in isolation. I have hundreds of these points in my head and I have great difficulty making connections between any of them.

If by a stroke of luck I manage to mentally connect A to B, I then have trouble communicating it because I often confuse left and right. (I've always insisted this is a form of dyslexia, but The Admiral says I'm just thick. In fact, he once said I was 'as thick as two short planks', and even showed me the planks in question.)

On one occasion I was walking over to The Admiral's when a car travelling in the same direction stopped and the driver asked the where-abouts of the Whitehall Restaurant. After thirty painful seconds trying to hardwire the two locations together, I said, "I think you need to turn around and go back up the hill."

"But the satnav is pointing in this direction," he replied.

"Well, who are you going to believe," I said, "me or a robot? I thought you wanted help." I was in no mood for a debate.

The car did a U-turn and I continued down the hill towards The Admiral's. Just before I reached his flat, I saw the Whitehall Restaurant. Hopefully they weren't keeping a reservation, because by the time he made his way back, it would be gone.

I think the ability to give good directions is creepy. If you can imagine moving from wherever you are now to another location without actually doing it, then you're having some kind of out of the body experience. I don't need out of the body experiences; I find *in the body* experiences hard enough, and if my mind is going to leave my body, I can guarantee it will get lost and be unable to find its way back.

"The Assembly Hall," I said, shifting my head left and right, then turning my whole body to face away from the stranger. "I think," I said, staring into the distance, "it's down that way."

"Are you sure?" he said. "Because I think it might be down this way."

"Oh, you do, do you? And you live around here?"

"No, but..."

"Well then, you don't want to be late for your, whatever it is," I said, straightening his tie.

"Meeting."

"All right then."

Over his shoulder, in the direction the stranger suggested, I could make out the distinctive outline of the Assembly Hall. But by this time I'd convinced him I was a trustworthy and knowledgeable local, so I gave him a circuitous route that would involve him walking the equivalent of three sides of a square when he really only needed one.

"Straight ahead, first right, then right again," I said confidently. "You can't miss it."

He strode off in the wrong direction and I wondered if I was a truly awful person or just twisted. It really wasn't such a bad thing to do on reflection. He would still come out at the right spot and it looked like he could stand to lose a little weight.

Before I turned the corner to continue towards LaFlamme's, I saw what appeared to be flaming torches at the entrance of the Assembly Hall, where several black limousines had pulled up and various guests in evening attire were being ushered inside. Someday I'd like to dress up in one of those penguin suits and be chauffeur-driven to a champagne reception with lots of other knobs. Who am I kidding – I might be able to afford a tie, but I'll never afford a ticket.

LaFlamme was rummaging in the kitchen when I arrived.

"Do you want a sandwich?" she asked. I assumed she was preparing a snack so I said yes. She tossed me a pre-packed supermarket delight that was several days out of date and looked as if it had been sat on.

"Haven't you ever heard of home cooking?" I asked her.

"I've heard of it," she replied. "But I thought it was just a rumour."

I sat down next to her laptop, which was displaying the Absolute Self page we had been discussing.

"Any theories?" I asked. LaFlamme was generally working on something.

She poured something bizarre into two glasses and handed one to me.

"It looks a bit like The Breakfast Club," she said.

"That stupid teen movie?"

"No, the networking thing you did at four in the morning."

"Oh, that," I said. "It was seven. It just felt like four."

The Breakfast Club left me traumatised for weeks. I only went once, coaxed along by The Admiral, who thought it would be a good idea to broaden our business horizons. Unfortunately, The Admiral slept in and I was forced to deal with a group of ridiculously enthusiastic self-improvers alone.

At its heart, the club was a business referral scheme whereby members found new leads and potential prospects for other members, which in theory meant more business for everybody. It seemed like a reasonable idea until I realised they met in the middle of the night.

I showed up at 7.15 and was ready to apologise to The Admiral when he inevitably gave me his 'tut tut' look. Seeing that he wasn't there, I made a mental note to berate him vigorously for his poor timekeeping.

"Welcome," said the host, who broke from addressing the gathered crowd to invite me in. "Please, take a seat." I stumbled in and headed for the back of the generic hotel conference room, which was alive with the smell of coffee and new shoes.

"That concludes the minutes of last week's meeting," said the speaker. "Now, who would like to begin? Charles?"

A solid-built professional with thinning hair stood up and walked towards the lectern.

"Thank you, James. Charles Fraser, Fraser and Co, Chartered Accountants. *You pay us so you don't have to pay them.*" I looked around the room, as this meant very little to me. (I may have been the only one present without a pinstripe anywhere on their body.)

"I have just one lead this week," he began, "but it's a good one." Fraser took a slip of paper from an inside pocket. "Stewart, could you come up please?" There was a round of applause as another suited drone rose from his seat.

"I have a client with a multimillion turnover and he's interested in trading NFTs. I said I knew just the man to speak to and he's awaiting your call." There was more applause and the pair signed the slip of paper.

This routine played out another twenty times as each member stood and listed all the suckers they'd managed to hoodwink into dealing with their club chums, by which time, it still being stupidly early, I had drifted off. Only when I was nudged awake did I hear the words 'would you like to introduce yourself?' reverberate in my head and realised all eyes were on me.

"Of course," I said, standing up, the silence of the conference room yawning open before me.

What am I doing here, I thought. I hate clubs. Especially clubs that meet early in the morning. If I ever do this again, I'll have to stay up the previous night for any chance of getting here on time. I looked at the faces gazing at me expectantly. How can they possibly be so chirpy at this hour? The Admiral would pay for this.

"Tony Boaks," I began. "Can you hear me at the back?"

"Yes," said a few at the far side of the room.

"Unlucky," I replied.

"I'm a graphic designer. I didn't really mean to be, it just sort of happened. I'd probably rather do something more interesting, but right now I'm not too sure what that is." Great start, Boaks.

"I generally work with people I don't trust, or like, for that matter. They're shifty and unscrupulous and always have a low opinion of me.

But I suppose that's okay because it's mutual. I have this one client, venture capitalist, likes anagrams – don't ask. And then the bankers. What a bunch. I try to shake them off but they always find their way back." Time to change tack.

"I have a great idea for the internet though, and my friend – who makes fuel from urine and molasses, tastes kind of sweet – he's putting that together, so watch this space. And there's this girl who's full of ideas. We're pretty inseparable, but I can't seem to get her to see me as more than a friend." Just can't seem to stop talking now.

"I'm not really sure what I'm doing. All I really want to do, I guess, is be left alone. And I suppose after this, I will be. Thank you."

I shuddered at the memory.

"If it's anything like The Breakfast Club," I said to LaFlamme, drinking from the chipped tumbler, "they're welcome to it."

"Well, there's only one way to find out," said LaFlamme, scraping hardened cheese off the worktop with a kitchen knife.

"Yes?"

"Infiltration," she said.

"I don't know. These clubs can be pretty exclusive."

"They let you into The Breakfast Club, didn't they? How exclusive can they be?"

"That was an open day. It costs hundreds to join."

"Who said anything about joining? All we want to do is slip in undetected and find out what they're up to."

"How are we going to do that?"

It turned out LaFlamme had been more thorough than I in gleaning information from the website, which is to say, she read beyond the home page. She demonstrated by clicking a link called 'Events', which led to a list of past talks and papers as well as the club's forthcoming programme. This revealed that the local chapter was gathering in town tonight – at the Assembly Hall.

"So that's where that stuffed shirt was heading," I said to myself. "If I'd known, I'd have sent him a much longer route."

"Security gets a bit lax around 10.00pm," said LaFlamme, with the authority of one who was used to slipping into places undetected.

"I'm not standing up and telling the group about myself," I insisted.

107

"God no, Boaks," she said, whisking my glass away for a refill. "Nobody needs to hear that."

"What is this stuff anyway?" I asked. LaFlamme raised her wraparounds to study the label.

"Kahlua."

"What the hell's that?"

"I don't know. Found it at the back of the cupboard."

LaFlamme's cupboards were impossible to fully explore or understand. Attempts had been made but all had ended in exasperation. On this occasion the result landed in my favour because after two rather hazy Kahlua hours, the coffee liqueur had lulled me into a sense of invincibility that made me think infiltration of the Absolute Self might be a good idea.

"Should we?" I asked LaFlamme.

"Get your coat, doll," she replied.

Huddling together for warmth, we walked the half mile up to the Assembly Hall. By the time we arrived, the flaming torches had died down to glowing stumps and the security guards were most likely preferring the temperature indoors. One of the double wooden street doors was bolted shut, but the glass fronted entrance beyond it was unattended and, as LaFlamme predicted, we were able to slip in unchecked.

Evidently knowing her way around the venue, LaFlamme led us upstairs to the grand ballroom where an array of round banquet tables draped in white silk tablecloths were spaced strategically across the hall and lit in a soft, muted ambience. Around five hundred assembled guests had just finished feasting, and by the looks of it, were well accustomed to rich fare. The stage was a focal point in this sea of semi-darkness, a raised platform with a polished wooden floor bathed in a pool of focused light. The back wall glowed with a projection of the 'AS' logo.

LaFlamme grabbed a plateful of finger food from an unattended buffet bar and led us to an empty table.

"That concludes the minutes of our last meeting," said the black-tied and tuxedoed host from the stage, echoing the words of The Breakfast Club. "Now, who would like to get us started? Sir Frank?"

Godalming – I should've known when I saw the box of earth in the cloakroom. I spotted the little gremlin at a nearby table as he untucked a napkin from his collar and took to the stage.

"Frank Godalming," he said into the microphone. "Bear Stearns. Not that Bear Stearns, the other one. *If it looks like a chicken and sounds like a chicken, it might be a turkey.*" The guests roared with laughter.

"I hate when they repeat their stupid slogans," I said to LaFlamme under my breath, whilst stuffing my face with smoked salmon and caviar blinis.

"Stop whining," said LaFlamme, lifting a bottle of wine from the table in front of us. "Get this down you."

Godalming removed a slip of paper from an inside jacket pocket.

"This one is for a certain Brendan Matlock," he said. "Matty, can you come up here?" This was greeted with enthusiastic applause.

"I can't believe this," I said. "It *is* just like The Breakfast Club."

"Told you," said LaFlamme, taking a hearty mouthful from the bottle.

"Matty's been 'resting' recently," said Godalming, making an inverted commas gesture with his hands. "But we're all glad to see him back where he belongs."

Matlock – so that's what 86 billion USD looks like. He could have passed for one of your dad's golfing buddies, if your dad had any interest in golf or indeed if he had any buddies. Sixtyish with shoulder-length white hair, he had an air of quiet confidence about him that clearly belied a psychotic personality. But that's enough about your dad.

"Brendan Matlock," he began, joining Godalming on stage. "Ex-Matlock Securities. A hundred and fifty years, served two – I used a stand-in. *Don't call me Ponzi, my name is Capone.*"

"Gibberish," I said, swigging from the bottle.

"That one wasn't bad," said LaFlamme, grabbing it back.

"Now, Matty," said Godalming, "this lead is so good I almost kept it for myself."

"Wouldn't be the first time," said Matlock, to more audience laughter.

"I have a client," Godalming continued, "who's so ripe for the picking, you could sell him the Brooklyn Bridge. In fact, he's already bought it – twice." Matlock's eyes lit up and there was an impressed 'ooh' from the crowd.

"He's been looking for an internet marketing guru to mentor him.

I realise you don't know anything about the subject, but since when has that stopped any of us before? Am I right? I mean, what do I know about banking?"

The laughter gave way to a full round of applause as the pair took it in turn to sign the slip of paper.

"This is making me nervous," I said. "If they're following The Breakfast Club model, then at some point they're going to ask the newcomers to stand up and introduce themselves."

"Oh, relax," she said, downing more wine.

With the business between the disreputable duo signed and sealed, the host returned to the microphone.

"Now, before we go any further," he said, "I see some unfamiliar faces here tonight."

"Okay, go," said LaFlamme. Unfortunately, as soon as we rose to our feet we were bathed in the heat of a spotlight.

"Please," said the host, "would you like to come up and introduce yourselves?"

The Kahlua may have emboldened me thus far, but the wine on top of it made me jumpy. Now, put on the spot, I was in danger of being swallowed up by panic.

"I can't do it," I said to LaFlamme. I looked around for the exit, spotted it, then realised that's where the security guards were tackling their buffet.

"Don't be ridiculous," she replied. "Follow me."

LaFlamme led us towards the stage, wine bottle in hand, encouraged by the symphony of appreciation from five hundred well-fed self-seekers.

It was a tall stage, and from the top of it, it seemed even higher. It reminded me of gallows, which was apt. I wondered if I could feign a heart attack, or even bring on a real one. Either would be preferable to this.

LaFlamme soaked up the applause and waited until the room was silent before acknowledging the audience.

"Thank you," she said, holding up the wine bottle. "This award means a lot to me." Fulsome laughter from the tables below.

"I'd like to thank Frank and Beans – gentlemen, you're an inspiration to miscreants everywhere. I wasn't sure what to wear tonight, but when Tony said you'd be here I wasn't going to waste much time on it.

"I see you've had quite a meal." She pointed to a portly gentleman at the front. "Especially you. Have you been here all week? Do they wheel you in to make the place look fuller? You better move before you put down roots. Do you want me to call a cab, or should I hire a crane?" To my amazement the guests were thoroughly enjoying this roast and LaFlamme, hitting her stride, took the microphone from the stand.

"You know what I love best about the Assembly Hall?" she said. "Leaving. Honestly, this place has as much atmosphere as the moon. The crew of Apollo 13 probably had more fun in their little capsule than anyone's had here. And the service? You usually have to be Griffin to be ignored this much. You know, *The Invisible Man*? They should bring back EU workers so I could at least be ignored in five languages." Most of the staff had stopped in their tracks to take advantage of the live entertainment, a rare luxury for those in the hospitality trade.

"But on to the business at hand. Settle down now." Once again, LaFlamme waited for silence before allowing the audience any more of her wisdom.

"By way of an introduction – LaFlamme. Goddess. *Too good for the likes of you.*" As a slogan this wasn't any worse than the others.

"I'm sensing a poverty of ambition here tonight," she continued. "Your self-seeking ways appear modest. It may be that your little club is in need of fresh blood, as indeed may be its members." (There were no mirrors in the room.)

"Internet marketing? Pah. Chicken feed. I may be the answer to your prayers because my assistant and I," she shot me a glance, "have leads for you all."

There was a collective gasp from all assembled and a brisk round of applause.

"I have been supremely self-centred since I left the womb. Before, in fact. And I have flown under the radar of all the relevant authorities by working in an unregulated field, providing a dubious service masquerading as a legitimate business interest. Through years of duplicitous chicanery, I have generated a seven-figure income simply by skimming the cream from an overbrimming cup."

111

There was a growing sense of anticipation in the room, and I really had no idea what LaFlamme was going to do with it.

"What is the nature of this field of endeavour which guarantees a cushy life with minimum effort? Ladies and gentlemen, hang onto your boners, because..." and the following was said in her best 'Ich bin ein Berliner' voice:

"I – AM – AN – ESTATE – AGENT." There was another gasp, followed by a general ruckus from the floor.

"Estate agency is unregulated?" said the host, aside.

"Bet you wish you'd known," said LaFlamme. He nodded enthusiastically.

"You're looking for suckers, people?" she asked the overexcited delegates in the hall. "You've hit the motherlode. Real estate is a chump magnet. Seriously, I wave my magnet and they come to me, thousands of them. They travel miles just to touch the hem of my clothes. I have to scrape them off and tell them to get their own hem.

"So here's what I'm saying." You could have heard a pin drop at this point.

"I'll set 'em up and you knock 'em down!"

This practically raised the roof in the Assembly Hall as five hundred ruthless, conniving grifters realised simultaneously that there was a regulation-free industry operating under their noses that they hadn't yet manipulated to serve their personal ends. I smiled nervously behind LaFlamme, knowing that we may have just conned our way into a new life of greed, self-advancement and phrases like 'bijou but elegant'.

I'd have been happy to bask in this reflected glory for a while longer, but LaFlamme dragged me from the stage and made for the exit. En route, she pilfered another bottle of wine, this time right before the eyes of seated guests, who looked grateful for the privilege of donating to such a wildly informative speaker.

14.
FACE THE DEVIL

I should have been in touch with Lyttleton to tell him his artwork was complete, but it's better to let him think these things take weeks to produce and are heroic acts of self-sacrifice. Lyttleton is the sort of client that makes me want to be bad to him. In fairness, he drives me to it. I can guarantee that when he uses phrases like 'corporate values', 'best practice', or 'core competency', he has no idea what he's talking about.

But the waiting game is a fine balancing act. Leave it too long and you'll notice your finances demand to be addressed. The bank is a ravenous beast.

"George," I said, when I picked up the phone. "Is this your lucky day?"

"I don't know," he replied. "Is it?"

"Yes, it is."

"Okay." He paused. "Thanks."

"Okay, bye."

Something didn't seem right about this exchange. Maybe I'd forgotten something. I called back.

"George," I said. "Is this your lucky day?"

"It must be," he replied.

"How do you know?"

"Well, the phone keeps ringing. That's unusual."

"Apart from that."

"You just told me."

"That's right. I did."

"Was there something else?" he asked.

"Yes, yes," I said, remembering. "Your artwork's ready."

"Ah! It *is* my lucky day."

I hung up the phone. Five minutes later, I heard the funeral march ringtone.

"Tony," he said.

"Yes?"

"I'm on my way round."

Not the result I was hoping for. Guess it wasn't *my* lucky day.

I never make preparations for client visits. I figure if they want to turn up at a minute's notice, and they always do, they can take the place as they find it. Besides, with clients like Lyttleton, any extra effort always goes unappreciated. You could have decorated the place specially with murals depicting scenes of his triumph over adversity in the music industry, and he'd just say it was 'artistic' – his stock description for anything he didn't understand. Lyttleton could visit the Sistine Chapel and describe it as 'artistic'. He's like Mr Jones in 'Ballad of a Thin Man' – he knows something's happening but doesn't know what it is.

The only preparation I'd make for a Lyttleton visit is counting the towels. Not that he's light-fingered as such, but he's so deeply entrenched in the '70s music industry culture of complimentary goods and services, he always assumes everything is laid on free of charge.

He was always known for complaining at dinner parties that the entrées were shoddy, or that the quality of the champagne was not up to scratch. Friends learned to tolerate this and put it down to eccentricity, though it didn't stop many of them giving him a good slap.

And champagne was something Lyttleton knew all about. Bubbly, and booze generally, had been something of an obsession for him in his touring heyday. Despite managing some of the most notorious hellraisers of the time, *they* were generally the ones bribing the police to keep *him* out of jail. Apparently in the old days, Lyttleton and Phil Lynott would have tanked a bottle of Smirnoff before they even put on their makeup. Other great soaks of the time recalled his enthusiastic pursuit of cocktails and described his rock'n'roll lifestyle as 'exemplary'. Some of these stories have become the stuff of legend.

Throwing the television set out the window? That was George. What the authorities never knew was that he was actually aiming for one of the band members on the ground below. Had it not been for his impaired vision at the time, 10cc might have folded there and then, and spared us their poor later work.

Driving the Rolls Royce into a swimming pool? That was George. Unfortunately, there was no water in it at the time, so it landed nose first with an almighty thunk.

But my favourite story was the infamous Christmas Eve when a hotel suite witchcraft ceremony got out of hand, and no bribe would ever be big enough to keep George out of the clink. It was an after-gig party and George had been tippling the Mexican spirit mezcal when somebody bet he wouldn't eat the worm at the bottom of the bottle. George had no problem with this, and even ploughing through the whole bottle to get to it was a minor obstacle.

Meanwhile the suite filled up with rock stars and assorted hangers-on and the scene degenerated into one worthy of Fellini. For whatever reason, they decided this would be a good time to try and summon the devil, right there in the London Hilton. Why anybody thought this was necessary is anyone's guess; clearly the devil is already well entrenched in most major hotel chains.

But as the ceremony progressed, George suddenly realised he was outside a circle of protection created by the attendees, and in his altered state, possibly caused by a full bottle of mezcal and a hallucinogenic worm, began to panic. He tore off his clothes, save for his socks and pants, sparked his lighter and insisted on standing on a chair in the centre of the circle. This nearly put everyone off the whole idea but they continued because at least George had stopped screaming.

As the group's High Priest reached the climax of the rite, the hotel room door flew open and a man dressed in red burst in, bellowing 'ho ho ho!' at the top of his voice. This was too much for George's fragile mind and he charged at Santa Claus, screaming bloody murder. The combination of the lighter and George's breath caused Santa's beard to catch fire and at this point George ran off, almost naked and quite hysterical, down the hotel corridor. They could place his rough whereabouts for the next couple of hours by the source of the screams.

It was a night that no one would ever forget – apart from George, that is, who had no recollection of it. This was shortly before he swore off booze altogether, having been shown the drink equivalent of a red card later in the '70s. The details are sketchy, especially to him.

Nowadays it's hard to imagine George the hellraiser, because the only colourful thing about him is his lime suit. I suppose sobriety takes its toll.

You know how this plays out. Ever since I – (delete as appropriate) – discovered our lord Jesus / took up amateur dramatics / learned how to roll cheese, I'm a changed man. But hell, I can still rock a lime suit.

In Lyttleton's case it's more like: Ever since I punched my best friend and slept with his wife / lost all sense of how to behave in public after two Babychams / assaulted a policeman and was court ordered into rehab, I've been forced to admit that I'm somebody who shouldn't drink. And no need to delete as appropriate, he did all of these.

God knows, I'm not here to mock anyone who manages the herculean feat of conquering addiction, because it's a relief to those who can enjoy a drink without serious consequences, when those who can't, manage to sober up. I have so many other reasons to mock Lyttleton.

Regardless, I found a half-empty bottle of brandy and opened it to air on the counter – look, I already said I was either a truly awful person or just twisted, so what did you expect? I knew Lyttleton's sensitive nostrils would pick it up the minute he arrived and this would keep him unsettled for the duration of the visit, thereby ensuring its brevity.

"Tony," he said, stepping through the door. His nose twitched. As I led him into the kitchen, he visibly stiffened.

"Courvoisier. Unmistakable. I used to drink but ever since I joined a Zumba group, I'm a changed man."

I decided not to torment him further and led him to the computer, where I showed him designs for Campbell Glen's *Midnight of the Mole People*.

"Aha," he said, with the faintest hint of a smile. "Very artistic."

"Funnily enough," I replied, "I trained as an artist, so I'm glad that comes across."

"Are these moles?" he asked, reminding me that, after 'artistic',

Lyttleton's subsequent response to any visual was to spend at least ten minutes asking about every single shape and dot contained therein, as if he had a blank paint-by-numbers version of the image in his head and could only fill it in by asking a series of unnecessary questions.

"Yes, moles."

"And this'll be the moon?"

"Yes, the moon."

"What's this here?"

"That's just paint, George. Don't worry about it."

He seemed happy enough with the artwork, though it was hard to tell with one so terminally subdued. The only way I would know for sure is if he asked me to start again, but he left without further comment.

It was time to prepare for print.

Later that day, LaFlamme barged in, followed by what appeared to be a walking cardboard box. Closer inspection revealed the box to have a person behind it, a small one in a floppy hat, and at this point, where the box ended and she began was undefined.

"Junior," said LaFlamme, pointing to a stack of clothes on the floor. "Over there." The box made its way to the clothes.

"Nice floordrobe," said LaFlamme.

"Floordrobe?" I asked.

"Is there an invisible wardrobe over there that I just can't see?"

I wondered how to explain that there used to be a wardrobe in that spot, and that since its owner reclaimed it, I was in denial about its absence.

"I guess not."

"Nice floordrobe," she repeated.

"Who's the kid?" I asked.

"Assistant."

"You call her Junior?"

"Well, her name's June, so Junior seemed about right."

"Isn't that a bit demeaning?"

"I was going to call her Minion."

"Does she speak?"

"I don't think so. But I don't really listen."

"If you don't listen, how do you know she doesn't speak?"

"If she said anything worth hearing, maybe I'd listen. She might be speaking now for all I know, but if it's not worth hearing, there's no point listening."

Junior didn't appear to be speaking but she was certainly perspiring, having single-handedly carried my computer up three flights of stairs.

"Publishing industry must be doing all right," I said with just a touch of pique.

"Keep your pants on," she replied. "The boys over at Vague had a trainee. They didn't know what to do with her – they don't know what to do with themselves half the time. That's why they're agents. They figured a trainee should be seeing how a writer lives at first hand, so they asked if I had any ideas."

"What did you say?"

"I said 'does she drink?'" Junior perked up at the Pavlovian mention of the 'd' word, but LaFlamme was quick to keep her in check.

"Now Junior," she said, echoing the words of the old song, "behave yourself." Junior relaxed back into her corner. "She's settling in just fine." It wasn't long before Junior drifted off, which was also a good sign.

I asked LaFlamme what Vague, Vague and Steadfast did to justify their commissions, as the role of literary agents in book publishing has always been obscure to me. In fact, I have no idea how books ever come together or how anyone can endure writing one. Even reading one seems an ordeal.

This journal alone has been a test of my patience. If I lived in a house with an open fire, I've no doubt that by now it would have made excellent fuel. The only thing sustaining its writing is the idea that, were it to be published and become successful, it might make excellent fuel for thousands and not just me. It would be my way of giving something back to the world.

"Well, you can't just have writers dealing directly with publishers," she explained. "Someone has to get in the way."

"Why?"

"Writers don't wash," she explained. "They sit in their little hovels tip-tappying away, chewing their nails and stroking their beards. That's just the women. They talk to themselves, laugh for no reason and eat with their mouths open."

"It sounds awesome," I said.

"Then there's the publishers," LaFlamme continued. "They know how the shower works and even what deodorant is. Naturally they don't want writers coming in stinking up their offices, but even if they have no sense of smell, this arrangement doesn't really work."

"Why not?"

"Have you ever tried talking to one? Sure, they know how to read books and even how to spot a good one, but once they do, it can be a real problem. When it comes to conversation, they're awkward – that's why they liked Junior. They sound like idiots on the phone, and even worse when they meet someone face to face. They try their best to avoid the outside world, but then a year goes by and the reading public is starved of possible literary gold. Platinum in my case."

"That's where the agent fits in?"

"Not quite. You see, this makes it sound like agents are facilitators and that the whole process would collapse without them. But actually, they're professional stumbling blocks."

"How do you mean?"

"It might be uncomfortable for writers to sit in the same room with publishers, but until the agents came in and built their Maginot Line around them, it was still possible. Now you can't get near a publisher without tripping over one."

"I don't see how getting in the way can be a useful part of the publishing process."

"Don't be so naive. Whole industries are built around getting in the way."

"Why can't *I* get in the way of something useful?"

"Not everybody is good at it. Do you know the first step to being good at getting in the way?"

"What?"

"Knowing you have no talent. Once you've crossed that bridge, you're on the right track. Whereas both writers and publishers need a degree of talent, you can be a full-time stumbling block without it. All you need is to be able to talk about books and have no sense of smell."

119

By now I'd decided that, with my lack of talent and slow-witted olfactory sense, a literary agent should be my next career move. But I wondered how useless Vague, Vague and Steadfast really were, given that there was a bidding war underway for *Help Yourself to Drink*. And just who were these publishers willing to commit several buttons for such a daring venture?

"They have a few lined up," said LaFlamme, fishing another well-worn scrap of paper from her purse. "Random Wailing, Feeble & Wither, and Out Damn Spot."

"That's great," I said. "But it sounds like you needed a literary agent to get this far," I said.

"You might not get a publisher without one," said LaFlamme, "but nobody needs a literary agent. Least of all, people who read books."

15.
TEN GAZILLION DOLLARS

I must get a dozen of these get rich letters every week. I don't know what made me check the sender's name on this one, but there it was – 'Matty'. I opened the email and was faced with a picture of a grinning Matlock showing off a cheque for ten million dollars, modest compared to his previous efforts.

Greetings Entrepreneur,

As you may know I have just closed the doors to my '10 Gazillion Dollars In 60 Seconds (2.0)' Training Program. There were only spaces for 100 students at my faculty, so doors were closed in a few short days...

There was only one problem. I forgot to tell anyone the doors were open. Hopefully you got in despite this, but if you had any difficulty, now is your big chance. Because for the next 12 hours only, you could be one of the lucky students ready to receive this invaluable, doctorate level, scientifically proven, cast-iron guarantee of super fabulous wealth authored by yours truly.

You will learn:

* How to find a profitable niche in a wide-open market that doesn't even exist yet.

* The hidden reason most online businesses don't reap the rewards they promise, apart from just being ill-conceived and generally tawdry.*

* The 20 traps 99% of internet marketers fall into that doom them to failure, 19 of which involve being money-grasping vultures.*

* How to make 10 gazillion dollars in 60 seconds.*

Friend, I have 10,000 video tutorials waiting for you the minute you join my supremely marvellous training course, but numbers are seriously restricted. I'm almost sold out already even though I just opened the doors 20 seconds ago. When I close them again in 12 hours, they will stay closed. I mean it. Not even the cat's getting back in.

Now, this may all sound a bit overwhelming and you might be thinking 10 gazillion dollars in 60 seconds is too good to be true. And that's why I can offer it to you at such a low price. So what is this going to cost? Well, if you added up the many thousands I've spent preparing this material you would reach a high number indeed. Something like fifty hundred million thousand dollars. But I'm offering it here for just $1.99.

Remember friend, the wisdom contained within my mentoring programme is completely reversible. Once you have made 10 gazillion dollars and become an internet marketing guru like me, you can go back to being a complete loser anytime you like. Don't miss this opportunity to stop being totally hopeless.

Act now before I change my mind and close my faculty doors again!

Yours,

Matty

I couldn't believe that having dabbled with Nigerian spam fraud, Matlock's new ruse was internet marketing, something I was certain he knew nothing about. Even worse, I'd already got my credit card out and signed up for it. I mean, $1.99 is a real bargain.

I downloaded his e-book, but thought I'd wait before trying out the whole 60 second gazillionaire bit, as I was in no hurry to become an internet marketing guru like him. Or anything at all like him. First I would send him a personal greeting.

Dear Brendan,

Just signed up for your latest scam, which is shaping up to be a peach. Yes, I'm a little overwhelmed at the sheer breadth of the material I've been promised, but I'm sure this will dissipate once I've seen the reality.

My knowledge of calculus is not great, therefore I hope you'll forgive my ignorance as to how much a gazillion is in earth money. Though it hardly matters, as the real benefit of '10GD in 60' will be the hugely inflated sense of self-worth that such a wheeze will bring to someone as hopeless as myself.

I am concerned about your faculty doors, and indeed about your faculties generally, but should I be one of the lucky 100 participants in this thoroughly disreputable wheeze, please consider me once again a most willing dupe.

Best,

Boaks (Tony)

PS I still haven't received the 86 billion you promised earlier, but again there's no rush.

Matlock's reply followed shortly.

Tony,

Congratulations on being accepted into '10GD in 60'. Your matriculation details will follow suit and you will become a fully-fledged student and virtual amateur drinker shortly.

Thank you also for the reminder – the 86 billion slipped my mind. There is much to discuss regarding this and other future plans; specifically, I have a new proposal that will assuredly be to our mutual benefit, and I have asked Sir Frank to liaise with you directly regarding the arrangements. For now, suffice to say that your appearance at the recent AS meeting was nothing short of revelatory – many eyebrows were raised and most have not lowered since.

*On a personal note, it may be time for us to take that fish-poling
trip, now that I have successfully evaded the authorities.
À bientôt!
Matty*

I could only imagine what ludicrous scam Matlock had lined up
next. And what was so revelatory about the meeting? Surely not the
fact that LaFlamme likes to drink. She says her problem is only having
one mouth.

I suppose I might get some answers in five to seven working days.

The last time I saw Sir Frank, I had just heard some shocking news.
Being stripped of a knighthood was not something that happened every
day, at least not to me, and I wondered how the failed banker turned
criminal mastermind would take it.

"Evening, Frank," I said with a slight snigger, when he arrived as
usual at midnight.

"It's still *Sir* Frank," he said defiantly. "I had my name changed by
deed poll some years ago. You think I didn't see this moment coming?"

"It's not like you to practise due diligence," I replied.

"Unfortunately, they've also stripped me of my deed poll. But this
is a mere technicality. Under Scots Law, all that's required for a name
change is to be registered with a physician and an orthodontist under
said name. I've had my doctor and dentist address me as 'Sir' for years.
Long before I was knighted, in fact."

"I suppose if your doctor and dentist call you 'Sir' it must be true."

"Exactly," he replied. "And I still have my knight's ribbon, which I
must say compliments my Ninja Turtle pyjamas beautifully. They can't
take that away from me."

But today's news topped this. I was on my way to the printer with
Lyttleton's artwork when I popped in to scan the day's main stories.
Normally I don't buy a newspaper, I just read one, and there are many
disgruntled newsagents in the area. Today though, I was forced to cough
up due to the power of the morning's headline.

'GODALMING DEAD'

There was no way I'd be able to take in the whole story at the newsstand because my fallen jaw was in the way. I paid for the paper and realised that all the hacks had to do to get me to buy one of their squalid circulars was to kill off someone I knew personally.

Sir Frank Godalming, disgraced former head of one of the country's largest banks, the Allied Uber Alles, has died. He was 320 years old. Despite his relatively advanced years, he was known to have been in good health and rumoured to be planning a comeback.

The unrepentant twister had become famously reclusive in his final days. Apart from being spotted in Monaco doing the dance that was named after him, and in New Orleans where he hosted a torchlit procession in the grounds of his mansion, albeit without his blessing, he had not been seen in waking hours since the collapse of his banking empire.

The news was broken by his close friend and business associate, Allen Stanthorpe. A distraught Stanthorpe emerged late last night from what some reports described as 'a troll's house under a bridge' and told the assembled press that his mentor had "gone and kicked the bucket". According to Stanthorpe, the banker had been agitated all day but appeared as normal for his Weetabix around 10.00pm. Tragically, he could only find Cheerios and this proved to be a tipping point, sending him into a rage.

Wild-eyed Stanthorpe, the troll in question, then described how Godalming had picked up a glass ornament, which may have been one of his priceless collection of crystal paperweights, and shuffled along the landing to the top of the stairs. In an apparent Dalek moment, he realised he could go no further by mere shuffling, dropped the crystal, whispered the word 'butthole' and collapsed at the foot of the stairs.

The exact meaning of his final pronouncement is unclear at this stage. Stanthorpe suggested it may have to do with his preference for Weetabix, and others have substantiated this, as Cheerios really are the most awful crap.

Police are anxious to trace the whereabouts of graphic designer and banking patsy Anthony Boaks. Boaks is known to have been

one of Godalming's closest confidants in recent days and it is
believed he may be able to help officers shed light on the matter.
There's certainly no point waiting for them to do it on their own.

It was terrible news – that's twice this week I've been called Anthony. Being wanted for questioning wasn't great either, and if my connection to Godalming was now public knowledge, it would scare off the respectable clients and increase my stock amongst the connivers and swindlers. Not that I like the respectable ones any better.

My professional life appeared to lay in the balance. At this stage I could either turn myself in and attempt an explanation that would distance myself from Godalming's underground banking operation, or I could continue to evade the authorities in just the manner that he and Matlock had taught me.

"I seem to be wanted by the police," I said to The Admiral. I often pay him a visit when faced with a dilemma because he can usually take my mind off things simply by annoying me.

"As a designer?" asked The Admiral.

"No. The people who want me as a designer tend to be on the other side."

"Passed over?"

"The other side of the law."

"Ah well," he said. "They're the ones with the real money."

"Do you have any painkillers?" I asked. "I have a brutal headache."

"I have Ovaltine. I don't really believe in painkillers."

"Do you believe in pain? Malt extract isn't going to cut it."

He went rummaging in the kitchen and reappeared with a box of Aspirin that had been worn soft through time, as if it had travelled extensively in a back pocket and possibly even been through a wash. It was interesting to see cardboard in such an advanced stage of decomposition. I suspected both the box and its contents may be from a past civilisation and was reluctant to disturb the site of a possible archaeological dig.

"How about a proper drink instead?" I suggested.

The Admiral led the way to 'The Cask', a local bar which he assured me would be a suitably hospitable environment for a case of headnip. En route I explained my dilemma.

It's never particularly satisfying telling my troubles to The Admiral as he usually just agrees that I'm in a fix and asks why I make such bad decisions. This time I told him I'd hit rock bottom and was considering switching allegiance to the dark lords of banking. He said I might have further to fall before I could really hit rock bottom and that this may be just the start. Which was at least different.

The Cask was mercifully warm and subdued. For a dive bar, the lighting and décor were surprisingly tasteful and there was light bossa nova coming through the speakers, which is always comforting. I thanked The Admiral for his sound judgement.

"They do have some excellent cask ales," he said. "I imagine that's why it's called The Cask Force."

"The Cask Force? That's an unusual name."

"Well, it's mostly frequented by the local constabulary."

"What?"

"Regional headquarters is next door." I looked around and imagined everyone present in uniform.

"Are you crazy?" I said. "Why didn't you just lead me straight into regional headquarters and be done with it?"

"I do apologise," he said, realising his error. "I didn't make the connection."

Being innocent, I had no reason to fear the police, but being the only one aware of it was making me nervous. It might take all night in an interrogation room to convince them of the fact, during which time I could confess to all manner of misdemeanours I knew nothing about.

I said we should drink up fast. (There was no question of The Admiral ever leaving beer behind. I would have to be patient.) Unfortunately, this being the time that many police officers completed their day shift, the bar began to fill up rapidly and some of the off duty looked like they were in serious need of lubrication. I suppose that's what real work does to you. I wouldn't know.

"Try to act natural," I said, knowing as soon as I'd said it that this was likely to cause all kinds of unusual behaviour in The Admiral. He immediately stiffened and looked suspicious. "Okay, forget that."

"Oh, thank god," he replied. "It's such a strain trying to act natural."

"We just need to blend in."

"How about a game of pool?" he said. It was an excellent suggestion but a surprising one. I didn't think he'd know what the large green table in the corner was, but then I remembered his extensive university education.

It transpired that The Admiral was reasonably proficient with a cue. He proceeded to sink everything in sight, including the beer. I was trying to remove mine from his clutches when one of the officers standing at the bar approached and said, "Doubles?"

"Thanks," I said, "but we'll get our own drinks."

"Doubles, yes of course," said The Admiral, before pressing coins into the table's payment mechanism and releasing the coloured balls. Not content with having taken me to within an inch of possible arrest, I couldn't believe he was now going to force me to have a game of pool with two of the arresters.

"I'll get them in," he said, heading to the bar and leaving me to line up the balls on the table prior to my inevitable incarceration.

"I don't play much," I said nervously.

"Looks like your friend does," said the first officer.

"Yes, he's quite the hustler," I replied, realising this was quite inappropriate. "I mean, he's never been to prison or anything."

"I've been to prison," said the second officer. "I was there today!" They both laughed at this.

"I told you to stop breaking the law," said the first officer.

"There's just something about that place."

Watching these two comedians enjoying themselves was not helping me relax and now, far from wanting to leave my drink, I wanted to consume more. Much more.

Several games and several beers later, it would be fair to say that The Admiral and I had taken the notion of 'blending in' to an extreme. Our new best friends, who introduced themselves as Whyte and Mackay, were clearly in the mood for celebrating. I'm not sure what they were celebrating, probably just that work was over, which is a fair cause for celebration in my book. And whilst it was clear from the level of play that there were no professional pool players present, the professional drinkers were most apparent.

I eventually loosened up about my wanted status and at one point returned with a round of drinks on what appeared to be the same metal trays The Admiral and I had put to good use at the Vigorous Dark Ale Festival.

"Look what I found," I said.

"Ah," said The Admiral, removing the drinks. "Allow me."

He lifted the tray and, with gusto, whacked me over the head with it.

"Wayhey!" chimed the policemen.

Unfortunately, the tray was not the same malleable sort at all and I reeled under its full force. On examination, the tray fared better. It was left without a dent, whilst my head rapidly began changing shape. This boisterous act of near concussion, though not in everybody's interests, seemed to endear us to the law and we whiled away several more hours in their company. Surprisingly, the headache I came in with had gone. In fact, all sensation had gone.

The following morning I vowed to stop waking up on strange sofas, telling myself should I ever do it again, I'd have my own sofa sent over first. This was not even The Admiral's sofa, nor was it a room I recognised. He must have moved house during the night.

To my horror, Officer Whyte from The Cask Force, now in full uniform, was offering me coffee. This was dancing with disaster on a major scale. Not only had I infiltrated the very place the local constabulary go to unwind, I was accepting extended hospitality in one of their homes.

"Couldn't let you drive," said Whyte.

"Drive?" I replied. "I don't have a car."

"Well, you tried to get into one last night."

"I did? Where's The Admiral?"

"He took his bike."

"He doesn't have a bike."

"You computer guys," he laughed. "You know how to party."

"We know how to party, but we don't know how to drive."

16.
THE DEAD DON'T LIE

"Anthony Boaks?" said Whyte.

"Yes?" I replied.

"Are you sure?" said Mackay.

"Well, I haven't checked today, but I think so."

I had immediately taken to the sofa on my return home, and was a little bewildered when a mere hour later, I was awoken by the same two policemen at my door.

They referred to a passport-style photograph, lining it up against my head. I thought there might be a discrepancy caused by the tray incident, but they seemed satisfied enough to proceed.

"We'd like to ask you a few questions." Their demeanour was in sharp contrast to last night. Now it was the cells for sure, but at least it would rid me of the stress of being on the run.

"Didn't you say your name was Tony?" asked Mackay.

"It is."

"Is that your middle name?"

"Yes," I said. "Anthony Tony Banana Fanna Fo Fony Fee Fie Mo Mony Boaks." I didn't care anymore. Just cuff me already.

"Did you know Sir Frank Godalming?"

"Yes," I said. "Apparently I was his patsy."

Officer Whyte read from his notebook. "Are you aware of his last words and any special significance contained therein?"

I wondered how I could convey the meaning behind the story Godalming had told me; how it was a treasured memory, a reminder of his lost youth, a family heirloom, an item of immense sentimental value which would forever be associated in his mind with childhood innocence.

"Butthole was his sled," I said, and was greeted with complete silence. Both officers stood poised to take notes, but clearly this was not considered noteworthy.

"His sled," said Whyte.

"That's right," I said.

"Why would anyone call their sled Butthole?"

"I don't know. Why would anyone call their sled anything? I had a sled once. I called it the sled."

They put their notepads away.

"He doesn't know anything," said Mackay. Both relaxed significantly.

"Oh man," said Whyte. "Hey, are you making coffee? I've got the hangover from hell."

I was ready to explain the whole issue and could probably have taken them to the Butthole in question, but they didn't seem inclined to pursue the matter any further. I went to make coffee. On my return I thought I'd try a different approach.

"What if I told you the sled could explain areas of Sir Frank's life that might otherwise go with him to the grave?"

"We don't care about that," said Whyte. "One butthole banker more or less makes no difference to us. This is strictly routine."

"It's not like this is a criminal investigation or anything," said Mackay. "He wasn't bumped off; it was just weird. The guy was found in a box of earth."

"If it was criminal, we'd be hauling you down to the station," said Whyte.

"You don't want that," said Mackay.

"You don't want that," said Whyte.

"I don't want that," I said.

"Anyway, it's pretty obvious what 'butthole' is all about," said Mackay.

"What?" I asked.

Both of them looked at me as if I was learning impaired.

"Didn't you see that guy Stanthorpe?" said Whyte.

"Case closed," said Mackay.

I felt vaguely snubbed by the law's lack of interest in my criminal connections, but not enough to protest. I knew it was only a matter of time before someone showed up with a real interest in the matter, probably a maker of biopics, and they would be most attentive.

Thinking back over the short time I'd known Godalming, he'd been such a vital and vibrant character that I might have said it was hard to imagine him dead. But as he'd spent much of our time together in a coffin, that wouldn't be strictly true.

It made we wonder. One man's life is harried by poverty and sickness, and cut short at 50. Another man's life is cushioned by vast wealth amassed through preposterous short term banking devices, and rolls on to 320. But is one life ever more valuable than another? I doubt it, especially in Godalming's case. Aside from the keyboard, his only talent was shamelessness.

But I reminded myself not to speak ill of the dead. I had to keep reminding myself for hours because so much ill came to mind. I was still reminding myself when he showed up downstairs, in his box, of course, and once again I had to help the courier bring him up.

Some hours later, I was spacing out to *Bride of the Monster* when I heard the familiar sound of the alarm clock within the box. After a commotion, the lid flew open and Godalming sat bolt upright in his nightcap, in one hand the alarm clock, in the other a copy of Men's Health.

"Boaks!" he exclaimed.

"Butthole!" I replied. "Sleep well?"

"I had a terrible dream. I was working for a paltry quarter mill. I didn't mind the wage so much as being expected to actually work. It was a nightmare. Anyway, I had you going for a while, yes?"

"You're meant to be dead."

"Technically I am. But there is so much more to life than the technical. And by the way, to celebrate my demise we're having a little cocktail party tomorrow evening. I'd be pleased if you could attend."

After a tomato juice, Godalming perked up further. He was in a garrulous mood and seemed only too happy to explain the circumstances behind his fake death.

"I've done all I can in order to cheat death and, who knows, I could probably cheat it out of another couple of hundred years. But the only way I can be sure of cheating death in the longer term is to actually die. That is, only by staging a version of my death can I effectively get the grim reaper off my back."

"Will he fall for that?"

"I don't see why not. And what makes you think death is a he?"

"Well, *she* must be quite hacked off with you," I said. "What with being undead and all in the first place."

"Indeed. But *they* can find somebody else to inconvenience. Death is like jury duty to me. It's most important that I am undisturbed by fatal citation for the foreseeable future, because now my real work must begin.

"You see, being one of the living has its disadvantages. One is expected to be accountable all the time, to be decent, to be fair, to pay taxes, to tidy one's room. It's so tiresome. By removing myself from the electoral register I can walk amongst the living without having to be accountable to them. Nobody expects a man to account for himself after death."

"Couldn't you have just skipped the census?"

"I tried that. But a missing form is just a missing form. It doesn't prove or disprove anything. They wouldn't say 'missing form – presumed dead', they'd just say 'missing form.'"

"I see what you mean. They definitely wouldn't say 'missing form – possibly skipped census in order to fake death.'"

"Quite. In this situation, what I needed was not *less* paperwork, but *more*. I wanted something that would mean I'd be free of the dreaded censi forever." From a drawer in the box of earth, he withdrew a roll of yellowed papyrus tied with red ribbon.

"It took an immense amount of planning, but finally I secured it."

"What is it?" I asked.

"My death certificate," he replied. His sense of satisfaction was palpable.

"But what difference will that really make?"

"Have you ever tried to prosecute a dead person?"

"Not that I can recall."

"It means I can fleece whomsoever I choose without fear of punishment. Hell, never mind punishment, nobody even wants to speak ill of the dead." He was lucky he'd been safely in the land of nod earlier, as I'd had no trouble with it.

I had to admire his efficiency. Godalming was the only semi-living person I knew who was travelling the world with a copy of his own death certificate. It would save a lot of time if he ever found himself with a stake through the heart.

Presently, the grinning buffoon Stanthorpe appeared at the window.

"Ah!" said Godalming. "The boys are back in town!"

Stanthorpe had a rucksack or suchlike strapped to his back. On opening the window, the rucksack turned out to be Brendan 'Matty' Matlock. They clambered in and fell to the floor, Stanthorpe drenched in sweat and out of breath, Matlock remarkably relaxed and adjusting his cufflinks.

"Tony," said Godalming. "I failed to divulge the true purpose of this evening's conference. How remiss."

"If this is going to turn into a conference," I said, looking at the window, "the others should probably use the stairs."

"That won't be necessary," he continued. "As we are all present, I'd like to introduce you to my colleague Brendan and turn the proceedings over to him."

Matlock dusted himself down with a silk handkerchief and looked around for a seat. I offered him the wonky office chair, knowing full well what the consequence might be. Stanthorpe stood guard at the back of the room whilst Godalming and I hovered by the table.

"Thank you, Frank," he said in his languid Manhattanite tones whilst making himself comfortable in the swiveller.

"Tony," he began. Already the chair had started to sink. "I'm sure you know me by reputation. And likewise, I have heard much about your work for the organisation. Sir Frank insisted you were a dullard, but I suspect there is more to you than meets the eye." He looked me up and down. "There must be." Godalming guffawed.

"In any political team there are those who are skilled in presentation and those who provide the substance, without which, presentation becomes a mere vacuum. I assume you work together in these matters and that your carefully choreographed presentation was the result of much planning." Did Matlock just suggest I was the brains of this operation?

"Your raven-haired companion," he continued, as the chair sunk gradually to the floor.

"LaFlamme," I interjected.

"She had rather a lot to say for herself. And frankly she lit a flame under our seats." I would love to have lit a flame under his seat right now but it would be difficult with only three inches between it and the floor.

"She's quite the fire starter," I said.

"And most appealing," said Matlock. "Her comments about the real estate industry provided much food for thought amongst the membership."

Suddenly the penny dropped. Matlock wanted a piece of LaFlamme's fictional scam. I suppose if you were working your way through the scam alphabet as he undoubtedly was, you'd get to 'R' eventually. I was going to have to break it to him.

"I don't think LaFlamme can help you in real estate," I said, preparing to explain a few things.

"You misunderstand," said Matlock. "Although this information was certainly welcome, especially to some of our less imaginative colleagues," he nodded towards Stanthorpe, whose grin had not shifted since he arrived, "it is of only secondary importance to me."

"It is?" I said.

"You bet!" said Stanthorpe.

"You see," continued Matlock, "despite her fine command of the audience, Ms LaFlamme made one fatal error that night."

"She did?" I said.

"You bet!" said Stanthorpe.

"Allen, please," said Matlock. Stanthorpe piped down.

"It was somewhat egalitarian of her to alert some 500 self-interested individuals from a variety of socially advantaged backgrounds to a largely untapped source of wealth. Now that the cat is out of the bag, as it were, they have no incentive to discuss any quid pro quo."

135

"It's true, Tony," said Godalming. "Many of them have already set up high street branches."

"However," said Matlock from a reduced elevation, "this is all somewhat by the by, as what we have in mind is quite unrelated." (If you're anything like me at this juncture, you'll be wishing Matlock would get to the point. But as you've managed to read this far, it's not likely you're anything like me.)

"Tony, the organisation is inordinately wealthy. And we have channelled some of this wealth into various advocacy groups that can help further our causes – free market thinktanks, if you will. *The Righteous Foundation* and *The Indignation Institute* are but two examples, both administered covertly by AS members.

"These bodies have been influential in shaping government policy for many years and their philosophy directly mirrors our own. However, we've come to believe they are no longer sufficiently influential for our purposes and that it would be preferable for the organisation to play a more direct role in capturing the political process.

"But here's the snag. Selfdom and charisma are not easy bedfellows. Many of us lack the appropriate public relations nous and may display our true colours to the media without the necessary filtering and translation required to make such thoughts palatable to a mainstream audience. Some are likely to turn to dust should they be in the presence of certain natural forces at inappropriate times. Others simply have no chin.

"In short, Tony, we are lacking the sort of personable, electable figureheads that would help persuade the public at large that we are a viable alternative to what is currently on offer politically."

"You want to run for office?" I said.

"Not exactly," he replied. He climbed out of the sunken chair.

"We would like to respond to what we feel is a groundswell of public opinion and unite grassroots support in a new and powerful movement for change. There is a rising tide of righteous indignation amongst the ordinary working classes and we believe we can capitalise on it."

"Surely the ordinary working classes wouldn't normally vote for a group of disreputable billionaire fraudsters?" I suggested.

Matlock and Godalming broke into broad grins and finally, Matlock spelt it out.

"That's where you come in," he said.

17.
THE WILLIAM TELL
UNDERTURE

I slept badly, the fox once again dominating my dreams. This time, when the bushy-tailed canid led me to the foundations of a new building, the sense of creative inspiration I felt previously turned to foreboding as a man in naval attire smoothed the cement surface of the base with a palette knife.

"No one should know what happened here," he said gravely, before accidentally dropping the knife in the cement and having to redo that section.

I nodded in agreement because I knew I was guilty of a terrible crime. There was no recollection of the crime, or any sense of a victim, but there was no question that I was responsible and the naval official complicit. The awful truth of the act, whatever it was, weighed on my conscience.

I awoke to the sound of the phone, and immediately thought the police had made the connection between the unknown crime and my number. My shame would soon be public. But instead of an officer of the law, it was somebody from the printers, which was only marginally better.

There is a certain pattern to dealing with printers. At some stage you go from being a respected client to an evil tyrant who makes their existence a living hell. The transition point usually occurs several days after you've left artwork in their hands and a day or so before delivery has been promised. The reason for the timing is that, as failed designers themselves, printers know a thing or two about procrastination.

This is when they head for the window ledge. I blame the chemicals. Those presses need feeding and the poor characters who have to do it are inhaling all manner of toxic inks and fixing agents all day. It's no wonder they're wired.

"Your artwork," said a 'Darren' on this occasion, when he called about *Midnight of the Mole People*. I was well used to these muted telephone tantrums and thought I'd make the most of this one. "It's a disaster."

"I'm fond of it too," I said.

"There's so much black in it."

"Yes, it was a radical decision for an album called *Midnight of the Mole People*, but I think black is the new beige, don't you?"

"I don't know if I can match all those deep tones."

"Well, you probably shouldn't be matching anyway. You're not really someone who should be anywhere near an open flame."

"Also, there's only 2mm bleed either side," he said, exasperated, "and not much slug."

"Surely as long as the slug's big enough to stop the bleeding, it'll be okay?"

None of this was helping to talk the poor man down, but if he hadn't been high on formaldehyde, he wouldn't be on the ledge in the first place. I think the fact that so many printers would rather jump than have to deal with my artwork is a testament to the power of my designs, and I had no more sympathy with Darren than with any of the other chemically-enhanced inkheads I'd tortured over the years.

I would have returned to slumber soundly after the call, were it not for the sudden appearance of LaFlamme and Junior.

"Bookcase over there," said LaFlamme. Junior headed to the corner of the room and took out a pad and pen. Methodically removing each book in turn, she examined the back cover and made a note before replacing it.

"What's going on?" I said.

"New business idea," said LaFlamme. "It's called 'Flops.'"

"Flops?"

"Flogging Other People's Stuff."

I did a quick count on my fingers. "Isn't that just Fops?"

"Flops," she said. "Fops are silly people. You ought to know."

"But flops are failures."

"Okay, Mr Successful."

"So let me get this right. Your new business idea is to sell my books?"

"Only the ones worth selling."

"Couldn't it be 'Sotts' – Somebody Other Than Tony's Stuff?"

"That would be 'Flosotts'," she said. "Look, I didn't come up with this plan, I'm just trying it out." I'm not sure why this justification for raiding my bookcase didn't elicit an objection. I guess I won't miss them.

"Then I hope you'll do the sensible thing," I said, "and buy us drink with the proceeds." Junior nodded enthusiastically. She was fitting in just fine.

Meanwhile I had to think of a way to present the BS boys' plan to LaFlamme, having already told them that getting her onboard for such a demanding role would be tricky. First there was the ideological issue. Then there was the logistical issue. Then there was the issue of LaFlamme being LaFlamme. It was going to be uphill all the way.

Matlock said that whilst they were not considering running for office themselves, they had a great deal of interest in helping to establish a political party that could advance causes close to their hearts more fully than their various advocacy groups. There would be unlimited funding for such an operation and its core individuals, along with substantial no-questions-asked pensions once they stepped down. They even had a dental plan.

Whilst I understood how LaFlamme could be valuable to them in this regard, I was less sure about the extent of my own usefulness. Matlock explained that, as well as my sound judgement and experience as an 'adviser' to LaFlamme, audiovisual presentations were crucial to any campaign, and my work to date had been more than satisfactory. And whilst any designer could fulfil this task, it was important to them to have a close-knit group of individuals whom they could trust.

Whenever I expressed any doubts, Matlock more or less repeated his sales pitch whilst swinging a pocket watch on a chain. Oddly enough, thereafter I was convinced it was the right thing to do. It's possible that George W Bush used a similar technique on Tony Blair all those years ago at Camp David, or just that Tony Blair was a complete divot.

"Dearest?" I said to LaFlamme. There was no response and the pair continued their inventory of my bookcase. I cleared my throat and LaFlamme looked around.

"Were you talking to me?" she asked.

"Well..." I said, testing the water. "Yes?"

"Nobody's ever called me that before," she said. "And I don't see why you should be the first."

"It's just that, you remember those nice people we met at the Assembly Hall?"

It took around forty minutes to explain what BS had in mind, partly because there was a lot to remember and partly because filtering their self-justifying drivel through my limited capacity brain was a challenge I wasn't particularly equipped for.

I explained how her charismatic performance at the AS meeting had endeared her to the group and singled her out as an ideal party figurehead, and that I had been suggested as a suitable deputy. I outlined the hugely beneficial remuneration package that was being offered and how it would mean neither of us ever having to work again. I thought, overall, that I presented a reasonably convincing case. But it's possible that I was merely blinded by the 'never having to work again' thing.

LaFlamme sighed.

"How can I put this?" she began. "I am LaFlamme. Goddess. She whose hem may not even be gazed upon, let alone touched." This probably wasn't a good start. I prepared to find the nearest rock to hide under.

"There are many paths open to *moi* at this particular juncture, and none of them involve becoming a front for a set of grisly grotesques, whose only talent is unconscionable avarice, in an unspeakably shameless and tawdry scramble for political office. My offence is such that I believe you should consider withdrawing the request, withdrawing the previous hour of your life or, best of all, withdrawing your friendship."

"Is that a maybe?" I said.

Nobody told me it was fancy dress, but I didn't much care anyway. I wasn't even sure why I felt compelled to attend this soirée – it was Monday night and everybody knows nothing happens on Monday night other than drudgery. Maybe when you're stupidly rich, every day is a Friday.

But the BS chambers were virtually underneath my tenement so I figured drudgery might be more acceptable in a less familiar environment. I also had to report to Matlock on LaFlamme's predictable response to the proposal and perhaps gather more ammunition for the challenge of persuading her further.

I was a little early for the party itself, but it was better to have any conversation before the guests arrived, as conversation was not likely to be the highlight of a party populated by bankers.

Stanthorpe, giddy and dressed as The Lone Ranger, met me at the door.

"Mr Tony!" he exclaimed, and then in a hushed tone asked, "Are you like one of them Hell's Angels?"

"Am I tattooed and beardy?" I said. "I'm just wearing a leather jacket. The one I always wear."

"Oh, I'm sorry," he replied. "I'm just so happy!"

I asked him if Matlock was around.

"Mr Matty's in his office," he said, escorting me there himself.

On entering the office, Matlock had his back turned and appeared to be dressed as a medieval huntsman, with green tunic, brown trousers, long black leather boots and a broad-brimmed cap. Strapped across his back was a quiver-full of arrows. I guessed this was Robin Hood and complimented him on his choice of costume, even though stealing from the rich to give to the poor was hardly his style.

I told him I'd had no success in persuading LaFlamme to front their political organisation and that I would need to find a way to make the idea more appealing.

"What seems to be the problem?" he asked.

"It's possible that she has principles."

"Principles? What do you mean?"

"You know. Morals. A sense of right and wrong."

"Oh," he said. "I see." He really didn't. And I wasn't sure principles were the problem anyway, as LaFlamme had worked in advertising and probably sold snake oil in a past life.

"Perhaps," he continued, "it would help if you explained where we have common ground. We are not so different, my friend. Our politics are more similar than you think."

"I think LaFlamme and I share a mutual apathy towards politics," I said. "We work for ourselves and mostly just want to be left alone. In fact, I only vote for someone if I think they won't notice me."

"Well, here you are, hitting the nail right on the head. All the regulation facing small businessmen like you and I is interfering with free enterprise, and interfering with free enterprise is interfering with personal liberty."

"Is that right?" I said.

"We are both liberals, you and I," he replied, "although personally I prefer the term 'neoliberal'. What we need is a leader who truly understands the value of individual autonomy and prioritises policies that protect our freedoms and privacy."

"Well, not having any money certainly limits my personal liberty," I said. "It doesn't matter how hard I work, I always end up with a stack of bills."

"I recognise the burden that high taxation places on working people. We should be fighting tirelessly to lower these levies across the board, allowing individuals and businesses to keep more of their hard-earned wealth. By implementing a fair and simplified tax system, we can stimulate economic growth, create jobs, and provide financial relief to struggling families."

"I guess so," I said. He brought out his pocket watch and began swinging it from its chain.

"Surely if you believe in the power of individual liberty and personal responsibility, you should be a committed and steadfast advocate for limited government, free markets and traditional values. In a world where big government continues to encroach upon our liberties, I believe it's time to reclaim our sovereignty and take back control. Do you think government was always this powerful?"

"It wasn't?"

"No, my friend. But together we can build a brighter future for our children, where freedom reigns supreme and is within reach for all who seek it. And to this end, we have crafted a distinctive and original campaign slogan which will accompany us to the hustings. A slogan so fresh and up to the minute that it is bound to gain traction at unprecedented levels and secure record numbers of votes."

"Which is?"

"*Power to the people*," he said, delighted with himself. Maybe these jokers need LaFlamme and I more than I thought.

"Perhaps this evening I can introduce you to other prominent neolibs who could reinforce our core values and encourage you to participate – Mr Blair, for example. He has been most supportive recently, although I find his toadying quite insufferable."

He took an apple from a fruit bowl, rose and called for Stanthorpe, who entered promptly and took the apple. In a routine he was evidently familiar with, Stanthorpe, unprompted, took ten paces to the far end of the office, turned his back to the wall, pushed himself flat up against it, and placed the apple on his head. Matlock produced a powerful-looking crossbow and removed an arrow from his quiver, which in fact was more like a heavy bolt. He placed the bolt on the crossbow, retracted the bowstring and pointed the instrument towards the top of Stanthorpe's head. Despite the obvious danger, Stanthorpe's grin remained fixed throughout.

Matlock took a moment to focus his aim, then with a single movement of his index finger, released the string, allowing the bolt to shoot through the air with a rapid whoosh. It pierced the apple crisply, splitting it straight down the middle and sending the two halves to the floor. Stanthorpe immediately gathered up the pieces, placed them on the desk and scurried out. There was a certain relief that it was the apple that was punctured, though I suspect any impact with Stanthorpe's head would only have resulted in deflection.

"Thank you, Allen," said Matlock, biting into a portion. He was an excellent shot.

"In any event, Tony, you need not be overly concerned about the minutiae of our individual policies because they will be clearly defined and determined by our various advocacy groups. *People for the Advancement of Wallet Girth*, for instance, would provide all the coaching and motivational instruction required to keep you and your team on the right track."

"Won't you and Frank be involved?" I asked.

"We will, of course," he said. "But discreetly. We'd like to be involved, as it were, from a distance."

"Like the song," I posed.

"What song?"

"'From a distance.'"

He took three steps back. "What song?" he repeated.

"From a ... never mind. It's a stupid song. So how demanding can we expect our roles to be? Will it be like having a full-time job?" The very mention of the term always made me shudder.

"There are two things to remember here," said Matlock. "Firstly, this is a grassroots movement which is effectively already running itself. It only requires minimum effort to appeal sufficiently to the electorate and deliver the victory that will bring it into office. Secondly, a politician's job becomes much easier after they are elected because they needn't waste time persuading voters their theories will actually work when put into practice."

Having said the magic words 'minimum effort', I was reassured that running for office and indeed running the country would be relatively straightforward. I agreed to give it another try and called LaFlamme.

"I've just been hypnotised by Robin Hood," I said. "Do you want to come to a cocktail party?"

"In Sherwood Forest?" she asked. "Well, I did promise Junior a drink." There was a scrambling at the other end. "Down, Junior, down!"

"What was that?"

"I'd say it was a yes. We might as well drink Robin Hood's booze."

"By the way, it's fancy dress and apparently I'm dressed as a Hell's Angel."

"Tattooed and beardy?" she said.

It was a mere twenty minutes before they arrived, no doubt due to a certain enthusiasm for imbibement in the agency's lower ranks, and by that time the party was already swinging. The diversity of costumes was boundless, from Venetian masquerade masks to Renaissance courtiers, futuristic space explorers to characters from beloved fairy tales. It was surprising to find that bankers could be imaginative.

On a small raised platform, a jazz quintet was playing a frenetic type of bebop and blowing a storm. I thought they'd be better off trying to make music, but I suppose jazz is always going to involve blowing.

"Watch this," said LaFlamme. "Junior – find drink!" Like a finely-tuned sniffer dog, Junior raised her nose to the air and led us immediately through the crowd to the nearest bar. Martinis were the order of the evening and Junior wasted no time in securing a tray's worth for our thirsty group.

"There's Robin Hood," I said, pointing to Matlock demonstrating his crossbow skills to admiring onlookers, and making what was likely to be the very best use of Stanthorpe's head.

"That's not Robin Hood," said LaFlamme.

"Well, I know it's not actually Robin Hood," I replied. "It's Matty Matlock."

"It's William Tell," she said.

"William Tell? What's the difference?"

"About five hundred miles, a couple of hundred years and a technological shift in small arms," she said. "And Robin Hood robbed from the rich."

"William Tell didn't?"

"No, he was whining about taxes," she replied.

I recalled Matlock mentioning something about taxes earlier, but the William Tell story was unknown to me.

"William Tell was a dab hand with the old crossbow," she explained. "But he was a pleb, and the Swiss government of the time imposed heavy taxes on plebs. He protested and was about to be thrown in the clink when the head honcho says, 'Okay, arrow boy, you're so good with that thing, if you can shoot the apple off your son's head, you can go free.'"

"So what happened?" I asked.

"Well, he wasn't stupid."

"He took the jail time?"

"Hell no, he shot the apple off the kid's head."

"It's really not the heartwarming story I was expecting," I said. "Did he go free?"

"Yes," she replied. "But he still had to pay his taxes, because you know what they say."

"Nothing's certain except death and taxes?"

"No, the scarecrow became a tax consultant because he was outstanding in his field."

I wondered what it would take to brainwash LaFlamme. Probably something much more powerful than Matlock had at his disposal – he could try swinging his pocket watch, but it was likely to melt in the face of a more powerful opponent.

"Have you ever thought about fronting a political party?" I said, still wondering how to persuade her that securing financial freedom and retiring to our respective mansions in the country was the way forward.

"Not that old chestnut again," said LaFlamme. Junior raised her eyes skyward.

"Matty says it really wouldn't be that much work."

"Matty says," said LaFlamme. "Matty, Matty, Matty. If Matty said it was fun to play on the motorway, would you do it?"

"Which motorway?"

"If you love Matty so much, why don't you marry him? Tony and Matty sitting in a tree, k–i–s–s–i–n–g."

"That's silly."

"Silliness is my birthright," she said. "I will be retaining my silliness into old age and carrying it with me to the grave. I want to be the silliest person in the cemetery. It's what separates me from the drones."

"You could be silly and have lots of money for a change," I said. "Look, these guys are deluded. Not only do they think they have enough support to form a popular political party, they think they can win an election. I guarantee nobody's going to even notice this movement, so why not take the money and be the drunkest, happiest, silliest people in the cemetery?"

"I have two problems with this," said LaFlamme. "One – why would I want to front something nobody's going to notice? Two – it wouldn't go unnoticed for long because I'd have to say something outrageous to alleviate the tedium."

"It sounds like problem two would cancel out problem one."

"Yes, but then I'd impersonate one of the other dreary MPs in order to deflect attention."

"But then you could say something outrageous again."

"I'm bored already," said LaFlamme.

Through the light martini haze, I recognised some familiar faces amongst the revellers. Sir Cliff Richard was present and had begun to trawl out 'Summer Holiday' for anyone who would listen. There were not many willing to make such a sacrifice and he stopped during the second verse. And, good as his word, Matlock introduced us to prominent 'neo-lib' Tony Blair, who was weighing up our options for fronting the party.

"Obviously, when it comes to a decision like that," he said, "I think it is important you take the decision, as it were, on the basis of what is right, because that is the only way to make such a decision. It gives you strength if you come to a decision, to hold to that decision, and that, as it were, would be my decision." But no one was listening to him either.

LaFlamme yawned. "I have the ennui," she said. "I feel jaded beyond the colour of jade."

"What colour is jade?" I asked.

"It's jade colour. Similar to jade. But with more jade."

Despite nobody taking any notice, Blair was still talking and had launched into an unsolicited defence of his decision to go to war in Iraq. That too was a decision formed, as it were, on the basis of what was right because that is the only way to do it.

I marvelled at his uncomplicated decision-making process and his ability to always know what was right. LaFlamme, however, was less appreciative of his evangelical tone and looked ready to preach some evangelism of her own, possibly by playing the spoons on his head. But while he was under the misapprehension that this was some sort of interview, I thought I might as well ask him an obvious question.

"Why don't *you* front the party?" I said.

"Oo-er," he replied, shifting uneasily in his seat. "I'd say my cover's blown – rather blotted my copybook the last time." He was right. No one outside of Bush's ranch was ever going to trust him again. I imagine even his mother counts the silverware before dishing up Sunday roast.

Mercifully, the bebop had ceased and a three-piece band took their place on the stage. On closer inspection, it wasn't just any three-piece

148

band. It was Godalming, dressed in white flared Elvis pantsuit, ridiculous hairpiece and shades, at the Hammond organ; a similarly bewigged William Tell Matlock on bass; and an oddly familiar drummer with an all but vanished hairline. With two wigs in the band, I can't imagine why they didn't give one to the bald guy.

Godalming stepped up to the microphone. "One two," he said. "One two, one two. Counting's not my strong point, as you know." Laughter. "Ladies and gentlemen, good to see so many of you here tonight. Now that the jazz is over, I'd like to get the entertainment started.

"We don't normally play together and this is strictly for one night only, so I hope you'll bear with us if we lose the plot – like we did in 2008, although on this occasion a complete bailout shouldn't be necessary.

"Allow me to introduce, by kind permission of the Pentonville State authorities, The Bossa Novians!"

They launched into their first number, the 1979 goth classic, 'Bela Lugosi's Dead', and surprisingly the trio powered their way through it beautifully. There's something special about hearing an Elvis impersonator wailing, "*Undead, undead, undead!*" over a brooding bossa nova backing, and it was all the more fitting given that Godalming's fake demise was the cause of the celebration.

Matlock took to the microphone for the second number, 'I Fought The Law', and with characteristic arrogance, had changed the words to '*I fought the law and I won*'. I suppose given that he was not breaking rocks in the hot sun and was instead at liberty to play bass in a bossa nova trio, he did. (Though that would never scan as a lyric.)

Their final number, 'Pretty Vacant', was an unusual choice. It's not normally the kind of song associated with a Hammond trio, or played as a bossa nova, but somehow they made it click, with Godalming warbling, '*We're so pretty, oh so pretty*', in a swaggering, Presley croon. The overall effect was like a cheesy Cabaret Voltaire.

I seriously thought the Bossa Novians should give up financial services and get into showbusiness, as they were definitely the most talented bankers I'd ever seen. Admittedly that wasn't saying much.

'*And we don't care*', he wailed, bringing the song to a close amidst rapturous applause. It was perfect. Godalming had never said a truer thing.

18.
SEDUCED BY MADNESS

Having had no success in persuading LaFlamme, or even Junior, that becoming proxy leaders for a disreputable political party would give us financial freedom, I believed my career in frontline politics to be over. It probably didn't help my case that the method whereby we'd be free from Godalming and his ilk involved being inextricably tied to them for at least another year.

I resigned myself to working instead, and the first thing I chose to do was avoid it. I spent the morning food shopping, something I normally try to do in short bursts, and today it was hugely enjoyable, dilly-dallying from supermarket aisle to aisle knowing I didn't have to be anywhere.

I was amazed by the countless varieties of cheese, the sort of amazement that only arises in the idle. I spent a long time just looking at labels – some other graphic designer's handiwork. It wouldn't be such a bad job, designing cheese labels. Why couldn't I get to design cheese labels instead of neon signs for underground banking organisations? I like cheese as much as anybody else.

All the while, I was aware of a presence shadowing me, slipping between aisles, making notes and, if I wasn't mistaken, taking pictures. He had a basket of groceries, but I'm sure this was a ruse because nobody buys five boxes of Cheerios. I carried on as if I hadn't noticed, wanting to be sure he wasn't the store detective, who's usually the one following me around taking pictures. Between the two of them they had enough to fill an album.

Each time I turned into an aisle he was there hovering right behind me. When I turned into the drinks aisle, I decided to fool him and immediately turned around again. This gave him quite a start – he wasn't expecting someone who looked like me to skip the drinks aisle.

I lifted a slab of gorgonzola from my basket, hovered it several inches from his face, adopted the most fake smile I could muster and said, "Cheese."

"I wasn't following you," he said, trying to hide his phone. "I just like supermarkets."

"And Cheerios," I replied.

"They're for a collage I'm making," he said. This was at least a more plausible explanation than wanting to eat them.

"Aren't there laws about taking pictures of people in public?" I said.

"Probably," he replied. "But I'm not a lawyer."

"Then what are you?"

"A filmmaker."

"Aha," I said. "It's about time you showed up." He seemed taken aback but ever since Godalming discussed his last words with me, I knew somebody would soon begin snooping around for information.

"Actually," he continued, "I'm a barista. But I *want* to be a filmmaker. I've got a thousand ideas for great movies, if only I could raise the funds."

"It's a tough business," I said. "You know there's a saying that discourages those with regular jobs from launching unreliable artistic careers?"

"Don't give up your chickens before they hatch?"

"Yeah, that's it."

He introduced himself as Lord Charles Tarantella. "Like the ventriloquist dummy?" I asked.

"That's what I said," he replied. "But they wouldn't listen. Mum loved that little guy. I'm not a lord, just call me Chas."

He was unusual. And I suppose he could be a filmmaker because he was geeky enough, in the grand tradition of Spielberg, Lucas and Landis – geeks of the first order.

"So is this my life and times you're working on?"

"Could be," he replied. "Filmmaking is a process. I follow leads and see where they take me."

"This one's taking you to the checkout."

After paying for my groceries, Tarantella asked me to wait for him as he settled his hefty Cheerios bill. Then he accompanied me to the exit and it was here that he popped the question. Not that question, this one:

"Did you know Sir Frank Godalming?"

"Actually," I said, rustling through my groceries to make sure I'd gathered up all my cheeses, "we were knighted together."

"Would you be able to help with my investigation into Sir Frank's life?"

"A biopic?" I asked.

"Could be," he replied. "Filmmaking is a journey. Like a jigsaw puzzle that keeps growing and there's always a piece missing." This sounded like a nightmare to me. A never-ending jigsaw was bad enough, a never-ending film would be worse (though both would be preferable to a never-ending journal).

Despite his undoubted knowledge of the filmmaking process, Tarantella explained that he had no access to a film camera, which some might consider an obstacle. He made up for this by creating viewfinder shapes with his hands, framing various scenes on our walk up the road. He also dictated ideas for film scripts on his phone wherever he went. No doubt one of these nuggets would be a future blockbuster, hopefully far enough in the future that I wouldn't have to watch it.

"So how much do you have on Frank?" I asked him.

"He was a 320-year-old banker who helped turn a billion-dollar operation into garbage overnight, skipped town with a sizeable payoff and used the words 'it wasn't my fault' a lot. I kept all the obits and ran up a draft script outline last night. Great story. It has everything – sex, money, death, the big three. It's got an enigmatic central character, a romantic subplot, a subterranean climax. It's rags to riches, triumph over adversity, good versus evil. It's Greek tragedy."

"A romantic subplot?" I said.

"Sure," he said. "We might think it's about bankers, but who cares about a bunch of bankers? It's not about them, it's about a man's struggle with his sexuality. What do you think his last utterance means?"

"Butthole? Whatever. Do you know about Monaco? New Orleans?"

"I've heard of them," he replied. "But I don't see how that helps." For once in my life, it appeared that I knew more than someone else on a particular subject. It's a pity the subject was Godalming and not astrophysics or something useful, but it was satisfying nonetheless.

"What are you going to call this opus?" I asked him.

"*Seduced by Madness*," he replied.

"Not *There's Something About Butthole*?"

"That's good too."

Something told me that a filmmaker with preposterous, puffed-up ideas could come in handy for a certain group of preposterous, puffed-up individuals of my acquaintance. Godalming wanted a propaganda piece to ensure his legacy, and he would need editorial control to pull it off. The best way to do that was to fund it.

"It just so happens," I said, "that I'm connected to a prominent group of capitalists with an eye for new projects. I'd be willing to bet that a sex, money and death movie with a romantic subplot would be right up their back alley."

"Who shall I say is calling?" said a receptionist when I telephoned BS headquarters. I was surprised to be greeted by a receptionist, but it was an improvement on Stanthorpe, who would often speak into the earpiece.

"Tony," I said.

"Calling from?"

"Upstairs."

"What is your call in connection with?"

"Stuff."

"Stuff," she repeated.

"Stuff," I said. "Old stuff, new stuff. Stuff."

"Stuff," she said, and put me through out of boredom.

Godalming sounded dazed, it being a little early in the evening, but he quickly perked up when I relayed the story of being approached by an enthusiastic young filmmaker.

"My biopic!" he said, after a sharp intake of breath.

"Yes. It may be time to set the record straight. Or even make the record."

"I have a draft script, you know."

"I think this guy has his own ideas about the script."

"Really? Does he have a title?"

"*Seduced by Madness*. What's yours?"

"*Triumph of the Will*. But no matter. With Matty as executive producer, script approval would be his prerogative. When can I meet him?"

"Remember," I said, "he thinks you're dead."

"Ah yes," he replied. "Very well. Have him send a script and Brendan can take the meeting."

"You'd consider funding it?"

"Tony, this is my life story we're talking about."

"It's just that films are expensive."

"Tell me what I do for a living."

"You run an evil underground bank."

"Exactly," he said.

It was probably the easiest fundraising campaign in movie history. If Orson Welles had been alive, someone could have introduced him to Godalming and made the poor man's life easier. But I suppose Welles was unlikely to be interested in making something called *Seduced by Madness*. *Seduced by Cupcakes*, maybe.

I called Tarantella and told him to send me his ludicrous script for appraisal by the executive production team. Several nanoseconds later, he was at the door with it. He said he'd made some improvements since we last spoke – he'd fleshed it out and honed it down. I told him he should have just fleshed it down and saved time, but I don't know much about filmmaking.

"It's going to be a cross-genre piece," he said. "Cinema vérité documentary meets fictionalised reconstruction." I asked him what this meant and he clarified it by saying, "Candid realism. Authentic dialogue. Naturalistic settings. Hand held cameras." Which didn't help.

"You want people to watch it though, right?" I said. Truth be told, I didn't much care either way.

I took the script down to BS and met their new receptionist face to face.

"Hello," I said. "It's Tony. From upstairs. Stuff. In connection with. You know."

"Yes," she said, less than delighted to put a face to the stuff.

"Can you see that Mr Matlock gets this piece of nonsense?" I gave her the script and toddled back upstairs.

When I returned to the flat, there was a hand-scrawled message from LaFlamme on my desk. I was only gone ten minutes, but in that time she had depleted the bookcase.

'Your tawdry book collection will fund several nights of debauchery,' said the note. 'BTW, I've changed my mind. Let's do the party thing.'

How interesting – not the prospect of several nights of debauchery, but the idea that LaFlamme would suddenly agree to front the party. What could possibly have happened in the last 48 hours to make her take such a complete U-turn? She had been adamant that the project held no interest for her. Now all of a sudden it did.

I puzzled over this for a while, but second guessing LaFlamme is a fool's game, and that's why I do it so often. She didn't necessarily have a rationale for decisions like this. One day she felt like doing something, the next day she didn't. I don't know why I was surprised to find my political career was back on track.

———————————

Matlock called, thanking me for the script and saying he was delighted there was a suitable creative to handle the Godalming story.

"Did you read it?" I asked.

"I'm not much of a reader," he replied. "But I'm sure it will make a fine motion picture. Bring him round at two and we can discuss the financing."

I liked his style. Most executive producers would at least want the story read to them or explained with puppets, but Matlock didn't need any of that. He was a film director's dream.

"By the way," I said. "I have more good news for you."

"Yes?"

"LaFlamme has agreed to front the party." I could tell these words made him sit up in his chair, assuming he was sitting in a proper chair and not one that would sink to the floor and make no difference whether you sat up or not.

"That *is* interesting," he said. "In fact, I may have to rearrange my plans accordingly, as this will require the mobilisation of our ground troops. We must be prepared for any eventuality."

"We're not going to war, are we?" I asked. I really didn't want to become a deputy head of state and pick a fight just to give the under-utilised elements of our overblown government something to do.

"Our field workers, Tony," said Matlock. "A political campaign requires ample preparation for strategic planning. I must attend to these matters immediately. Watches must be synchronised, wheels put in motion."

"What about the meeting?" I asked.

"Don't worry," he replied. "You and Allen can take it."

I wasn't worried before, but I was now.

I arrived prior to Matlock's departure in order to receive instruction on how the interview was to be conducted. He directed my attention to a list of questions, a selection of wax crayons, a trio of coloured lights behind a chair where the interview subject would sit, and of course, Stanthorpe.

"Are you sure Allen can handle this?" I said, taking him aside.

"Yes, yes. Frank will also be present."

"Won't he be, you know, resting?"

"Frank is generally indisposed at this hour due to his dermatological condition, but is not necessarily sleeping. He has agreed to be conscious at the prearranged hour and so long as he remains within the confines of the rest area in his chambers, he should still be able to partake in the proceedings."

"Skype?" I asked.

"I believe the communications will be adequate," he replied.

I marvelled once again at Godalming's efficiency. Not only did his wooden casing have ample storage facilities, it must have a phone with sufficient data allowance.

"Here's how it will work," Matlock continued. "You will ask a question. The interviewee will supply an answer which will be judged remotely by Sir Frank on a system similar to traffic lights." He pointed towards the coloured lights on the wall.

"A green light signifies approval, amber ambivalence, red disapproval.

These ratings will be behind the subject, therefore unseen. Allen will record Frank's responses using the crayons provided." Stanthorpe had already begun playing with the crayons, one of which had melted in his palm.

"That's quite a plan, Matty," I said. "Are you sure you can't stick around for another hour to see it implode?"

"Alas," he replied, "Monaco beckons. My plane departs shortly."

I heard the muffled sound of an alarm clock coming from an adjoining room. Godalming was stirring.

"Allow me to demonstrate," said Matlock, pressing a number of buttons on a small mixing desk and clearing his throat.

"Good afternoon, Sir Frank," he said into the table-mounted microphone. "Are you reading me?" A green light flashed on the wall. "Have you slept well?" Again, the light responded in the affirmative.

Matlock retrieved his jacket from a broom closet and prepared to leave.

"Of course," he said, "whilst your questions can be phrased in such a way as to spark a conversation, you must remember Sir Frank's response can only be a simple yes, no or maybe, and you must note agreement or otherwise accordingly. But the beauty of the system is that although Frank can hear our every word, we cannot hear him. For example, if I were to ask him presently, Frank, is it true you prefer to wear ladies' undergarments?" A red light flashed defiantly.

"As you can see," said Matlock, "we have a visual response, but are mercifully spared the sort of language that only the Scotch can articulate.

"Frank, would you agree that as a young man you were rather effeminate and liked to press flowers like a little girly-girl?" Matlock smiled to himself amidst the glow and rapid flashing red of the traffic lights.

"It's a very good system," I said.

Shortly after Matlock's departure, I heard what I assumed to be the doorbell, chiming to the tune of 'Money Makes the World go Round' in a ponderous, minor key. Stanthorpe sprang to attention and a moment later returned with Chas Tarantella. The aspiring filmmaker was clearly impressed with the gothic splendour of his surroundings and was framing shots with his improvised viewfinder.

"This would be the perfect location for a sci-fi script I'm working

157

on," he said. "It's about these creatures called Morlocks who work underground and never see daylight."

"Are they graphic designers?" I said.

"It's based on *The Time Machine*, except not really. I mean, I've taken the important stuff and dropped the whole time travel bit. Now it's like a fantasia on the theme of *The Time Machine*." It may have been the stupidest thing I'd ever heard, but I reminded myself that the interview had not even begun.

"Chas," I said, "the principal players in this interview have been called away on more urgent matters. I know it may be hard for you to imagine what could possibly be more urgent than *Seduced by Madness*, but I've been instructed to conduct it on their behalf. As long as you have no objection to being interviewed by someone who has no idea what he's doing, then we can proceed."

"Okay," he said, making it sound like a question.

"Ahem," I said, making sure Godalming could hear from the confines of his box. "Is everybody ready?"

"Yes, ready," said Tarantella.

"You bet!" said an overexcited Stanthorpe.

An amber light flashed behind Tarantella. Stanthorpe reached for the orange crayon.

"Not yet, Allen," I said.

There was an awkward silence and I had no idea how to fill it. I wasn't going to try making chitchat with Chas because all he ever talks about are movies and stupid script ideas. Luckily, just as I was almost forced to ask what else he was working on, the green light flashed. Maybe Godalming had been fixing himself a drink.

"Right," I said. "Let's discuss budget. What is this project likely to cost?"

"Well, I've drawn up a budget that brings it in at just under half a million, but I think I might be able to trim it further." This elicited a red light behind the subject. I noted the figure and Stanthorpe, clutching a red crayon in his fist, branded a red cross next to it.

"I think that might be a little high," I said. The light flashed red again. "I'm sorry, my mistake. Perhaps we could go higher?" This time there was a green light.

158

"Higher?" said Chas. "You'd prefer a bigger production?" Once again, the green light flashed.

"Yes," I said, interpreting the signs. "I believe my client feels the subject matter warrants a lavish treatment."

"Well, the cinema verité techniques I had in mind wouldn't normally justify it, but I can tailor it to a higher end treatment if you'd prefer. Say somewhere nearer three quarters of a million?" Red light.

"Higher," I said.

"A million?" Red light.

"Higher," I said. This continued until Tarantella reached four million, by which time an amber light flashed.

"Just a little higher," I said.

"Five?" he suggested, sounding more confused than delighted. Finally, this drew a green light.

"Yes, I think that's closer to the figure we had in mind."

By now, Tarantella had become aware that Stanthorpe and I were continually referring to a point somewhere behind him, and I daresay he knew something was up by the intermittent coloured glow on our faces. He turned to face the lights but at this stage was still unaware of the behind-the-scenes communication taking place.

"Who do you have in mind for the lead role, Chas?"

"Well," he said, "I'd always planned to use an unknown." Red light. "But of course, that was partly driven by budget. With less constraint, we might think about approaching a name actor, perhaps one with some stage credibility in order to up the ante. How about Hugh Jackman?" Red light.

"I'm not sure that stage credibility would be high on my client's list of priorities," I said. "Unless we could include deceased actors, in which case, ahem, Marlon Brando might have been more suitable." Predictably this received a green light.

"I think what my client has in mind is someone with rugged good looks, still in the prime of life with a steady stream of hot available women falling at his feet." Green.

"Brad Pitt?" he suggested. Red. "Tom Cruise?" Red. "Matthew McConaughey?" Red, red, red. "What's with the flashing lights?"

"We're having a rave here later," I said. "You're welcome to join us.

Meanwhile I don't think any of those actors are quite suitable. We need someone who can really bring individuality to the part."

"Well, there's always Johnny Depp," he said. This was met by an initial red light, followed closely by amber. Chas studied our faces as we waited for a decisive response from the wall behind him. There followed an emphatic green. I was ready to step on the gas and take off at this point, but remembered just in time that I wasn't in a car and couldn't drive anyway.

"I think that's a distinct possibility," I said, and made the following point specifically for Godalming's benefit, "although he'd probably want to play the role in heavy, grotesque makeup." A red light.

"Moving on," I continued, "what do you think the return on investment is likely to be?"

"A subject like this is box office gold," replied Chas. "Even with its arthouse treatment, there's no way it won't appeal to a wide audience, so I'm thinking the returns could be substantial." Allen and I stared at the back wall apprehensively but no signal was forthcoming. Chas, too, turned to check the back wall reaction.

"Could you be a little more specific?" I asked.

"Well, I think box office gross could reach ten million." Red light.

"Hmm," I said. "I think my client would be more enthusiastic in his backing if that figure were higher." Again we went through the routine until Chas suggested nineteen million and we received an amber light.

"Just a little higher," I said.

"With the right star and saturated marketing, perhaps twenty million?" Green light.

"Yes, that sounds about right."

By now we'd given up any pretence that this interview was being conducted without third party participation. Chas had turned his chair to face the back wall, where all the decisions were being made, and I had stepped from behind the desk to perch on the front of it. Stanthorpe had long since given up noting the answers and was drawing, and I made a mental note to check these images later in case there was anything suitable for a forthcoming Lyttleton album sleeve.

I pressed on with the list of questions but by this time it was clear they were not Matlock's, but Godalming's. The whole project was after all a vanity project for him. He considered himself a misunderstood genius and this little folly would be his way of swaying public opinion to his perspective, so it was important that he had a sympathetic director in his pocket.

"Do you think Frank Godalming was a nice guy?" I said.

"That's where the documentary sections will come into play," said Tarantella. "By interviewing those close to him we'll be able to develop a consensus and maybe the truth will reveal itself. Filmmaking is a process. It's like archaeology. The truth doesn't just appear, you have to keep digging until it's uncovered."

There was a short pause before the amber light flashed. I felt Chas's answer had not been fully satisfactory to Godalming so I decided to rephrase the question.

"But do you think Frank Godalming was a nice guy?" I said, nodding my head in a deliberate attempt to encourage an affirmative response.

"Um, yes. Yes, I do," said Tarantella. A green light flashed.

"Good," I said, ready to move on, but as the next question was 'Who do you think is better looking – Frank Godalming or Matty Matlock?' I decided to exercise my right as interviewer and veto it. Godalming was starting to wear me down.

"What do you think about flared trousers?" I said, dispensing with the questionnaire. "Do you think they're the fashion that should have stayed in the '70s or would they be welcome in your wardrobe?" There was a series of abrupt flashes of red light. Godalming was not amused.

"Do you think wearing flares, bright red flares with decals, would have improved your chances of securing funding today? Big epic flares with turn ups? If you were stranded in the arctic tundra and had nothing but dozens of sets of flares, would you be tempted to wear a pair on your head?" More red flashes. Had there been any music I might have been inclined to dance.

"Are you saying, great and powerful Oz, that you would prefer me to return to the script?" Green. "Fine. Are you now or have you ever been a butthole of the first order?"

Mysteriously this was greeted with an amber light, which left me momentarily confused. All the while, Chas could only look on and guess the exact nature of this game.

161

"Are you reasonably satisfied that this ambitious and creative young man can handle the project in a manner that would do justice to the subject?" Amber. "Are your reservations to do with the lack of detailed financial projections?" Green.

It was clear what Chas had to do in order to finally secure funding. I began to feel superfluous and rose from the desk.

"There you go, Chas," I said. "This is your chance to convince a row of flashing lights that you can make them wealthy."

It brought a whole new meaning to the idea of getting a project green lit.

19.
MEDIUM OR LARGE

There was a message on the answerphone when I returned. It was Darren the printer calling to say that *Midnight of the Mole People* was ready for collection. He sounded close to tears. I wasted no time in heading over there, as a man in such an emotional frame of mind might jump, and then I'd be forced to deal with some other inkhead.

I asked for Darren himself but the receptionist informed me he had left for the day. "Stairs or window?" I asked.

I was disappointed, not because he had indeed taken the traditional method of exiting the building, but because I had missed an opportunity to torment him further by pointing out some non-existent flaws in the printing. It was only fair that someone who made such heavy weather of what was essentially loading paper and pressing a few buttons should in turn be given a hard time over the results. But this would have to wait for another occasion.

The receptionist led me through to a storeroom where the prints were stored. I hadn't been sure how much space 100,000 CD sleeves were likely to occupy. Would they fit in a box or should I have brought a wheelbarrow? It's not something you really think about when designing a sleeve, but I suppose if they press enough buttons, those little slips of paper are going to add up.

I was not prepared for the Volkswagen-sized pile of boxes to which the receptionist led me. Even a wheelbarrow wouldn't cut it.

I asked to settle the bill whilst I considered how to shift this monument to my creative genius. She placed one of the boxes on a set of scales and said their pricing structures had changed; from now on they'd be charging by the truckload.

"So what do I owe you?" I said. "About a transit van?"

This was going to need some lateral thinking, as there was no way I wanted to be responsible for moving this colossus. I called Lyttleton.

"George," I said, "I'm at Darren's with the artwork."

"How's it looking?" asked Lyttleton.

"Heavy."

"That sounds good."

"Well, it won't blow away in a storm."

"I haven't seen the weather forecast," he said.

"If you could get down here with a van and a couple of slaves, you could take it away and shed a few pounds at the same time."

"What if there isn't a storm?" he asked.

"There will be when you get here," I said.

LaFlamme asked to meet me in a well-known coffee house uptown, an unusual choice of venue in that it wasn't dark, dingy or catering to a lowbrow clientele. I would generally steer clear of chain stores like this, not because I'm concerned about creeping globalisation or the imperialism of large international corporations, but because I find their menus intimidating. I usually have no idea what I'm ordering, and if the barista confuses my order with another, I wouldn't know. I can just about tell the difference between black coffee and white, but that's about it.

"How can I help you?" I was asked.

"I'd like a Caffe Misto, I think."

"You think?" she said.

"Yes."

"You're not sure?"

"No, I'm not," I replied, "but life is short and I don't want to waste any more of it reading about coffee."

"Medium or large?" said the girl.

164

"Medium or large?" I replied. "Whatever happened to small?"

"We don't do small," she said.

"Then how do you know what medium is?"

"Because of large."

"Why don't you just call it small and large?"

"We don't do small," she said. Life may be short, but I had a feeling this conversation could last forever.

"Okay," I said. "I'll have the small-*est* size available. But put it in a big cup."

"To stay or to go?"

"Should I?" I said.

"Should you what?"

"Stay or should I go?"

"It's your choice, mate." She was probably too young to know the song. I ran through it in my head wondering if the band had come to any conclusion that might give me an idea how to respond. But nothing rang any bells.

"Better make it to stay," I said. "I'm not sure what I'd do with a large Caffe Misto in the street."

I paid with a five-pound note and she returned the change, far from interested in my dilemma.

"Should I put this change in the tip jar," I asked, "or should I keep it for myself?"

"It's always tease, tease, tease," she said, moving on to the next customer.

Judging by the vast number of laptops in the shop, there appeared to be a considerable number of writers present. I'm not sure why it seems essential for writers to escape the quiet of their home-offices and find inspiration in noisy environments with multitudinous distractions, but what do I know about writing.

From time to time, staff would chase the writers with a broom, but little by little they'd sneak back in, look for a moment as if they were going to order something, then start tippy-tapping on their notebooks. There was virtually no place to sit when I arrived, but after a vigorous sweeping of the authors by an irate employee, I found a table and sat down. My legs crashed into something soft below. It was a writer, cowering underneath, typing like fury.

"I've told you a thousand times," said the employee, dragging the writer from below the table and sending him on his way. "You know better than that." The writer scurried away. "It's good for them," the employee said to me afterwards. "Makes them feel tortured. They need that."

"Tough love," I agreed. "They'll write better books this way."

I watched them huddle together outside the shop, bracing themselves against the cold and waiting for their moment to slip back in undetected.

I wondered how many of these characters were published authors and how many just liked the lifestyle and thrill of the chase, but then I recognised a couple of familiar faces. One hunted-looking individual was the internationally renowned author of all those boy wizard books, who could surely afford a dedicated writing room of her own by now. (I have no idea whether these books are any good, as I would rather read *War and Peace* than a thousand pages about boy wizards.)

On the other side of the room was the guy who'd written all the hardboiled Edinburgh police inspector books that were clogging up TV schedules with their innumerable adaptations. I can't imagine what a policeman could do that would be so interesting to fill an entire bookcase and at least a year of solid viewing with his daily plods. But again, I am no judge of the books' worth, as I'd sooner bite off my own hand than read one.

After fighting her way through the horde of authors in the doorway, LaFlamme arrived with Junior. They dispensed with the process of ordering coffee altogether, something I wish I'd thought of before being overcharged for what was essentially steam. Junior appeared disappointed with the choice of venue too, presumably because her idea of steaming didn't involve coffee. But it was probably no bad thing that she be deprived of her precious bourbon at this juncture, partly because it wasn't good for someone so small to have built up such a tolerance for strong drink, and partly because it was midafternoon.

"Are you ready?" asked LaFlamme.

"For what?" I replied. "Don't you want to torment the staff first?"

"Certainly not," said LaFlamme. Junior shook her head. "These people work long hours in sweaty conditions for slave wages. Sometimes they have two or three other jobs as well, because most of them are paying their way through college. If it weren't for places like this, nobody could afford college. We'd have a nation of dumbos." She knocked her knuckles against my head implying that I could be their leader. "You think they need difficult customers on top of that?"

"Why did you want to meet here if you don't want coffee?" I asked.

"They need my signature next door," she replied.

"At the bank?"

"The bookstore," she replied. I couldn't imagine why anyone would have to sign for a book, but it didn't sound like it would take long and then we could begin plotting our strategy for a life without work.

Junior pushed several authors aside to clear a path for our exit and the three of us strolled along to Bohnhead's bookstore, where a line of avid readers had accumulated some way down the street. In the window was a large cardboard display advertising *Help Yourself to Drink* with a picture of LaFlamme and bold lettering announcing a book-signing event. 'The number one bestselling author – live in person. The book that has captured the nation's feeble imagination.'

What LaFlamme neglected to tell me was that her self-help work had become an overnight sensation and that the bookstore 'needing a signature' was actually more like several hundred new fans wanting to meet her. It was indicative of her ambivalence towards the publishing industry and her new celebrity status that it had slipped her mind.

"I didn't know it was an event," she said. "I figured it was a contract to sign or maybe someone wanted my autograph."

"This could take a while," I replied.

A fawning manager approached and introduced himself as Daniel Bohnhead. Naturally, LaFlamme wasted no time in addressing him as 'bonehead' and in return, made an effort to present us.

"My personal assistant, June," she said, "and my manservant, Tony."

"Excellent," said Bohnhead. "First I should lead you to the representatives from the publisher and the PR agency handling the event, before getting down to business." LaFlamme groaned but agreed and was whisked away, leaving Junior and I standing.

Junior, who by now had the scent of bourbon in her nostrils, grabbed me by the arm and led me through the store to where they had set up a makeshift bar (there was no shortage of willing sponsors for such an alcohol-positive event). It was a little early in the day for me but as the central theme in LaFlamme's tome was throwing off the shackles of conventional thought and embracing a life of indulgence, it was in keeping with the spirit of the event to at least have a white wine. Besides, what else was I going to do?

I took a high stool by the window and rested my wine on the shelf. As twilight set in, snow began to fall, and on the opposite side of the front doors where the queue of book enthusiasts maintained a steady presence, a smaller group of protesters with placards gathered, and a more miserable looking throng I've never seen. On closer inspection, one banner read 'Success to Temperance'. No wonder they were miserable.

I looked on as Bohnhead introduced LaFlamme to several suits hovering around the bar, guys I had pinned as publisher and PR reps from the start, as professionals from these industries are never far from the nearest source of alcohol. LaFlamme's body language spoke volumes, and it wasn't long before she broke off and walked across to the window.

"This is hideous," she said. "Apparently I have to greet all these dorks one by one and write stuff in their books."

"That's generally what book signing is about," I replied.

"I'd never have agreed if I'd known. You have to get me out of here."

"Maybe you should have thought of that before becoming a best-selling author." I have to confess to enjoying her discomfort in this situation. There's very little scope for pleasure in your friends' successes and I needed to take what I could find of it here.

"Who are the guys with the placards?" she said, eyeing the joyless mass in the snow, which had started to fall as if it meant business.

"The Temperance Society," I replied.

"They look like they could use a drink."

"Apparently there are people in the world who think drinking is a bad thing, and that your book encourages others into bad habits."

"It's a *self-help* book. It could save thousands of people from a life of stultification and near-certain early death from tedium. They're promoting it in the Mind, Body & Spirit section next to *Chicken Soup for the Soul*, but obviously it's way more fun."

A flustered Bohnhead came to retrieve LaFlamme and led her to a desk in the centre of the store, where the signing was to take place.

The moment LaFlamme was sitting comfortably, the first in the queue was ushered forward.

"I love your book," said a fair-haired young woman, presenting LaFlamme with her copy.

"You do?" said LaFlamme. "Did you read it?"

"Yes," she replied. "Twice."

"I'm impressed. I only read it once. Maybe *you* should be doing the book signing." LaFlamme seemed unsure how to proceed, probably the first time I've ever witnessed such a thing. "What do you want me to do?" she asked.

"Could you sign it please?"

"Sure," she said, writing a barely legible 'LaFlamme' in her inimitable scrawl on the inside cover. "Is that it?"

"Yes," said the woman, clearly thrilled. "Thank you."

"Okay, bye," said LaFlamme.

Mr Bohnhead stepped over and suggested she may want to speed up the proceedings in the interests of getting out before spring, then ushered the next signee forward.

"I'm a big fan of your work," said a perspiring young man with a square physique.

"And I of yours," said LaFlamme.

"You are?" he said.

"Yes," replied LaFlamme. "What do you do?"

"I work for the roads department."

"I love roads. I don't know where I'd be without them. I guess I'd be in a field or a meadow, somewhere that didn't have roads, if there weren't any." Bohnhead cleared his throat and LaFlamme signed the young man's book. "There's a road just outside, I used it to get here," she said. "Keep up the good work."

Junior stepped in with a tumbler of bourbon for LaFlamme, who was immensely grateful. "Am I doing it right?" she asked. Junior nodded enthusiastically then made a twirling motion with her index finger to signify haste.

My secret pleasure in LaFlamme's discomfort began to wear off as she got into her stride. I didn't feel right about leaving her to it and wondered if there was some way of speeding up the process. Junior too

169

seemed to be thinking along the same lines, and after getting a sample signature from LaFlamme, dashed off with some scheme in mind.

She returned ten minutes later with a sheet of tracing paper, an ink blotter, a chisel and scalpel, and what looked like a thick rubber sponge, all of which she dumped on LaFlamme's desk.

"This better be good," said LaFlamme.

Junior traced the signature then reversed it, placed it on the sponge and drew over it again, leaving an imprint on the sponge. Using the chisel and scalpel, she gouged around the fine lines until they were the only remaining raised areas, then pressed the carved face into the ink blotter and stamped the sponge several times onto a sheet of paper, leaving an excellent impression of LaFlamme's signature. Testing the resilience of her ink stamp, she printed the pattern first onto the back of my hand and then onto my forehead, and this seemed to confirm that it would indeed be an excellent aid. It certainly raised our chances of getting out this year.

"Nicely done," said LaFlamme.

Bohnhead was less enthusiastic and questioned whether an ink stamp was diminishing the personal touch of a book signing.

"Nonsense," said LaFlamme. "It's a limited edition print. This lino is creating history."

There was a certain rhythm to the customary greeting and stamp, and with Junior shooing her fans in and out, they had a revolving door process that kept the line moving at a rapid pace. Despite his doubts, Bohnhead probably didn't mind the idea of shifting around five hundred books in record time.

The Temperance Society remained and I certainly feared going out there alone – not because of the threat of aggression, but because I didn't want any of their misery to rub off on me. But by the time the line dwindled, daylight had gone and so had they. Junior and I had settled into playing gin rummy by the window and were sufficiently well oiled to have stopped caring anyway.

When LaFlamme rose suddenly and announced she had had enough and would stamp anything presented on her way out, we followed directly behind without question. Outside in the street, several inches of snow covered the ground, but the fall had let up and Christmas lights shone brightly all around us. We huddled together, Junior with a bag of craft tools, me with a LaFlamme signature on my forehead, as we made our way home through the cold.

LaFlamme was silent, perhaps realising for the first time that being a writer might be hard work.

20.
SNOW ANGEL

'You are cordially invited to a midnight feast,' read the handwritten invitation. 'Bring your own cordial.' Godalming's sense of humour was an acquired taste and I wasn't sure I would ever develop it.

'Admits LaFlamme plus one,' it continued. 'Where's my neon?'

Without a nudge from Godalming, this might have become another in the long line of leads I'd failed to follow up, something that won't make reading this journal any easier. Therefore, in the interests of public relations, I will take this opportunity to seek out a neon emporium, if such a place exists. If it doesn't, you can use your imagination, which won't be the first time during the course of this descriptively woeful tome.

First, I wondered if I might be able to make the sign myself, thereby retaining more of Godalming's cash. I mean, how hard can it be to make a tacky sign?

A quick search revealed that the process involves bending heated tubes of glass into shape, attaching electrodes to the ends of each piece, using a vacuum pump to remove air from the tubes and subjecting them to high voltage electricity, pumping them full of something called argon gas, connecting them to a transformer and allowing them to age for several days before fixing tube supports onto a backing panel, wiring the separate sections together to create a circuit, and connecting the cables to a second transformer. So I guess I'll stick to Plan A.

I managed to locate a neon emporium, oddly enough called 'The Neon Emporium', on some godforsaken industrial estate five miles out of town (it had probably been banished to the outskirts for crimes against good taste). I considered calling ahead to explain what I wanted, but as what I wanted was an 8-foot sign that read 'The Bank of BS', it was probably best just to show up.

I donned my usual gear – I like to think it's similar to Brando in *The Wild One*, without the motorbike and silly hat, and with a bobbly black jumper, given the time of year – and set out into the icy cold day. Light snowflakes were falling and even my far from salubrious part of town looked pretty.

By the time I boarded the bus and asked the driver to let me know when we approached the Dryburgh Industrial Estate, flakes were thicker and falling with more of a sense of purpose. It added to the picturesque quality of the city centre streets, which were alive with Christmas shoppers.

Traffic was slow on the main thoroughfare and I spent the time gazing blankly out the window. All of human life mixes on this street, rich and poor, young and old, the executive, the delinquent, the drunk and destitute. On one corner a brass band played 'Hark the Herald Angels Sing', on another, a rockabilly band knocked out 'Summertime Blues', apparently without any sense of irony. (They dressed like Brando too, but carried it off with less panache.)

In the doorway of the most exclusive private members club in town, a homeless man and his dog sat on a blanket, beneath which was a polythene sheet. He held a sign that said, 'I am not a junky'. Further on, another man lay slumped in a corner, passed out or asleep. He had no sign.

The whole street was a circus, a terrible, occasionally beautiful circus with jolly old Santa Claus as ringleader. And Santa was everywhere. I can't imagine what Christmas must have been like before Coca-Cola invented him.

Past the city centre, the tinsel-coated façade of the glamorous part of town slipped away to reveal the positively unglamorous reality of its outskirts. Here the snow was lying deeper and obscuring road markings, making driving difficult. It was obscuring pretty much everything, and as the light begins to fade around 3.00pm at this time of year, there was precious little to see out the window now.

An hour into this journey to oblivion, I was the only passenger left on the bus. The driver called out "Dryburgh" and, relieved, I jumped to my feet. Now I could place my stupid neon order and catch the next bus home.

When the vehicle doors opened, I stared out into total emptiness.

"There it is," said the driver, pointing at the emptiness. I stepped out.

"You're kidding," I said. "Can we go back?"

"There's another bus in an hour," he replied.

"I mean now."

"You want me to turn the bus around for you?"

"Can you?"

He closed the doors and drove off silently.

The snow was above my ankles and showing all the signs of meaning to accumulate further. There were no other cars around and once the bus disappeared into the void, the road was difficult to discern. I could make out the shadowy forms of buildings in the direction the driver pointed and only hoped one of them was The Neon Emporium.

For an industrial estate it wasn't what you might call industrious. Trudging through the snow towards the cluster of units, I saw no signs of life. Shed after shed was closed for trade, cars embedded in carparks as if abandoned. Surely, I thought, a purveyor of neon is going to have a huge flashing sign outside announcing their presence. But not only was there no neon, there was no electric light of any kind and the natural light was in its dying moments. I turned back and followed my tracks in the snow but the further I walked, the more the tracks were obliterated.

Taking shelter in the alcove of a unit doorway, I assessed the situation. If the neon factory was here, this wasn't going to be the time I would find it. I cursed Brando. Not only was it completely inappropriate attire for these conditions, if I hadn't decided his hat was stupid, I'd have had some warmth for my frozen dome.

I raised my jacket collar as high as it was willing to go and folded it in towards my chest, then looked up at the falling flakes, dark against the sky. Above me were strips of grey glass tubing mounted onto a backing panel and I wondered why this image seemed familiar. Stepping a couple of feet out from the doorway, I began to make out the twisted shapes that formed the neon logo I'd seen online. At that moment I realised there is nothing uglier than unlit neon.

I started to panic, a familiar claustrophobic panic that's never pleasant. The snow was suffocating. I huddled back into the doorway and breathed deeply. Okay, calm yourself. I can't imagine there's ever been a case of suffocation from falling snow.

Apart from avalanches.

What if I faint from hyperventilating and wake up trapped beneath a ton of the stuff? What if I don't wake up at all due to inhalation of snowflakes? At times like this, many will turn to God. I needed a shrink.

I dragged myself over to where the bus would supposedly pick me up in an hour and looked up and down the road. A handful of streetlights covered the immediate area of the estate but a few hundred yards beyond was complete nothingness.

If the road were to close and the bus failed to arrive, I could perish here. If I tried walking back into town, illuminated by snow alone until I reached the edge of the city, I could easily stumble and perish that way. Was it time to choose how to die?

I started walking and hoped a bus might appear.

Beyond the industrial estate, the streetlights were left behind. In normal conditions, drivers would be guided through these stretches by cat's eyes in the road, but tonight there were no cat's eyes because there was no road, and consequently no drivers. There was a certain elegance to this, but I failed to appreciate it fully at the time because it wasn't likely to help me survive.

There were no pavements either. They were never going to build them here because nobody would ever be stupid enough to attempt walking this road, let alone walking it in a snowstorm. But I tried to keep to what I guessed was the verge in case a bus should appear, as the only thing worse than the bus not showing up would be the bus running me over.

I kept stumbling from what must have been this verge, the distinction between it and the road now heavily blurred, and before long I ended up taking the path of least resistance in the centre, guided by the distant glow of the city.

I cursed everybody and everything I could think of. I cursed the elements. How could this much snow accumulate in the time it took to get out of town? I cursed neon, its tackiness and its incredibly complex construction process. I was beyond cursing Brando; I was onto the whole Actors Studio and its stupid founder, Lee Strasberg. Most of all I cursed Godalming for commissioning the job in the first place. Butthole. But then I began cursing myself for accepting, and that must have lasted for a good couple of miles.

When I checked my watch, I noticed I'd been walking for over an hour and hadn't seen a single vehicle, let alone a bus. But then I realised the watch had stopped. So now I had no idea how long I'd been out in the wilds and no idea where I was, other than on the fringes of the city.

I slipped and stumbled here and there; it was impossible not to. But this time I went down, falling backwards into the snow and cracking the back of my head against something hard. (Only I could find something hard to fall on amongst this abundance of soft powder.)

I put my bare hands in the snow to raise myself up and slowly got back on my feet. Then I turned, crouched down and replaced my hands in the snow because it was warmer there than in the open. I could see black drops of blood where I'd hit my head.

By the time I reached the first streetlights of the city, I was overcome by a peculiar warm sensation flowing through my body. I felt serene. Invincible. And sleepy. I figured I could lie down here in my snow bed and sleep until the storm blew over. In the morning it would be easier to get home. And that's what I decided to do.

Just as I lay back in the drift and folded my arms across my chest, resigned to relaxing into the blizzard, a tall, black-cloaked figure approached from out of the relentless powdery white.

"Are you an angel?" I asked.

"As far as you're concerned," he said, "yes."

It was Aloysius Spore.

Like coming out of a general anaesthetic, I was first aware of a low reverberating sound which slowly became recognisable as voices. Then I was struck by the smell of soup and wet clothes, and eventually when I opened my eyes, I found I was on a stone floor by a log fire, covered in blankets. As my brain struggled with the process of decoding visual information, faces began to take shape. One of them was Spore's.

"Your logo's nearly ready," I said.

"Ah, Mr Boaks," said Spore. "Welcome to our hostelry."

"Hostelry?" I said, though it may have sounded different as most of my face was numb. I was in a warm hall lined with tables, the tables lined with people – many people, eating. "A youth hostel?"

"Alas, you betray your middle-class upbringing," said Spore. "The shelter opens its doors to anyone in need of temporary accommodation, and in conditions like these, our intake tends to be inversely proportional to the number of staff and volunteers available." I wasn't sure what this meant, and not simply because I had just regained consciousness.

"Busy and short-staffed," he explained, placing a steaming bowl of vegetable soup on a table above me.

"Why am I here?" I asked.

"You had a moderate case of hypothermia and seemed intent on sleeping it off," said Spore. "Had you slept where you planned to, however, you would not have made it here. Or anywhere."

I stepped slowly up to the table and cupped my hands around the bowl, but the contrast between the icy tingle in my fingers and the radiant heat of the bowl was too intense, painful to the touch. Instead, I hovered my hands above it and let the gentler warmth of the rising steam attempt a thaw.

"It was touch and go as to whether we could open tonight," said Spore. "Only two of our regular workers could make it and around six volunteers. But as you can see," he cast his eyes around the hall, "there are about thirty souls in need of food and a roof over their heads, so it was vital to make the effort."

I looked out at the many people milling around the hall and recognised the man I'd seen on the street earlier with the sign saying, 'I am not a junky'.

Only then did I become aware of the wild incongruity in this scene.

Just what was a multi-millionaire venture capitalist – a man I had pinned as the epitome of the Absolute Self ideology – doing in a homeless shelter, apparently helping others? I tried to form a comprehensible question but, although my fingers were beginning to thaw out, my brain was still frozen.

"Why are *you* here?" I said, after much consideration.

"I know," said Spore. "I should be serving the sweet by now, but we're running late."

"You work here?"

"I help out," he said. "Once upon a time I was the general manager."

"The shelter has a general manager?"

"A shelter needs to be managed just like any other hotel. You think thirty beds make themselves?"

"But aren't you an investor?" I asked.

"Indeed," he replied. "And mankind is one of my investments."

He rose. "Excuse me. Rice pudding waits for no one."

I felt a sudden pang of guilt. What have I ever done to help anybody out? I'm as egalitarian as the next man, but unfortunately in recent days the next man has tended to be Frank Godalming. Maybe I'm no better than the rapacious profit-mongers I've been associating with. Maybe I too am inordinately selfish. I might feel a kinship with the common man, but would that ever extend to giving up my time to help him?

Maybe it was the 'middle-class upbringing' Spore referred to, though I would strongly contest such a label. When I was growing up, we were too poor to have a class. My father was a factory storeman and my mother a sales assistant. My brothers and I were brought up in a cramped, 3-bedroom flat with asbestos walls and rusty metal-framed windows you couldn't see out of because of running condensation. If that was middle class, I'd hate to think what any class below had to contend with.

Perhaps it was my profession, sadly not my preferred profession of idler, but the design profession I fell into, that led Spore to his assumption. Or perhaps it was having had further education, which allowed me to fall into such a profession in the first place. Certainly, further education is what gave me the imagination to see that the daily grind endured by most working-class people is a shockingly bare faced con by the rich. Recognising that is most definitely a middle-class trait.

An unshaven, dishevelled man opposite struck up a conversation. He said it was his birthday and he'd just turned thirty. He looked a good deal older. He had dried blood on his shirt. I asked him about it and he explained that he'd been stabbed.

"You should be in hospital," I said.

"It was three days ago," he replied. "What happened to you? You have blood on the back of your head."

"Do I?" I said, examining the area with my fingers and finding a crusted area on top of a substantial lump. "I can't think why."

I asked him about the shelter.

"It's not bad," he said. "It's warm, has hot showers, and they'll teach you how to cook if you want. Keeps you off the streets." He was right, it was warm. Not quite the sort of warmth Spore was accustomed to, but plenty warm enough for the non-reptilian.

And this led me to the second major incongruity here. How was the lizard king Spore, someone who appeared not to have any natural body heat of his own, able to brave last night's freezing conditions and sweep me to safety?

"The streets are dangerous," the man continued. "Nothing but addicts. One of them stole my watch and one of my shoelaces."

"Why would somebody steal one of your shoelaces?" I asked.

"Somebody stole one of his," he replied.

It occurred to me that as long as Spore's mankind continued to suck so badly, this vicious circle might play itself out indefinitely until one of the unfortunates was able to buy new laces. In the meantime, everyone on the street would be guarding theirs for the foreseeable future.

"I used to have a job," he continued. "Before the recession. Then my marriage broke down."

"What was your job?" I asked.

"Storeman," he replied. "I'm one of the lucky ones here."

"You are?" He didn't look so lucky.

"Some of these guys are old and frail. They won't survive too many winters like this. Some of them are sick in the head. I might be homeless but I'm not mental." It wasn't politically correct but I took his point.

179

"See that guy over there?" he said, pointing to a gaunt man with an unfortunate tic which made him grimace and snarl in an alarming fashion. "He used to work at the AUA. When the banks went under, he was out on his ear. Been in and out of treatment ever since. Gets himself back on his feet for a while, then it all kicks off again."

I considered telling him I was working for Sir Frank Godalming, but thought it was probably something I should keep to myself. Instead, I wished him a happy birthday.

I spent the rest of the evening washing dishes under Spore's direction. After being immersed in hot water, my hands were red and swollen with the increased blood flow, but by now the tingling sensation was pleasant. There was much that I wanted to ask him about his dual role as shelter volunteer and Absolute Selfer, but it could wait till morning. I was tired and, given events and the ongoing blizzard, he insisted I turn in.

I was allocated a bed and spent my one and, with good fortune, only night in a shelter dormitory with a number of other strangers. Normally this might have made me and my middle-class upbringing uncomfortable, but I was thankful to be sleeping here and not where I had chosen to lie down in the snow.

21.
THE IMPOSSIBLE JOB

I slept deeply. So deeply that I was not disturbed by other residents rising and making their way out of the shelter dorm. A couple of staff members began stripping down the beds and were none too happy at my appearance at this hour, whatever hour it was. Spore was nowhere to be seen. I slipped my jacket on and found my shoes and socks still drying by the fire next door. One of my shoelaces was missing.

I set out into the morning, the streets unfamiliar at first because of the snow, which had stopped, and mercifully not settled to the extent it had outside the city centre. I quickly got my bearings and realised I was only a mile or two from home, replaying the previous night's events in my head as I walked.

Had Spore saved my life? Maybe he was some kind of guardian angel and had been shadowing me the whole time. Maybe now he would get his wings and I'd have some vision of how life would play out had I not been born.

I called LaFlamme. "This is Tony Boaks," I said. "Do you know me?"

"I've heard of you," she said.

"If I hadn't been born, would your life have been different in any way?"

"Yes," she said. "I might have been more successful without your anchor-like presence weighing me down."

I judged from this response that I was not going through my own *It's a Wonderful Life*, and was instead still stuck in my own 'it's a pointless and exasperating life'. It was hard to know which was preferable, but at least this way we'd avoid all that schmaltz at Christmas.

Despite this, I began to wonder what the world would be like had I not been born.

For one thing, there would be no one to write this journal, which would spare you the effort of reading it. This would save a good deal of paper, and perhaps allow a more worthwhile book to be printed. A more worthwhile book might have something meaningful to say about contemporary life, perhaps a devastating ecological satire that wins a literary award celebrating the comic novel and has tanktop-wearing types stroking their beards and saying, without a trace of a smile, 'This is funny'.

Critics would describe the book as 'gently satirical', 'quietly humorous', or 'witty and wry', and by these terms, people like me would know it wasn't going to be any fun, and take appropriate evasive action.

The beard-strokers would move on to the next award-winner and sooner or later the abandoned book would return to pulp. The pulp might be used to create blank journals like this one, bursting with potential for a brilliant and gifted first-time author to let loose on its virgin pages. Instead, someone like me would fill it with a vast sea of twaddle.

So I don't suppose it makes much difference.

"I'm glad my life has had such a profound impact on you," I said to LaFlamme. "I nearly died last night and I know you would be stuck without me hanging onto your ankles."

"What happened?" said LaFlamme.

"I lost a shoelace," I said. "Where can I buy a new one?"

"At the shoelace shop."

"Helpful."

"How does anybody lose a shoelace?"

"It's a long story," I said. "In the meantime, I might need your assistance."

"Didn't you learn in primary school?"

"Learn what?"

"How to tie them."

"It's not about shoelaces," I said.

"There's no shame in it. It can be a form of dyslexia."

"I know how to tie shoelaces."

"You can always get slip-ons," said LaFlamme.

By the time I got home, I was already feeling the predictably debilitating effects of having a non-functioning watch strapped to my wrist. I hate not knowing the time. Despite the fact that I'm generally never required to be anywhere at a specific hour – and I actively encourage this – I like to know which particular hour I'm currently frittering away. Without that security, I'm on edge. There's a fuzzy void where there should be rigid lines of nothingness. Today it was compounded by the disorientation caused by a near fatal run-in with ten tonnes of white hell.

When LaFlamme arrived with a bottle of wine, my mental state had deteriorated to the point that I was running taps and switching on electrical implements in order to interfere with my chaotic inner thoughts.

"Have you seen yourself lately?" she said, taking a folding corkscrew from her leopard skin purse and tackling the red. Apparently my hair had formed into two horn shapes at the sides of my head after clutching bunches of it for a prolonged period.

"Time is standing still," I said in an ethereal tone. "I have no frame of reference for worldly events. I simply exist in a nebulous space, a series of physical sensations without an external framework." I held my hand out before me, rotating the wrist slowly.

"It is time out of time. These fragmented movements are all suspended in a space beyond that dimension."

LaFlamme sighed, recognising familiar symptoms, and set the bottle down.

"What have I told you about this?" she said. "Where's your watch?"

"Watch?" I said. "I am unaware of any watch. All instruments of time are but artificial impositions on the continuum of our life flow."

LaFlamme unfastened my watch from my wrist, held it by the strap ends and rapped it sternly against the table's edge. Then she held it to her ear, gave a satisfied nod and, consulting her own watch, reset it to the appropriate hour.

"Here," she said. "It's 3:00pm."

"3:00pm," I repeated. "Are you sure? You wouldn't just say that?"

"Put it on," she said. "Then look at the second hand going round." I did as she suggested and was immediately comforted. "See? It's not time out of time, it's time being wasted on twattery."

This certainly brought me back down to earth with a thud, and after a few more minutes staring at the second hand, I felt ready to relate last night's unusual events; specifically, how the shadowy figure of Aloysius Spore had been there to prevent my premature cryogenesis.

LaFlamme listened patiently whilst continuing to tackle what had proven to be a troublesome red. The corkscrew had broken off in mid-flow, leaving a stump of metal still engaged below the surface of the barely dislodged cork.

"Metal fatigue," she explained, plunging the cork into the bottle with her thumb – a method much favoured by desperate art students, and proof that art college education is extremely practical.

In fact, this was not my favourite art college non-corkscrew method of opening a bottle of wine, because the cork would invariably send streams of vin ordinaire back into my face. My preferred method involved using a screwdriver to thread a 2-inch screw halfway into the cork, then removing the cork-embedded screw with a pair of heavy pliers. (Screwdrivers and pliers were handy art college tools, but really, a corkscrew would have been handier.)

I told LaFlamme about my confusion at being faced with a case of suspected benevolence on the part of one of my lowlife clients. I'd only just resigned myself to the idea of being doomed to work for profi-teering, narcissistic, over privileged self-seekers, and now one of them was volunteering to help the less fortunate. What was I to make of it?

"Your life may be in danger," said LaFlamme, setting up two glasses and pouring the cork-infested wine.

"What?" I said.

"Or not. Just thought I'd throw it out there. You see," she continued, in a manner that suggested she was working on a potboiler, "your client may not have been entirely honest with you."

"My clients are never honest with me," I said. "If they were, I'd know they were up to something."

"At this very moment Spore may be planning your death."

"Murder?" I asked.

184

"No," she replied. "Something worse."

"Something worse than murder. It's a great title, but might be a bit radical for self-help."

"I'm bored with self-help," she said. "I thought I might try a thriller. Like Dan Brown, but enjoyable. Your story has all the makings of a good one."

"Funnily enough, I've never really considered my life in terms of thrills."

"Think about it. This Spore character could have walked off the page of one of those airport fillers. Maybe he gave you the world's worst logo knowing you could never work with it. Nobody could. It was 'the impossible job'. He figured the case would make you crazy and you'd be driven to suicide."

I was familiar with 'the impossible job'. The impossible job is not a difficult job, it's a job you can't possibly hope to complete. Either the client wants you to build him an empire in a day, has failed to supply you with vital information, is generally being awkward, or any combination of the three. A difficult job may be tricky but the impossible job is stressful. In my limited experience of these matters, hard work alone doesn't cause stress – it needs an unhealthy sprinkling of the impossible to do that.

"Why would my client want to kill me?" I asked LaFlamme. "I'm not that bad a designer."

"Maybe he has you heavily insured," she replied. "You might be worth more dead than alive to him."

"Without my knowledge?" I said, confident that I could get LaFlamme's plot idea to unravel like one of The Admiral's bobbly cardigans. "Wouldn't I have some say in that?"

"Clients have all kinds of rights these days," she said. "They need to protect their investments. It's become standard procedure." She paused to take a healthy glug from the troublesome red, tamed now in her hands.

"In fact, the underwriters treat it like pet insurance. But I don't think Spore would have insured your talent."

"That's a pity, because he could have made a significant claim by now."

There was a pause before the significance of her last words struck me.

"So what would he insure?" I asked. LaFlamme looked up.

"Your soul," she said.

It was hard not to feel humiliated by the notion that my life could have been insured alongside a hamster's, even if it was just a suggested plotline for a hypothetical thriller. And I didn't like thinking my pointless existence could inspire something that frequent flyers would find hard to put down. If they knew that not only are there no car chases in my life, I have no car, they would surely return to Arthur Hailey. It didn't sound plausible, but I suppose that never stopped Dan Brown.

"Hang on," I said. "Why would he save me from freezing to death, only to let me bump myself off?"

"Bigger payoff," replied LaFlamme. "I don't know. What is this, *Double Indemnity*?"

My phone started buzzing and I answered reluctantly. "I have Sir Andrew Lloyd Webber on the line," said the caller.

"What the hell does he want?" I demanded.

"Are you the author of *Help Yourself to Drink*?"

"Just a minute," I replied and handed it to LaFlamme. I can't imagine how they got my number, but as LaFlamme never had the same mobile for more than a month, she probably offered this one.

"What?" said LaFlamme, an unusual opening gambit to a knight of the realm. "I suppose so." She raised her eyes skywards, then made a 'blah blah blah' gesture with her hand. "Okay," she agreed finally, "let me think about it."

"What was that about?" I asked.

"We're working on a musical based on *The Omen*," she replied. "He's not sure about my title."

"Which is?"

"*Antichrist Almighty*."

I didn't mind the title, but groaned at the basic premise, as I suspect source material for musicals is chosen by throwing darts at a movie channel schedule.

"So anyway," said LaFlamme, returning to an earlier thread. "The insurance premiums on your soul would be a much-debated topic down at Standard Life…"

She was unstoppable. The only problem was that reality, especially the reality of my humdrum life, would always pale next to anything she could conjure up. It could never compete. Reality for LaFlamme was something she just dipped into occasionally, and the problem was not so much hers as mine.

Her literary forays were not helping. I would have to figure out Spore's story myself, which might mean having to immerse myself once again in social media and the murky world of The Anagrammatics. I might even have to take another stab at his logo.

But first, we were wanted at The Bank of BS.

Hovering around the banquet table with a film camera was the budding auteur Chas Tarantella, presumably filming the dinner party for inclusion in his grand opus, *Seduced by Madness*. I asked Frank why Chas was allowed to witness him being very much alive, when the idea of a fake death was to let people think you were very much dead.

"The pretence was exhausting," said Godalming. "I felt sure it would give me an undead heart attack and bring about an actual undead death, rather than just a fake real one, so it was best to bring him into the fold. He's taken the sacred oath."

"What sacred oath?" I asked.

"Well, maybe he hasn't. I can't remember if we had a sacred oath or not."

"We don't do oaths," said Matlock.

"I had oaths this morning," said Stanthorpe. Dinner was off to a fine start. I already wanted to punch everybody.

Several waiters of decidedly blanched appearance began serving appetisers and Godalming wasted no time in coming straight to the point of the dinner.

"Friends," he began, "we are embarking on a great adventure. And whilst we are confident not only of success but of the increased opportunities that the participation of our guests here will bring, I would first like to ask Ms LaFlamme about her understanding of the Absolute Self's core values. We are an organisation built on the solid rock of self-absorption, avarice and opportunism. We thrive on our own sense of self-worth and have very little regard for those we may trample. In short, I'd like to ask, is Ms LaFlamme selfish enough for this role?"

Laflamme took one of the newly opened wine bottles from the centre of the table, drank straight from it with gusto, marking it for her sole consumption, and belched loudly.

"Keepsies," she said.

"Just thought I'd ask," said Godalming. "Let's eat."

Beef carpaccio was followed by apple-stuffed pork loin, and both were exquisite. Although I consider myself a vegetarian, I have a total inability to resist meat if presented to me. I suppose you'd say that means I'm not a vegetarian at all. Well, what's it to you? It's my stomach. Do I care what you eat?

Actually, my real problem with vegetarianism is vegetarians. Have you ever spoken to one about it? If 'being a vegetarian is one of those little things you do that helps the planet', I can only marvel at how the elimination of meat from your diet could result in such a massive surplus of self-satisfaction. Maybe you could help out the planet by being less sanctimonious. Or exist purely on your own hot air. Attach a little turbine to your head.

"What do you think, Tony?" said Godalming.

"Absolutely," I replied. "Vegetarians can be twats."

"I mean about the policies."

"Yes, of course," I said. "Sound."

Tarantella's handheld camera appeared to be halfway inside my ear as I spoke. When I turned, we collided. This was going to be quite a movie.

"Very well," said Godalming. "This brings me to a question which we have yet to address. Our new political party is going to need a suitable moniker; something memorable."

"How about 'Twat Vegetarians'?" said LaFlamme.

"I don't think that would be a true reflection of our values," said Godalming.

"Can we work the word 'pyramid' in there somewhere?" said Matlock. "I've always been drawn to it."

"The Pyramid Party," I said.

"Well Matty," said Godalming, "you might as well call it The Ponzi Party and be done with it."

"The Ponzi Pyramid Party," said LaFlamme. "PPP for short."

"How about The Wild Party?" said Godalming. "Then we'd have an excuse to practise what we preach."

"I like parties," said Stanthorpe.

"You need something which is really going to engage the voters," I said.

"The Engagement Party," said LaFlamme.

"What would best sum up what the party is all about?" I asked.

Godalming looked thoughtful. "We can't very well call it The Me Party," he said.

"The I Party," said Matlock. "The First Party."

"It's My Party," said Godalming.

"If you want ordinary plebs to vote for you," said LaFlamme, "best not sum up the party. What you want is the opposite, a name that disguises what it's all about. Like The Thoroughly Decent and Morally Upstanding Party."

"That would be dishonest," said Godalming. "I like it."

"Or something that addresses our historical origins in some way," said Matlock.

"The Toxic Debt Party," Godalming suggested.

"Toxic for short," said LaFlamme. "Or just Tox."

"Tocks is an abbreviation for buttocks," said Matlock. "I heard it on my exercise video."

"That really would sum you guys up," said LaFlamme.

I wasn't sure this was going to be resolved in one night, but LaFlamme had been watching Junior silently ploughing through the wine.

"Why don't we call it Lush?" she said. "Toxic Lush." Junior appeared vaguely offended. "Or if you want to reflect the candidate in question, Luscious."

Suddenly Godalming rose. "Luscious," he said, slowly and thoughtfully. "Of rich, sensuous beauty."

"The Luscious Party?" said Matlock.

"Just Luscious," said Godalming, his gaze fixed on LaFlamme.

"I admit," said LaFlamme, "I'm hot."

The suggestion was greeted with approval from everyone present. I'd have felt better about it had it not been directed at LaFlamme, as I was guarded about my tortured longing; I didn't want anyone else moving in on that. But it was a good enough handle for now and unless one of us came up with something better, the political wing of the Absolute Self would be known as 'Luscious'.

With discussion of party business complete, Godalming spent the remainder of the evening berating me for taking so long to fulfil his neon order. Butthole.

22.
HONEY I SHRUNK THE
GOVERNMENT

We were ready to take some initial steps into the political arena, and the BS boys certainly had a busy schedule lined up for us. Soon, Luscious would be hitting the campaign trail and there was much to be done. But first, Matlock, along with the intellectually untroubled Stanthorpe, insisted on driving LaFlamme and I to the 'Institute of Cognitive Neuroscience', where our brains were to be scanned for signs of political leanings.

"Studies have shown," said Matlock on the way, "that there is a significant correlation between the size of two particular areas of the brain and the individual's political views. Those leaning towards the right side of the spectrum tend to have a more pronounced amygdala, whereas those on the left tend to have thicker anterior cingulates.

"This is open to interpretation, of course," he continued. "Some would portray the conservative's enlarged amygdala as a negative, as it is responsible for fear and other so-called primitive emotions; whereas the anterior is responsible for empathy and reasoning, so-called higher functions.

"But I would suggest that, for example, replacing the word 'fear' with 'caution' might produce an alternative interpretation. Is it fear that drives a mother to keep her child out of harm's way, or caution? Is it fear that keeps us safe on a busy road, or caution?" I don't remember Matlock being so cautious with 80 billion dollars of investors' money, but perhaps this too was open to interpretation.

I asked him how the scans of Sir Frank and himself turned out. I assumed their amygdalas were epic.

"Predictably we were somewhat lacking in the anterior cingulate department, whilst our amygdalas were highly developed. In fact, poor Frank is often forced to walk with his head bowed due to the weight of his."

I had no doubt that this study was further evidence of the marvel of modern science, but found it hard to see what possible use it could be in the real world. I mean, a person's political views are generally borne out by their actions, and I don't need to see a scan of Godalming's brain to know he's a rabid right-wing loon. Matlock conceded the point.

"Call it a hobby," he said. "Such scans are limited in their practical use, but they are rather fascinating, and I've built up an impressive private collection. I have one of Jeff Bezos!" Clearly his underdeveloped anterior was responsible for this shoddy piece of reasoning, but it was a good enough answer for me, probably due to my overdeveloped lack of interest.

After a series of scans and a short wait at the Institute, we were introduced to a Dr Fogg, who had the results of our tests. My immediate concern was that I hadn't failed.

"Both cases are quite remarkable in different ways," said Fogg, a fair-haired young man wearing an open white lab coat over his t-shirt and jeans. Aside from the lab coat, he didn't look like a doctor, but he was wearing a nametag, and if you have a nametag in a place like this you probably have initials after your name.

"Allow me to present the results one at a time," he said, raising the first pair of scans onto a wall-mounted lightbox. "These are Ms LaFlamme's."

Fogg pointed to two circular shapes on an overhead plan view of the brain, and identified them as the amygdala. Then, on a side elevation view, he pointed to a curved, tube-like shape and identified this as the anterior singulate.

"The unusual thing here," he said, "is that the amygdala and anterior singulate are both very large, much larger than average, and this

192

would tend to suggest a highly developed political mind – typically one belonging to a shrewd and calculating individual, such as a great wartime general. The result goes beyond anything we have encountered in this study. All other cases have shown a distinct tendency towards an either-or scenario.

"From these results, I would not care to hazard a guess as to Ms LaFlamme's political leanings, but suggest she would make an excellent case study in her own right for any future research into the workings of brilliant minds." LaFlamme shrugged, unimpressed. "Would you consider leaving your brain to medical science?" he added.

"She might need it," said Stanthorpe, wide-eyed and concerned.

"Not right now, obviously," said Dr Fogg.

"I don't think you deserve it," said LaFlamme.

"We can offer you Allen's in the meantime," said Matlock. It was clear this was of limited interest.

"Moving on to Mr Boaks," said Fogg, replacing one set of scans with another. "In this case, the complete reverse is evident." He circled the shrivelled shapes of the amygdala and the barely discernible tube-like anterior singulate.

"As you can see, both areas would appear to be equally underdeveloped and are similar to results we have seen in the pre-pubescent to early teens age group. This underdevelopment would suggest an individual with little experience of the world, or a lack of engagement with it. From this I would deduce that Mr Boaks has a limited interest in politics, or understanding of the subject, and therefore no particular political allegiance. He is what we might consider an open book.

"Of course," he continued, "what we cannot be sure of is whether the brain structure determines our political outlook, or whether our political outlook, shaped by life experience, determines the brain structure. That too will be an interesting topic for future study."

Fogg certainly knew how to keep those research cheques coming in, but if I had any say in it, he'd be cut off from any and all funding herewith. This wasn't further evidence of the marvel of modern science at all, it was a spurious pseudo-scientific method of humiliation, and I can't believe I consented to it. It was as close to a fail as I could ever have imagined.

The only consolation was that scans of LaFlamme's overdeveloped brain seemed to confirm she would be a formidable political force, capable of manoeuvring to a necessarily high degree. The fact that they concluded I was an 'open book' was neither here nor there, even if the implication was that the book was empty.

"I can't believe this government," said an agitated Godalming, clutching a newspaper with the bold headline, 'Majority think Godalming should keep knighthood'.

"They thought they were bowing to the weight of public opinion by rescinding my knighthood. But they're so spectacularly out of touch with public opinion, the very act of rescindment has shifted it back in my favour."

"Isn't that a good thing?" I asked.

"It might be if I cared," he replied. "You forget that, although I may have no formal banking qualifications of my own, I've spent a great deal of time around bankers. And since when do they give a flying fig about public opinion?"

He had a point. If the bankers ever listened to public opinion, most would be beating themselves with wet fish – the hoi polloi's preferred alternative to bonuses.

"The thing is, Tony," he continued, "I'm finding all this to be quite a distraction. How can I be expected to expand my evil empire with public opinion behind me? Do you think Blofeld had widespread public sympathy when he was intent on world domination?"

"Well," I replied, "maybe if you suggest you'd like to be known as the Blofeld of banking from now on, it would redress the balance."

"What's so funny?" he asked.

"Nothing, I suppose," I said, tears running down my legs. "But you might want to reconsider that title before attending the conference for failed bankers turned criminal masterminds."

"Too aggressive?" he said. "You know the conference is next month." It was typical of my current predicament that the most outlandish theme I could imagine for a social gathering turned out to be a real event.

"In those circles there may be stiff competition for the title," I replied. "You can at least expect a challenge from Matty."

"You could be right. He's never forgiven me for amassing my fortune without breaking the law. But I don't think he has any real claim to the title, as he's not technically a banker."

"He's hardly a mastermind either. He got caught."

"He's technically a criminal though. A hundred and fifty years in Pentonville State is fairly conclusive."

"That's only one out of three."

"Yes, but he deserves bonus points for effort." This was indisputable. It takes a monumental force of will to sustain an 80 billion dollar fraud over thirty years.

"I suppose," Godalming continued, "I should probably start focussing on my speech. I'll be announcing the formation of our new underground operation, which I expect to raise eyebrows, and probably much more."

"Yes," I said. "It won't just be the competition that's stiff."

"Did someone call me?" said Matlock, appearing from the hallway with Stanthorpe, and followed by LaFlamme and Junior. "It's my middle name, after all. Well, technically Stiff-Matlock is double-barrelled, but I dropped the Stiff some time ago because it seemed rather close to the bone."

"You've certainly stiffed more people than most," said Godalming.

"And I'd do it again in a heartbeat. In fact, I'll be doing it this very afternoon."

Matlock explained that the reason we had gathered today was to attend a rally organised by *Honey I Shrunk the Government*, a loosely organised advocacy group, or 'free-market thinktank', who they were coaching and motivating along with other undercover Absolute Selfers.

Similar to *The Tea Party* in the United States, the group had been campaigning for smaller government and lower taxes for some time, but lacked any real focus. Without a figurehead, he said, their influence was likely to be limited and therefore our task would be to galvanise them. I thought galvanising them was a bit strict and that we should at least hear what they had to say first, but LaFlamme seemed to understand what was required.

He also mentioned that we should not be surprised by the number of young families present – not their traditional demographic, he said, which was generally old buzzards.

"We're trying to broaden our appeal to include small 'C' conservatives. The *Honey* group may have been able to influence certain policy decisions, but without sufficient numbers they are unlikely to have any staying power."

"They've already influenced government policy?" I said.

"Certainly," said Godalming. "Along with our other advocacy groups, they've helped stop new environmental laws, cut social spending, refrained from taxing the rich and ended the ridiculous notion of wealth distribution."

"Why would a young family want that?" I asked.

"Well," Matlock explained patiently. "They may not *know* they're doing it. You see, in order to get sufficient numbers to support our causes, we have to convince them it will be good for them."

"How do you do that?"

"By appealing to their basic self-interest. And this is where the Absolute Self has a great advantage; we've been appealing to the selfish for decades. For example, if you tell the common man in the street that he is paying too much tax in order to support a bloated, wasteful government, he will most likely agree with you. It's a very popular concept."

"How does that tie up with what you want?" I asked.

"It's actually quite simple," said Matlock. "The freedom from higher taxes and government interference that the common man seeks is the same freedom we and our various corporate interests seek. We are not so far apart."

I couldn't quite see how the freedom to end wealth distribution would be in the interests of the man in the street. In fact, I thought this sort of freedom would turn out to be the freedom for Matlock and his corporate interests to trample him into the dirt.

I pretty much lost the thread of the discussion after that because, as my brain scan testified, I have a limited understanding of politics, and even less interest. But LaFlamme, who'd sat silently throughout the conversation, had a question.

"It sounds like you're already getting everything you want," she said. "Influence is bringing in the desired results. Why push for more?"

"We're tired of merely *influencing* the government," said Matlock. "Now we want to *be* the government."

I had prepared some 'inspirational' slides for the presentation, culled from the surreal world of stock photography – overly staged and stereotypical images of happy families, people in business, construction workers, all contrived to illustrate the idea of a fair and free society that political parties like to present, but few actually believe in.

It was after seeing one such image used recently in an email from my energy supplier that I was inspired to try something similar. 'Tony, your latest bill is ready to view', it said, alongside a picture of a classic breakfast table scene – classic, that is, in stock photography land. A glamorous young woman sits in a pristine kitchen next to a cafetiere of coffee and a vase of tulips, viewing her month's gas and electricity charges. The idealised setting gives a clue to the image's artificiality, but the fact that she is smiling, rather than crying or screaming, is what really gives it away.

I asked The Admiral how best to project these behind LaFlamme as she addressed the audience. The Admiral had worked in theatre, mostly as a sound engineer, but he'd also gotten to grips with most of the workings of the stage itself, including curtains and trap doors. Indeed, it was his curiosity into the mechanics of the latter that led to his banishment from The Kings Theatre after the untimely exit of Madame Butterfly.

The Admiral explained how modern projection carousels work – they don't use a carousel. I won't trouble you any further with it because it's not interesting and I didn't understand anyway. Suffice to say that, unlike old projectors, there is no need for cartridges or slides – just hook up the projector to a laptop with a USB stick or DVD. It was already too technical for me so I asked him to hire the appropriate equipment and be a part of the operation.

I wasn't expecting Godalming to join us for the rally; I assumed he would be indisposed due to it taking place during normal waking hours. However, he explained that, after extensive research 'in the old country', he had discovered a vaccine that was ideal for someone with his condition. Taking it would allow him to appear in broad daylight without turning to dust, and at the same time let the author out of the corner he had painted himself into by having to exclude him from key scenes. I congratulated him on his find.

At the appointed time, Godalming, wearing his original false nose and moustache, Matlock, also travelling incognito beneath a felt fedora and dark glasses, and Stanthorpe, wearing a paper hat and blowing a party horn, joined LaFlamme, Junior, The Admiral and I on the campaign minibus and, along with filmmaker extraordinaire Chas Tarantella, we prepared to set off.

Initially there was some confusion as to who would be driving the 10-seater vehicle. LaFlamme, Godalming and Matlock immediately sat in the back, assuming it was someone else's responsibility. Tarantella was intent on filming the entire journey. The Admiral and I had no licence. And no one would ever be comfortable with Stanthorpe behind the wheel. It therefore fell to Junior to act as chauffeur, a task she seemed more than happy to carry out.

The short drive to the auditorium was uneventful, and I spent most of it wondering what I'd done wrong in life to be stuck on a minibus with such a collection of degenerates and oddballs. Given an alternative roll of the dice, I might have had a nice undemanding and financially secure position in accountancy or, with training, become a data entry worker, even a banker. But the latter brought me to the conclusion that contact with idiots like Godalming was inevitable. There was no escape.

Several hundred people had gathered in the auditorium and, as Matlock suggested, many were couples with young children. I overheard more than one discussion regarding the brilliance of this offspring, a topic unique to the current generation of young parents – when I was a child, parents generally just consoled one another. I mentioned this to LaFlamme as she prepared to step up to the stage.

"They don't look so brilliant," she said.

Matlock handed LaFlamme a speech, 'written especially', with the instruction to stick firmly to it, and as The Admiral's slideshow kicked into life with a classic stock shot of a smiling young family seated around a dinner table, she was introduced to the audience as 'our inspirational new libertarian candidate'.

The reception was warm as LaFlamme stepped up to the podium, tossed Matlock's speech to the floor, took a deep breath and stretched out her arms on the lectern. She was in no hurry.

"Friends," she began. "I thank you for your generous welcome, and suspect you may be even more generous on my exit.

"As I look out onto this sea of shiny faces, I can only wonder where all the powder puffs went. But I'm delighted that I can I see my hopes and fears reflected in all of you, as well as my own features.

"I want to keep this simple, as I can see you're an uncomplicated bunch. I stand before you as someone pushed to the edge by the current administration and the equally hopeless opposition, and I don't push easily. Never have I seen such mismanagement in or out of office. They should have let me mismanage things and then they'd know something about mismanagement.

"The mainstream parties – centre, right, further right, and not right bright – have kept up an endless stream of empty campaign promises, and although I never heard what they were, they're unlikely to be as empty as mine. I know for a fact that they held off making keynote speeches because, understandably, they wanted to hear mine first. So let me say to them..." At this point, she addressed Tarantella's camera directly.

"Up yours, muppets! How the other parties are ruining this country is not my concern. My concern is I how I plan to ruin it, and that I haven't decided yet. But I share your frustration at the length of time it has taken to get this far, the length of the current incumbent's sideburns, the length of a piece of string, and indeed the length and breadth of a rectangular field, should you choose to fit a fence. We are tired of propping up this stuffed shirt of a government. Let's stick the bloater on a treadmill until it's shed at least sixty pounds!"

"Seventy!" cried Godalming, from under his disguise.

"Sold," said LaFlamme.

"We're all agreed the government needs to be put on a diet – and frankly so do you. I haven't seen this much blubber since the whales came down the Forth. But how are we going to do it? I'll tell you. Some

199

of you are going to march straight down to WeightWatchers, and if you march via the perimeter of the island, it won't do you any harm. Take your brilliant kids with you, tell them there's an ice cream shop just round the corner.

"The government, on the other hand, needs pushing, it needs agitating, it needs poking with sticks. And that's where I come in. You may be wondering where I've been all your life, and to be honest, I'm wondering the same.

"I don't hear any of the other parties saying they're going to cut your taxes. That may be because I'm not listening, or because they're not saying it. Or both. But here's what I am saying. A vote for me is a vote for common sense. And judging by your gormless expressions, you could use it.

"So let's all stand together under the banner of Luscious, the only party with me in it. Whatever the other parties promise you, they can't promise you me. Only I can promise you me, and only I can fail to deliver.

"We have the support of many fine free-market thinkers. These unusual men have been willing to part with significant sums of money in order to fund this magnificent new venture. Why? Because they firmly believe in liberty. And they're lucky to *be at* liberty. All they ask in return is that you continue to call for lower taxes and don't come crying to them when you have to pay for a hospital bed.

"And with that, I suggest we reach accord, ink a pact, put our best foot forward and otherwise consign the current government, and indeed modern politics as we know it, to the bin. Vote me."

This brought the over-stimulated ground troops of *Honey I Shrunk the Government* to their feet, ready to wage war against any imagined foe LaFlamme cared to name. The accompanying slideshow ended with an image of LaFlamme herself, arms crossed and to my mind as nonchalant as ever, but to an audience of eager young voters, easily misinterpreted as the epitome of determined, strident leadership. In a word, electable.

The success of the event was living proof of three things: 1) LaFlamme is indeed a charismatic performer who would make an excellent party figurehead; 2) as Matlock suggested, all you have to do to get the common man to help further the interests of large corporations is tell them you'll cut their taxes; and 3) politics is in a bad way.

23.
THE CENTRAL HEATED SUIT

Today I made a second attempt at engaging The Neon Emporium, not because I felt any professional obligation to fulfil the task, but because if Godalming continued to point in a reprimanding way to the blank space where the sign should hang, I was likely to punch him.

Rather than leave the city limits and risk ending up in Narnia again, I found a number and telephoned ahead.

"Neon," said the brusque male voice at the end of the line.

"Do you exist?" I asked. "I mean, I know where you're meant to be, but unless you were somewhere else when I was looking for you, I'd be inclined to think you don't, and if you do, it might be somewhere other than where I looked."

The line went dead. I wasn't convinced I'd handled the call as effectively as I could.

"Neon," said the gentleman, on my second attempt.

"Hello," I said. "I'd like to order some neon,"

"Certainly," he replied. "What did you have in mind?" This was more like it.

"I have artwork," I said.

"Can you bring it into the store?" he asked.

"Oh no," I said firmly. "I tried that before. I have nothing against

Dryburgh but at this time of year, it's probably easier to get to Middle Earth."

"We have a city centre store," he said.

"What? Why doesn't it say so on your website?" At this point I spotted the city centre address above the Dryburgh one.

"It does," he began. "It's just above the…"

"Never mind. Look, let me email this to you." My frustration with subcontractors had just hit a new peak.

He stayed on the line as I prepared the email, all the while wondering how a company that specialised in electric signage could have failed to make it clear where I could find them.

Sighing deeply, I drummed my fingers on the desk and waited for him to pick up the message.

"Got it," he said. "I'm just opening the file." There was silence at the other end of the line and I assumed that, like Darren the printer, there would now follow some laboured consternation at the complexity of the task.

"The Bank of BS," he said slowly.

"Yes?" I had little patience in these situations, especially after the subcontractor in question had already lured me to Greenland.

"Are you sure?" he asked.

"Of course I'm sure," I replied. "I do this for a living, you know."

"Okay," he said. "Do you want me to quote for it?"

"No, I don't," I said. "Just do your little glass tubey thing and bill me when it's done."

I realise now that this may have come across as irritable, and not the way you should talk to someone you're entrusting to bend a selection of heated tubes of glass into an 8-foot design of your making. The truth is I was exhausted. The party schedule had gone way beyond the hour or two a day I'd imagined, and sometimes I found myself putting in entire afternoons. If I wanted to work that hard, I could have stuck with graphic design.

LaFlamme continued to impress the various free-market thinktanks, as well as the party donors who lined up to meet her and were unanimously delighted at her selection. Her blatant disregard of Matlock and Godalming's preprepared scripts concerned their authors at first, but they seemed happy to go with the flow so long as LaFlamme continued to achieve the desired effect with her own take on political rhetoric. (Audiences didn't know how lucky they were to be spared the turgid monomaniacal ramblings of two of the world's greatest twisters.)

In fact, in terms of the party's prospects, things could not have been much better. There was only one hiccup along the way, which occurred at a meeting of *The Tax This Institute*, another pressure group who it will not surprise you to learn, are less than fond of government levies.

It was a clear, crisp day, albeit one climatically more familiar to Muscovites, and once again our dysfunctional family had gathered for a minibus outing with Junior, remarkably sober and controlled, in the driving seat. She would insist on being rewarded later, and I don't mean with cocoa.

Beside her, accidental billionaire Allen Stanthorpe still believed these events were parties, and bobbed up and down under his restraining jacket like the idiot son I never had. Behind them was the techy row, otherwise known by LaFlamme as 'the help' – Chas Tarantella, The Admiral and myself. This was probably the only time Tarantella's film camera had stopped rolling in the whole campaign, but that was only because The Admiral insisted on examining it.

Godalming and Matlock, both in their respective disguises and acting for all the world like the dorks they were even without them, took the back seat. Between them sat the star of the show, LaFlamme, and from the loud snoring that emanated therein you would not guess she would play such a major part in the proceedings. But conversation centred on strategy and the key Absolute Self players who would be present at the event, so it was probably inevitable that slumber beckoned.

At the hall, The Admiral began assembling the audiovisual equipment, closely shadowed by Junior, and it occurred to me that Junior might have less of an interest in how the equipment was set up and more of an interest in how The Admiral was set up. (I'm always surprised when women find my friends attractive, and in The Admiral's case, doubly so. But given that The Admiral had enough verbiage for two, perhaps they were not such a bad match.)

Shortly after LaFlamme began her address, it became clear, to me at least, that there was something far wrong with the projector. I'd left this entirely in The Admiral's control, knowing that if there were buttons to press at crucial moments, it was not wise for me to be the one doing the pressing. However, it appeared that he was not infallible in this regard either, and instead of being treated to a selection of uplifting images of hardworking families about to have their taxes lowered, we were instead shown images of what was clearly an excellent selection of dark ales – in kegs, in glasses, and in various stages of pouring between the two.

Stepping backstage, The Admiral – and Junior – were nowhere to be found. I looked for controls on the projector, but thanks to the glory of the digital age, could only see a cream-coloured polycarbonate box without anything resembling buttons. Meanwhile the comprehensive range of beverages had been superseded by shots of The Admiral sampling each. By this time, LaFlamme had noticed the incongruity and adapted her speech accordingly.

"Let's talk about beer," she said. "Frankly there isn't enough beer in this campaign. Or the world. Lager, stout, pilsner, brown ale, pale ale, fael ale, McPhail ale, witbier, wheat beer, root beer, porter, snorter, contorter. Hey, I don't need to tell you about beer, you look like you had a skinful last night. And let's face it, you deserve it. We all do.

"Here's another thing about beer – it's expensive. Never mind adding a penny to the pint, it's time the government subsidised it. Why not? If you'd seen the people we're working with, you'd understand why I consider beer medically necessary."

For a while it seemed that, far from spoiling the effect of LaFlamme's address, the errant slides seemed to enhance it – being unashamed of enjoying the finer things in life tied in nicely with LaFlamme's general message, and apart from The Admiral and Junior, who I finally spotted playing cards in the far corner of the hall, the audience hung on her every word. It's likely they were in need of a hair of the dog.

Even when the finer things in The Admiral's life tipped him into inebriation and apparent rowdiness, resulting in an altercation and some of the silliest expressions ever seen on a human face, the audience stayed with us. In fact, we received the best reception of the campaign. There were many offers of drinks and, in the absence of a bar, many demands to find the nearest one. Luckily Junior always carried divining rods in case of moments like this.

But today was marked as a day off and, although largely an inactive one, I was restless due to two niggling preoccupations. First there was LaFlamme. I pined for her more than I've ever pined for anything, and I'm someone who does a lot of pining. I didn't know where she was today and I didn't want to call for fear of appearing clingy. I worried that she might be with Streatham. It was torture.

Then there was Aloysius Spore and the logo that had evaded all attempts at artistic reinvention. It had become a thorn in my side, and whichever way I turned, it was there to remind me that thorns were a bad thing.

I suspected the cause of the mental block that had built up around it was the number of unanswered questions. Spore turned out to be a mass of contradictions and not simply the religious symbology scholar and lowlife VC client I'd imagined. His AS connection led me to assume he was affiliated with Godalming and Matlock, but what was someone whose core ideology centred around stiffing his fellow man doing helping out in a homeless shelter? And how was somebody with no natural body heat of his own able to brave freezing conditions and sweep me to safety?

I'd long since given up on following his encrypted insults on social media, partly because of my inability to solve anagrams, and partly because I prefer to be insulted without encryption. But I imagine he's still there, leaving little clues, playing stupid word games with other Anagrammatics, and falling in and out of favour with Stephen Fry.

It was time to admit defeat.

The snow had been compacted into ice by the footsteps of a thousand Christmas shoppers as I crunched my way over to Spore's neighbourhood, occasionally shielding my eyes from the low afternoon sun. I wasn't exactly sure what I was going to say, but I knew I couldn't continue with his infuriating project. It had become a millstone around my neck, an icy cold millstone that I felt certain would eventually pull me down into the snow and bury me. It had tried once before. Was I to give it more opportunities until it succeeded?

But somewhere between the flat and Spore's villa, my mood changed. I don't know what triggered it, but there was a moment, and in that moment, I let go.

As I turned the corner into his street, I felt oddly contented. A sense of helplessness came over me – not a negative feeling of being unable to act or make decisions, more of a submission; a realisation that I had no control over anything. Forces of nature, politics, my own creativity, LaFlamme (who was herself a force of nature), all were beyond my control, not subject to my influence.

Having no control is liberating. If nothing I do makes any difference then I can be free to simply exist, like the trees or Stanthorpe. Maybe submission is the true meaning of freedom. I welcomed it.

But what exactly was I submitting to? Here I was less sure.

I wouldn't suggest anyone who follows a religion is out of control, but doesn't 'it's in the hands of God' or 'I put my faith in a higher power' sound like devolving responsibility? Well, why *not* put someone else in charge? We take certainty wherever we can find it, and if this is what it feels like to believe in God, no wonder they're so happy-clappy. (I made a mental note to consider joining a cult that believes a middle eastern freedom fighter was the son of the world's creator and emerged saint-like from his mother's womb without anyone having sex.)

With this perspective, Spore's residence lost the murkiness that had etched itself in my memory. Under a blanket of snow, it glistened in the weak sun like a crystallised Graceland.

Approaching the front gates, I heard the wailing of a solo saxophone, and whoever was playing was a virtuoso, flying high in the manner of Charlie Parker, though hopefully without the swagload of hard drugs Parker needed to do it.

I pressed the intercom and immediately the saxophone stopped.

"Hello?" said Spore's unmistakable plummy voice.

"Mr Spore," I said. "Tony Boaks."

"What a delightful surprise," he replied. The gate swung open and I stepped briskly up the frozen walkway.

But then I slowed my pace to take in the beauty of the garden. What a sight to behold. How could I ever have considered this a place of deep gloom? Perhaps a French author might look at those snow-covered holly and ewe trees and think they're out of control, but to me they're beautiful.

Spore opened the front door with a saxophone strapped to his chest.

"I find it restful," he said.

"You could be a professional."

"Bless you. But those days are over."

I stepped into the steamy, tropical rainforest conditions of his home and, having already shed my responsibilities, prepared to shed several layers of clothing.

Those days are over? Did that mean he once *was* a professional? I had many questions, but first there was something I had to do.

"I'm not really sure why I'm here," I said. "Apart from returning this." I handed him the world's smallest laptop. "And this." It was an envelope of cash. I had decided to repay his advance.

"What seems to be the problem?" he asked, furling his brow.

"I don't understand the commission and think it's best that I stand down."

He led me to a lush green conservatory and offered me water, which was timely as I'd already lost a pint through perspiration.

"Can you be more specific?"

"For reasons of your own, you wanted to distance yourself from your logo, and were even willing to change your name in order to do it. That was before I knew that AS wasn't Aloysius Spore but the Absolute Self, a brotherhood of the self-interested. Or was it? Maybe it was just a coincidence that you used a similar logo. Anyway, at that point you were just another client to me and as such I'd already formed a low opinion of you. No offence."

"None taken."

"You seemed to cement this by posting scrambled insults directed towards me on social media. Luckily, I'm very good at anagrams and solved them immediately.

"In the meantime, I became involved with Absolute Selfers who also wanted to distance themselves from AS, but in a different way – by forming an arm's-length political party. I now appear to be doing their bidding by deputising someone running for government on a neoliberal ticket, and I'm only able to do so because the person who was insulting me ended up saving my life.

"So when you ask what seems to be the problem, I'd have to say all of the above. And it started with this logo. The sooner I'm free of it, the sooner I can return to my humdrum little life."

Spore took a deep breath.

"I was wondering when we would have this conversation," he said. "In fact, I applaud your tenacity in the face of such odds." He raised his gangly frame and took two steps to the window. It would have taken me four.

"Had you been as good with anagrams as you say, however, you would surely have found that what began as gentle teasing to test your mental agility evolved into a series of clues which would have made clear all of the information I'm about to relate.

"It's no coincidence that our respective insignia bear more than a passing resemblance. You see, Tony – I was the founder of the Absolute Self."

Although I'd initially suspected as much when I assumed he was just another self-serving vulture client, I was dissuaded of this theory when he displayed signs of benevolence.

"As I'm sure you know," he continued, "the Absolute Self was a freeform jazz band. But in its purest form, it was a spiritual movement; a branch of Buddhism which proposed that our shared collective consciousness was absolute and infinite. That is to say, individuals may die and others are born, but the collective self remains.

"This is the nature of our belief in reincarnation. It's not simply a case of my telling you I was once Kaiser Wilhelm and you telling me I am a fruitcake, which is the norm for discussions of this type. After I pass on, my spirit will not return in the form of a future Queen of England, much as I may delight in such a role. Collective consciousness, however, ebbs and flows like the sea, and will continually regenerate. It is this regeneration which was central to the philosophy of the Absolute Self."

"So how did a movement rooted in spirituality become a society of total bastards?" I asked.

"That is a long story, but I can probably sum it up in one word," he said.

"Good," I said. "It's been a long day."

"Hijack," he replied.

"Hijack?"

"Messrs Godalming and Matlock, fine jazz musicians by the way, were both victims of a political polarisation that occurred in the late

1960s. Finding the self-righteous bleating of the revolutionary left insufferable, they tragically succumbed to something far worse."

"The LibDems?"

"Radical conservatism. The symbolic pillars and steps no longer suited their outlook and, rather than develop their own insignia, they perversely developed a new meaning for the existing one."

"Me me me," I said.

"Indeed," said Spore.

"Is that what happens if you play jazz for too long?"

"My point is, that just as the unfortunate equilateral cross was hijacked by the National Socialists, our symbol of collective regeneration has become an unacceptable reminder of individual and corporate greed. Which is why I found it necessary to engage your services before too much damage is done – and why it is essential that you persevere with the task.

"Therefore," he said, returning the envelope, "I cannot accept this."

I was sweating profusely, which reminded me that the last time I saw Spore, the temperature was at the opposite end of the scale. It was time I asked how a man with an obviously reptilian disposition could have survived the cold and swept me to safety.

"Occupational hazard, I'm afraid," he said. "Venture capitalists are all cursed with cold blood. You don't think we go to Palm Springs for the golf, do you? No, dear boy, we need constant heat, hence I hope you'll forgive me for your current discomfort."

"But that night in the snowstorm," I said. "Why weren't you the one close to perishing?"

"Are you familiar with hand warmer technology? Come with me."

He led me through the house to a candlelit bathroom upstairs. The bath was full of hot steaming water and in it was a deep red plastic suit made up of small bulbous compartments of liquid stitched together.

"It's something I had one of my developers create especially for me," he explained. "The liquid is a saline solution which, when immersed in hot water, crystallises and generates a temperature of forty degrees centigrade for up to eight hours."

"A centrally heated suit," I said. "Amazing."

"Isn't it?" said Spore, holding up the suit by its shoulders. "It's brought a flexibility to my life that other VCs can only dream of. However, I must be very careful not to outlast my eight hours grace period, because once the saline solution begins to cool, it shrinks and solidifies. It could be most embarrassing if I was in the supermarket and suddenly seized up, not to mention the pain of constriction."

"I can see how that could be awkward," I said.

It was a perfectly rational, if barking mad explanation and Spore added to its credibility by offering to let me try it on. I declined, as the heat was already so intense it would likely have resulted in my instant liquefaction.

"Mr Spore," I said, preparing to tell him something I've never told a client before.

"You seem like a nice person. You're obviously talented, your nearest anagram rival is probably the computer that beat Kasparov, you're the only spiritual man I've met who doesn't appear to believe absolute drivel, and you seem to genuinely care about other people, regardless of whether or not you can profit from them. So I have to ask…"

Spore's eyes shifted sideways in an uneasy manner.

"How did they ever let you become a venture capitalist?"

"Your confusion is understandable," he said, relaxing when he realised I wasn't having some kind of temporal fugue.

"It's true I may be a little unusual amongst business angels, and at first, was regarded with a degree of suspicion in those circles. But anyone with a passion for jazz has a love of invention, and the doubters have seen my love of invention sustain me through many successful projects."

"But those projects made you wealthy, and in my experience, the wealthy tend to tune out the pain and suffering of the rest of the world. It's like a right they've earned."

"I may be wealthy," he replied, "but I'm not a scumbag. Unlike Sir Frank."

"Just how well do you know Frank?" I asked. "You must have spent a lot of time together in your jazz band days."

"And before," he said. "You see… Frank Godalming is my brother."

Campaigning for Luscious may have been tiring but my afternoon with Spore was starting to drain me. Mostly this was just dehydration, but the revelations added a drama to my day that I didn't necessarily need. I get enough drama just staring into space.

The idea that he and Godalming were siblings was particularly surprising because they were like chalk and cheese. Admittedly they'd both had to find ways of dealing with cold bloodedness, but whereas the no-reflection Godalming was out and out creepy, the only sinister thing about Spore appeared to be that he was left-handed.

"Half-brother actually," he said. "We have shared paternal parentage."

"Is there much of an age difference?" I asked.

"About 250 years," he replied. "But we needn't dwell on that. His arrogance will be his downfall, not his age."

I asked Spore what he meant by this – not that I was questioning Godalming's arrogance, which was as plain as the false nose on his face, but Spore seemed to be hinting at something specific.

"I've been following the Count's progress for some time. His banking operations, his interest groups, and now his foray into politics. I'm also aware of the upcoming premiere of *Seduced by Madness*, which, knowing our friend Charles Tarantella, ought to be highly diverting. Let's just say that I await the inevitable."

I was surprised that Spore was up to date with his brother's activities, given the bad blood between them. Very bad blood. Perhaps theirs was a symbiotic relationship where one sneezes and, miles away, the other says 'gesundheit' without knowing why.

And I had no idea Chas had come so far with *Seduced by Madness*. It made me wonder what kind of a film it was going to be, because as far as I was aware, all the material he had gathered centred around the formation of Luscious, and it was hard to see how that would fit in with the Godalming story.

But according to Tarantella, filmmaking is a process, and presumably the process had led him to a conclusion of some sort. The process felt more like an ordeal to me, but that's probably because I don't know much about film. In fact, The Admiral once called me a 'philistine' because I refused to read subtitles at the cinema. That's why I thought *The Seventh Seal* was a gay romcom.

Sure enough, when I returned home, I found an invitation to the Assembly Hall press launch. I could only imagine how Godalming would react to whatever Tarantella had concocted, but I knew there was little chance of him seeing a cut before the launch. Chas was guarded about 'work in progress', and it would remain in progress until the house lights dimmed because he would obsess over every frame until the last possible moment. I doubt this obsessing would ever result in a better film, and suspect his guardedness was unnecessary – few people are interested in the 'work in progress' of crap filmmakers.

So the invitation was a mixed blessing, but nevertheless I looked forward to it. Events on the horizon didn't have the portent of doom they usually had, and in fact, I was feeling upbeat.

I knew I was still charged with tackling Spore's rebrand, but something had changed. The spell was broken. There wasn't the grey cloud of despair hanging over the prospect, and with this in mind, I put aside my memories of previous failed attempts and set to work on the logo.

24.
CHERCHEZ LAFLAMME

It's over. I have triumphed over blank canvas syndrome and general lack of talent to create a work of stunning genius. And whilst there aren't many logo rebrandings described as such, I consider this a descriptive failure on the part of unimaginative hacks, who will soon rectify the error once they clap eyes on this.

It's hard to know what the problem was. I shuffled the pillars and columns around, changed 'AS' to 'PS', twisting the forms of the letters so they were totally unlike the original, and generally lifted the whole design out of its rigid framework. I think it took about three hours. If you count it from the time I was first commissioned, I guess it was about six weeks and three hours.

When they write my obituary, they will describe this as a high point, a watershed, a defining moment. He came, he saw, he went into creative decline. He was almost cryogenically frozen. He was hypnotised into believing those in less privileged sectors of society have a chance. He was seduced by madness. He was touched with the electricity of a moment's inspiration and fashioned the insignia that changed all our lives for the better.

Yeah, yeah. Since when did graphic design change anybody's life? Whoever designed the Coke label might have had *their* life changed, but the rest of us just got bad teeth. Nevertheless, what's important is that I found my way out of the creative wilderness. To think I only had to resign in order to get here.

LaFlamme called and asked if I wanted to have coffee at Flanagan's Bar; she had something to tell me. I don't normally ask questions when LaFlamme calls, but I couldn't remember ever having coffee at Flanagan's. I wondered if they'd know what it was.

"The clue's in the name," said LaFlamme.

"Coffee?" I said. "I'll just have a beer."

"Flanagan's," said LaFlamme. "Irish. What happens when the words 'Irish' and 'coffee' come together?"

"I get a sore head."

I set off for the bar and wondered, as always, if LaFlamme was about to announce that she had finally dumped Streatham. This wasn't the first time I'd wondered and I'd always been disappointed. Today might be different. She was coming from the dentist. Irish girl. Tiny fingers. You might remember from before.

"She said just a scale and polish, nothing exciting today," LaFlamme recounted. "I said I didn't really look to my teeth for excitement, I'd probably look elsewhere for that. But it made me wonder what exciting teeth would be like."

"Surely there's a limit to how exciting teeth can be," I said.

"There's only a limit to the imagination," she said. "Yours more than most. What if you were a velociraptor? Even a scale and polish would be pretty dramatic."

"Did you bring me here to talk about teeth?" I asked.

"Not unless you want to," she said.

This was it. LaFlamme would explain how there was an amicable break-up. Streatham was gone, no hard feelings. Now we could be more than friends. We'd embrace passionately and spend several glorious hours making out in the bar whilst getting gently tipsy. Then we'd make our way home with the taste of whisky and each other and finally I'd be able to lovingly caress her delicious naked body and praise the lord I was a man. I'd probably faint at that point.

"Let's talk about the party," she continued.

My heart sank. Again. I don't know why I don't give up this epic quest ('cherchez LaFlamme', The Admiral calls it) and take up with a nice uncomplicated girl. Maybe one who works in an office. And likes it. My face must have echoed my inner pain because LaFlamme looked concerned.

"What's the matter?" she said.

"Nothing," I replied. "I didn't sleep well."

It didn't sound convincing so I risked boring her with my recurring dream of being led by a fox to deflect her from the real problem.

"Didn't I tell you about the kitsune?" said LaFlamme. "Trickster fox. They can enchant and bewitch, sometimes in human form, and often do it just to make mischief."

"You said the fox was a good omen."

"It *can* be. But sometimes they only want to mess with your head. The trick is to know which."

There was no way I ever would. And now there was no disguising the real problem in my life. I was aching for LaFlamme and it was time she knew just how bad the ache was.

"Actually," I began, "there's something really big the matter. The matter is now the size of a house. The house is growing. It has extensions, an attic conversion. It thinks it's a hotel. With a pool. The matter is in the way. I can't move for the thing. It's taking me over."

"What is it?" she asked.

"I think it's love," I said finally, "and I don't like it one bit."

I sighed deeply before continuing.

"I am so much in love with you that it's become an existential threat. My intellect is regressing because of love for you, and in my case that's very bad news. At this rate I'll have the mind of a three-year-old in weeks.

"I am in pain. I am physically hurting because of my love for you. Every day I wake up with a lump in my throat and knots in my stomach. My body has made a decision and nothing I tell it about how impossible my love for you is, makes any difference. If I moved to China, at some point in my sleep my body would get up and bring me back here. There's nothing I can do to keep my body away from yours and frankly it needs to be closer.

"In short," I said, realising my all or nothing position was risky, "nobody in the world loves you as much as I do."

LaFlamme stared at me blankly, having a terrific poker face that belies the intricate complexities of her great brain. It took a few seconds before she spoke and they were the longest few seconds of my life.

"Okay," she said. "But I want to talk to you about the party."

"I could have sworn I just poured out my heart to somebody. Wasn't it you? Was that the voice of a man who wants to discuss politics?"

"Later," said LaFlamme.

"It's all work with you," I said, knowing it to be not remotely true.

"You know it's a game, right?"

"The party?"

"Yes."

"It's all a game," I said. "My life's a game. A cruel and pointless game with no end in sight."

It wasn't the time for it, but I was reminded of when The Admiral taught me how to play chess. He explained the parameters within which each piece was permitted to move and we spent several hours shuffling around the board. This was amusing for a while, but soon I wondered where it was going and asked, 'How do I actually win?' Little did I know at the time that this was to be the pattern of my future life – I understand the basic moves but never get anywhere.

"Do you play chess by any chance?" I asked LaFlamme.

"Don't be ridiculous," said LaFlamme. "Look, I'm serious. These guys are dangerous and I don't want you to get hurt."

"Chess players?"

"Frank and Beans."

"I don't think they can hurt me," I said. "You, on the other hand..."

"We only did this to make money, right?"

"Yes?"

"Well, how much money do you need?"

"What do you mean?"

"At some point you need to let go. Are you really going to stick around and start believing the things they say? Right now, we're convenient for them. But soon they'll find some other dummies. Do you think they'll give you a gold watch for loyal service and send you a card on your birthday?"

"I don't need another watch," I said.

"You don't need *them*. And soon they won't need you. Then you're in trouble because it'll be too late. If you get to that point, you'll remember this conversation and wish you'd made arrangements."

"I'm pretty sure I won't forget this conversation," I said. "What kind of arrangements?"

"Contingency plans," said LaFlamme. "Once this film gets out, the game will change. You need to be ready."

"*Seduced by Madness*? How bad can it be?"

"Voltaire said 'It's not enough to conquer, you must learn to seduce'. That's why they brought us in – they don't know how to. The word is Latin. It literally means 'to lead astray'. Well, there's leading astray and there's leading astray. You don't win friends by telling them what's in it for you."

"Are we still talking about the film?"

"Everybody's selfish to some extent. I'm selfish. You're selfish."

"I'm selfish?"

"You just spent an hour telling me how much you want me. I want, I want, I want. Selfish. It's a survival instinct. But these guys are off the scale, and they don't know how to dress it up. If we don't do it for them, that's going to be a problem. Private greed is one thing, public greed is a definite vote loser. And there's nothing more public than a press launch."

"I'm confused," I said. "And depressed. I just told the love of my life that I couldn't live without her and she's talking about greed and contingency plans."

LaFlamme took my hand across the table. She leaned over and kissed me gently on the cheek.

"I won't hurt you," she said softly. "But Frank and Beans, on the other hand..."

I know sexual attraction is all in the mind, but the merest suggestion of having LaFlamme's body just about brought a tear to my eye. And my own body, so consumed by my feelings for her, had a very definite reaction to her touch. It wasn't just that things were looking up – I blushed.

"Everything is going to be alright," she said, recalling the neon artwork at the gallery. "But now I have to go."

These were the words I heard most often from LaFlamme, and the saddest. I looked forward to a time when she didn't have to go, when there was no place to go but back into my arms.

"Contingency plans," she repeated, finishing her Irish coffee.

"Now drink up. And remember, life's too short for chess."

If I was smitten before, now the situation would probably need medical attention.

25.
BUZZING

I may have addiction issues. Well, issue, singular. I'm addicted to LaFlamme and apparently the only way to tackle this kind of thing is to go cold turkey. So far, I've managed twenty minutes without thinking about her – it's a start. There are probably other men in my position who could help; it wouldn't surprise me if LaFlamme had a dedicated support group.

Everything is going to be alright, she said. But what did that, and the accompanying kiss, actually mean? I don't know. I'm still stunned. What about contingency plans? Maybe dumping Streatham was part of that – dumping Godalming and Matlock certainly seemed to be.

All in all, I had no idea what happened yesterday and couldn't stop replaying the conversation in my head. Each time I did, I considered different nuances, came to different conclusions, and ended up spiralling downwards into smaller and tighter circles. Surely that's the face of addiction. I needed to get out of the flat, and didn't care where.

As I was about to leave, The Neon Emporium called.

"Just to say your sign is ready to collect." Now I had somewhere to go.

There seemed to be a buzz in the store when I mentioned my name, not just the electrical buzz of several dozen neon signs, but staff peaking round corners to see who I was. I suppose there was a certain curiosity about what sort of person orders an eight-foot neon sign that reads 'The Bank of BS'. One of them scurried off to retrieve it.

"Nasty stuff, neon," said a tall, dapper man who appeared from under the counter with a recipe book, introducing himself as 'Armstrong, Gavin'. I took this to mean his name was Gavin Armstrong but I couldn't be sure.

"Dangerous if it explodes," he added.

"I nearly died the first time I tried to order some," I said.

"We've all been there," said Armstrong. "Cooking's my passion. French, Spanish. Do you like quesadillas?"

"Very much," I replied.

"I tried many recipes without an awful lot of success. It's possible that prior to venturing into the kitchen I'd had a martini too many, but that's never really been a problem before. Eventually I abandoned the recipe books and did a little experimenting. Finally, I cracked it."

"You did?" I said.

"Yes," he replied. "The perfect martini."

A tiny assistant appeared with the bubble-wrapped sign, struggling under its bulk.

"Thank you, Gregory," said Armstrong.

"What's a man who loves cooking doing in a neon store?" I asked.

"Selling neon," said Armstrong, revealing the sign below the wrapping. "Nasty stuff. The real torture is that most of our customers are restaurants."

The sign was just as I'd imagined it. The twists and turns of its glass tubes folded beautifully into place and I expected Godalming would be pleased. Armstrong plugged it into the wall socket and it flickered into life.

"If I wanted to write 'Everything is going to be alright' in metre-high letters, would it pose you any problems?"

"Didn't the last time," said Armstrong. "Only a few explosions."

"You did that?" I said.

"Not me, personally. But yes, we *are* The Neon Emporium. We sell neon. I shouldn't think you would go to a bookstore for that, you'd go to The Neon Emporium, somewhere that sells neon."

"Of course," I said, settling up the bill.

"Did you know refried beans are not actually fried, let alone refried?"

"You should be a chef."

"Yes," he said with a sigh. "But I sell neon. At The Neon Emporium. Most of our customers are restaurants."

It struck me that 'Suave Gav' Armstrong would make the perfect dinner party guest, if I were the sort of person who threw dinner parties. I can cook well enough to stay alive, and I always insist that my problems in the kitchen are just about presentation, but I don't suppose I'm fooling anyone.

Maybe someday I'll be sophisticated enough to invite company and have Armstrong make his perfect martinis whilst we all trade witty banter. This would make a delightful change from the afterhours crashing into walls that The Admiral and I recognise as a party.

Although not particularly heavy, it wasn't the easiest parcel to get home, especially with the crunchy ice underfoot, and with hindsight I should have asked them to deliver. But thinking straight was not on my list for today, so I attracted some peculiar looks and suffered the awkwardness of its bulky cardboard covering. I couldn't wait to try it out at home before delivering to Godalming, and I knew The Admiral would love it. (I'd have to ensure he wouldn't be attending any Vigorous Dark Ale Festivals first.)

So now I'm trying to psyche myself up for tonight's press launch. The neon is helping, buzzing away in the corner, reminding me of a bar and how nice it would be to have a drink. I should probably switch it off as it's only noon.

I called The Admiral. He said he was very busy today but would pop over after the soundcheck. I said I was busy too; I was planning on taking turns watching TV and sleeping until it was time to go out.

After five hours of exactly that, the daylight faded and the neon really kicked in, saving me from having to get up to switch on a light. I was glad I'd frittered away the day rather than trying to be productive. Work is overrated.

I did have to get up to let The Admiral in, but it was worth it to see his glasses, steamed up from having come in from the cold, completely filled with dense reflected blue. I told him he was interrupting my schedule and that I still had several tasks to accomplish before I could possibly see anybody. But that didn't faze him.

"It's just as you described it," he said, transfixed by the sign. "But much more blue."

"I'm thinking about keeping it," I said. "As a motivational tool."

"Really?"

"Yes. I've been looking at it all day and now I really want to go to the pub. How was the soundcheck?"

"Everything in readiness," he replied.

"Good," I said. I still had no desire to attend this stupid premiere, but at least LaFlamme would be there. "Can you assure me it won't be deathly dull?"

I waited until 8.00pm before setting off, and by the time I arrived, the Assembly Hall was packed. It looked to me like hacks rubbing shoulders with Absolute Selfers, a nightmare combination, but the atmosphere was convivial, as Matlock and Godalming had been smart enough to lay on a free bar.

There was no sign of either of them, of course. Matlock was meant to be serving 150 years in Pentonville State and Godalming had been reported dead – it wouldn't be such great press for them if it turned out they were throwing a party.

There was no sign of LaFlamme either. I hadn't seen or heard from her since I let slip that I might die without her, and I could only hope it wasn't something I said.

George Lyttleton spotted me and approached. I tried to pretend I didn't have a champagne glass in my hand, but that's a very difficult trick to pull off, so I drank heavily from it instead.

"Tony," said Lyttleton.

"George," I replied.

"Have you seen Glen?" he asked.

"Glen who?"

"Campbell."

"Glen Campbell's here?"

"Campbell Glen."

"Oh," I said. "No, I haven't." I wondered what the sudden trend for reversing name order was all about – Armstrong, Gavin. Glen, Campbell. All it does is confuse me.

"He's meant to be here," said Lyttleton, George. "But he's a funny guy. He might not show." I was hoping Lyttleton might not show but it was too late now.

"I'll look out for him," I said.

"Is there a band?" he asked.

"Looks like it."

The stage was dressed for Godalming's Hammond power trio, and I assumed The Bossa Novians, in heavy disguise of course, would be opening the show – only they would be arrogant enough to risk exposure by holding a public event like this. But they were a hell of a band, and that might take the sting out of having to watch the movie.

The Admiral and Junior milled around the stage area testing microphones, Junior tapping them with her index finger rather than saying 'one, two', although she did actually mouth the words 'one, two' in time to her tapping. Then the house lights dimmed.

"Ladies and gentlemen," said The Admiral, "welcome to the launch of *Seduced by Madness, the Frank Godalming Story*." Round of applause.

"Chas Tarantella will be introducing the movie shortly and we'll have a screening in the adjoining hall for your delectation and delight. Meanwhile, I see you've found the bar. There's also a buffet for anyone who likes that sort of thing." The Admiral would not have been my first choice as MC. He should probably have stopped at 'one, two'.

"We'd like to get the show started now, so please welcome – the exquisite stylings of – The Bossa Novians."

Godalming and company burst onto the stage wearing 1950s Russian issue space suits and dark glasses.

"We are The Bossa Novians from the distant galaxy Bossa Novia!" Godalming bellowed. "Take me to your leader!"

He fired up the Hammond organ and the band launched into something I began to recognise as 'Take Me To The River', but set to a Latin groove. And a tight groove at that – Matlock played a mean bass and the oddly familiar bald drummer was rock solid. Then Godalming sang in his inimitable Elvis croon.

"*I don't know why I love you like I do, after all these changes you put me through*." He must have messed with the lyrics after that because I don't remember all those references to Yuri Gagarin.

"Marvellous," said The Admiral, when he and Junior joined me.

"They're very tight," I said.

"I mean the sound," he replied. The Admiral liked music well enough, but was more interested in its technical delivery. I once asked his opinion of a song and he studied its wave form on the computer before offering one.

"Is she here?" I asked Junior, and with a slight shake of the head I knew she was not.

"Is she coming?" With wide eyes and shoulders high, she shrugged.

I got the feeling Junior was almost as concerned as I was. Why would LaFlamme miss a night like this? I started to worry that maybe I'd really messed up. Maybe she'd decided we couldn't be friends. I needed more drink.

I spent the rest of the set by the bar. I wasn't in the mood for The Bossa Novians now, although the entire Assembly Hall was at their command. Even the hacks put their glasses down to applaud, which must have taken a supreme effort of will. When Godalming announced this would be their last number, I checked my watch: 8.50pm.

When the band launched in to 'Low Rider' (a perfect choice of song for an Elvis impersonator, with its crooning "*All – my – friends – know the low rider*"), the trio were accompanied by what sounded like a duck call. Then the duck call got more tuneful and distinctly less duck-like. It was in fact a saxophone, which was good news for those of us who feel the duck call is out of place in a Hammond bossa trio.

Though I'd heard him playing saxophone recently, it still came as a complete surprise to see Aloysius Spore emerge from the shadows and step onto the side of the stage. Now he was coming through the PA loud and clear.

"What's happening here?" I said to The Admiral, who was fiddling with the settings on the mixing desk.

"Guest appearance," he replied. "He asked for a radio mike earlier."

Godalming and Matlock exchanged nervous glances as Spore, stepping in time to the music, joined them centre stage. Then Godalming made a slashing motion to his neck, gesticulating wildly and still never dropping a beat. He was truly wasted in banking.

"Unusual way to treat a guest," I said, as he proceeded to leave his Hammond station, put his hands around Spore's throat and begin throttling him.

The rhythm section continued the groove without the organ and Spore too did his best to maintain the integrity of his solo with limited airflow. It sounded a bit like Ornette Coleman.

The hacks all thought this was great theatre (it was probably the only theatre they'd ever seen), but when Spore and Godalming started rolling on the ground like wrestlers, their bodies entwined in a frenetic dance of aggression, I was more than a little concerned. The rhythm section finally petered out and Spore managed to clamber free, hurriedly exiting the stage. For a moment, we thought that was it.

Then Spore returned, retrieved his saxophone and unclipped the radio mike.

"Ladies and gentlemen," he said, holding it to his chest. "I'd like to introduce the band."

There was panic on stage as Godalming and Matlock realised the full horror of what might happen should they be introduced. Godalming scrambled for his own microphone but the scuffle had resulted in a disconnected lead somewhere and he fumbled aimlessly.

"On the drums," he continued, "it's the best band he's ever been in, please welcome – Mr Phil Collins." So that's why he seemed so familiar. It made sense that Collins was hanging out with Absolute Selfers, probably taking advice on how to avoid tax in Switzerland. He took a bow.

"On the bass," Spore continued, "serving 150 years in Pentonville State at this very moment, but miraculously able to be here tonight – Mr Brendan 'Matty' Matlock."

A collective gasp ran through the hall. The hacks were taking notes and camera flashes lit up the stage. Matlock undocked his bass and edged shiftily off the stage.

"On the organ, and looking remarkable for a man who is 320 years old and technically dead, your friend but not mine, Sir – Frank – Godalming."

The organist looked set to lunge at Spore once again but the journalists, recognising a scoop, rushed the stage, stopping him. Many of the Absolute Selfers headed nervously toward the exits and some appeared ready to draw arms. Collins was still bowing.

"Most interesting," said The Admiral, as if he'd been watching a particularly arresting version of *Waiting For Godot*.

"Do you just give out radio mikes to anyone who asks?" I said.

"He told me he was Stan Getz," he protested.

I felt my phone vibrating in my jacket pocket and wondered if it was LaFlamme. I didn't recognise the number but made for the hallway where I might stand a chance of hearing whoever was calling.

"Hello?" I said into the phone, plugging my other ear.

"Boaks," said a man's voice.

"Yes?"

"It's Justin."

"Who?"

"Justin. Streatham." He didn't sound happy, but at least he had his name in the right order.

"Streatham? What's up?"

"You've got some explaining to do," he said.

"I do?"

"Is there something you want to say to me?" I considered asking him what his girlfriend saw in him but decided now was not the time.

"You and I need to have a little talk," he added, before hanging up abruptly. Well, which is it, Streatham? Do you want to hang up or do you want to talk? Idiot.

By the time the audience was ushered into the adjoining hall for the second half of what was turning out to be a memorable night for all the wrong reasons, I was none the wiser. Maybe LaFlamme had done the smart thing and finally dumped Streatham, and naturally he wanted to direct his anger towards me.

People always blame the third party when their relationship breaks down, as if the ex had no say in the matter. You think your girlfriend left you because of somebody else? It's far more likely she left because she realised you're a knob. I mean, LaFlamme wasn't here and was obviously in no great rush to see me. It was possible she had tired of us all and moved on to somewhere she could torment a whole new set of individuals.

The Admiral took to the stage once more for what would undoubtedly be another triumph of public speaking.

"Ladies and gentlemen," he said, "I'm sure you all enjoyed that hugely. I know I did. Almost as much as the last time I saw Gong. Obviously,

I'm more *Radio Gnome* than *Gong Expresso*, but nevertheless we all had a jolly good time." Junior gesticulated from the wings and The Admiral thankfully took the prompt.

"Now, to introduce the film please welcome to the stage – Chas Tarantella."

Tarantella stepped up and I prepared to hear a treatise on modern film techniques, something I'm sure you can imagine I was just in the mood for. I thought this would clear out the majority of the hacks, as they already had tomorrow's headlines in the bag, but they remained – such is the lure of the free bar.

"Thank you," said Tarantella. "When I began researching this story, my knowledge of film history was sketchy. I mean, I thought *Star Wars* must be one of the first movies ever made, but it turns out it was only the first *Star Wars* movie ever made. Obviously when I saw *Alien 3*, I realised cinema had a past. But I had no idea the past was so old."

I began involuntarily checking my watch every few seconds, as if by doing so, something might have changed when I looked back up. But each time I did, Tarantella was still talking.

"That's when I realised that cinema is an evolving art form and that filmmaking is a process; a gradual unfolding, or revelation. And that was my starting point for the film you're about to see, which I think may also be a revelation.

"When I began writing about Frank Godalming, I thought this would be the greatest story ever told. Even better than *The Karate Kid*. Certainly better than *Karate Kid 2*. But the process took me on a journey. I was introduced to a group of people who began to shape the narrative, and I had a choice of following the rigid storyline I'd developed painstakingly, or allowing the process to influence the film's development.

"You can be the judge, but I hope you'll agree that I made the right decision in allowing it to follow its natural path. Ladies and gentlemen – I give you – *Seduced by Madness*."

It was mercifully brief, but any time at all spent listening to Chas is a reminder you've made some bad decisions in life.

As the opening credits played over a theme song reminiscent of *The Godfather*, it became clear that Tarantella's intention was to create an epic tragedy. And it would indeed be an epic tragedy if I had to sit through it. There were reconstructions of Godalming's childhood, including scenes with his sled, Butthole. It reminded me of *Citizen Kane*, but only in that they were at opposite ends of the quality scale.

In the style of a latter-day Jean Luc Godard (which is to say utterly incomprehensible), Chas had intercut these with documentary scenes and interviews. There were secret AS meetings, which ruffled a few feathers in the crowd, informal shots of all of us on the Luscious tour bus, scenes of the rallies at *The Tax This Institute* and others, and choice selections from LaFlamme's speeches, which made me all the more aware of her absence.

But it was when Tarantella included candid scenes of Godalming and Matlock discussing party policy that the embarrassment factor began to rise. Specific policies such as 'dismantling the state', 'letting the sick fend for themselves', and 'sterilising the poor' were mentioned. These are not things that other political parties haven't considered, but it's generally agreed that voicing them isn't terribly good for business.

Then Godalming and Matlock got into an argument over who had the most money.

"It takes more than a passing interest in money to amass eighty billion," said Matlock.

"But you had to break the law to do it, you great nit," said Godalming. "*I* could have done that. In fact, I'm doing it now and it's not a measly..." Godalming paused to count on his fingers, "...ten digits. It's more like..." Again, he tried counting on his fingers, but fumbled after ten and became flustered.

"It's a lot, all right? It takes much more talent to skim a fortune without breaking the law, and once we roll into office, phase two will bring me even more."

"That's my money too, you Scotch pygmy," said Matlock, before the two began squabbling like ten-year-old girls.

It was clear their interest in politics was not about furthering the common good, and now there was a general sense of unease in the audience. This would all have been deeply embarrassing for the party's figurehead had Chas not included several lengthy one on one interviews with her, and one in particular was damning for the bankers.

"Hello tubes," said LaFlamme, directly to the camera. "By the time you see this, the two sad desperadoes behind this pitiful exercise in eye-watering avarice will probably have made off. You can try and track them down and who knows, you might even catch them, but soon they'll be free again.

"Because they're smart – smart in a really stupid way. Should a miracle happen and you manage to outsmart them, give yourselves a pat on the back, but whatever you do, don't send them to jail. No, no, no – make them regulators. As the saying goes, it takes one to know one, and only a true reprobate will spot another. So put their supreme and incomparable deviance to work and nail some of the others. Because, my little drones, in order to defeat people who are smart in a stupid way, you have to be one of them."

So that's why she wasn't here tonight. LaFlamme was always at least two steps ahead of me, and I suppose she planned to expose them all along. The Selfers shifted uncomfortably in their seats – this was not the PR exercise it was meant to be, and they could only wonder how much worse the revelations could get for their arm's length party. I was uncomfortable too, and when I saw my own face up there, staring at LaFlamme adoringly as she took the floor at one of the rallies, I decided I needed some air.

I made my way through the grand corridors of the Assembly Hall, with its opulent stairways and chandeliers. Somehow I found my way into the kitchens, which were deserted now and silent but for the hum of the overhead lighting and something rustling in a cupboard. It might have been a duck. I explored a little further and saw an unassuming little man in a pork pie hat.

"Hi," I said.

"Hi," he replied. I soon recognised him as Lyttleton's protégé, Campbell Glen.

"Do you know where I can find some food?"

"There ought to be some here, this being the kitchen."

It sounded facetious, but between us we could only find the sum total of a single tin of sardines and two cans of Heineken. He seemed quite pleased with the sardines though, as the tin had a ring pull top which allowed him to open it easily and pick out the little guys with his fingers.

We cracked open the beers and sat on a kitchen worktop staring into space. He certainly wasn't a talkative sort, but there was an air of calm about him that was appealing, especially to someone who had more issues than The Times.

It's hard to know what to say to celebrities. On the few occasions I've met one I've always said something stupid. I was determined not to repeat that mistake here and tried to make conversation in the manner of someone who was unfazed by celebrity status.

"Do you know Justin Timberlake?" I asked.

"I don't think so," he replied. "What does he look like?"

"You *are* Campbell Glen, right?"

"Yes?"

"Aren't you a big star?"

"I don't know," he said. "I've never really thought about it."

"I designed your album sleeve," I said a little guiltily, knowing that idiot savant Stanthorpe had done most of the work.

"You did? Why?"

"That's a very good question," I replied, and fell silent when I realised I couldn't think of a good answer.

Of all the arts, graphic design has to be the most pointless; its only purpose is to sell stuff, and a lot of the time it's stuff nobody needs. It's probably causing untold environmental damage, clogging up landfill sites and recycling centres with its stupid serif fonts and unnecessary flourishes. We should all buy white label goods, keep the clutter out of the system and spare designers the existential angst.

"I thought this might happen," he said.

"You mean that the whole party thing would backfire and we'd all end up back where we started?"

"No," he said. "That I'd get hungry."

I smiled. I realised that no matter how big a deal a collapsed political adventure and a case of unrequited love might be to me, they wouldn't mean much to anyone else, and mattered even less on the grand scale of things.

There was a commotion in the corridor; angry voices and scuffles had broken out.

"Looks like the game's up," I said, heading towards the door.

"I'm sorry," said Glen.

"It doesn't matter," I replied.

"Did you want one?" he said, offering me a sardine.

26.
GOING GOING GONE

The neon sign had served its purpose, in that it enticed me out of the house last night with the promise of beer. But now it was time to deliver it to its rightful owners. I repackaged it in bubble wrap and cardboard and headed across the canal to BS headquarters, passing the newsagent en route.

'GODALMING UNDEAD' read the headline, and this time the hacks had really nailed it.

The heavy wooden door to the underground chambers was ajar and the nameplate missing. I shuffled through with the neon and, unable to find a light switch, made my way downstairs in darkness. There was a light coming from the main hall and I continued in that direction, finally backing through the doorway and parking the neon safely against the wall.

Only when I turned to face the hall did I realise it had been completely gutted. Gone were the rococo artworks, the pipe organ, the furnishings, fittings, and appliances. Gone, in fact, was every trace of the entire BS operation. Godalming had been thorough. There wasn't a sink, cupboard, tile or skirting board left in place. He must have been well prepared for skipping town.

I stepped towards the great staircase – it was surprising it remained

– and to the cupboard below, where Godalming had kept his prize possession. But even the sled was gone.

My footsteps echoed through the great hall and soon I became aware of other steps approaching from an adjoining room. I froze in my tracks, fearing the state of mind of the chambers' erstwhile occupants. But emerging from the dimly lit space was the unmistakably floppy hatted, diminutive frame of Junior. With a nervous look in her eye, she stepped briskly towards me and hugged me tightly.

"What are you doing here?" I asked. She waved a sheaf of papers and I assumed she was gathering materials on LaFlamme's behalf. But then something miraculous happened.

Junior spoke.

She had a little scratchy voice that sounded painful to produce. Each word was uttered as if through dry sandpaper and it was evident why she did not do it more often.

"You better go," she rasped. "They're saying it was all your idea." It was a minute before the shock passed, but then her words sank in.

"Me?"

"Have you checked your bank account?"

"I don't think they'd be interested in emptying my bank account."

"They're not going to empty it. They're going to fill it."

With that, she waved the papers in a farewell salute and scurried back upstairs to the street.

I took a last look around the hall and at the cardboard packaged neon sign that I'd propped up by the door. This package had nearly been the death of me. I wondered if I should take it home, a souvenir of my time with degenerate fraudsters and a reminder that I should probably be doing something better with my life. But this was where it belonged. It should really go down with the ship.

Emerging from the vaults, I immediately headed towards the nearest auto teller machine and requested an account balance. When the slip of paper printed, I grabbed it furtively and stuffed it in my jacket pocket. Only when I turned into a side street did I examine it, and then it was with a mixture of horror and incomprehension.

I had never seen such a large number before and had no idea how to say it out loud. I counted the digits. There were eleven in all, and three commas. Either I had mistaken the combined account number and sort code for the balance, or I was filthy rich.

By the time I reached home, I'd put two and two together and formed a picture of Boaks, Tony in jail. What was a graphic designer doing with eleven digits in his bank account? It was unprecedented. Who did it even belong to? I didn't have much time to weigh up my options.

I fell back into a chair and gazed out the window. So this is what LaFlamme meant by contingency plans. Godalming and Matlock had stitched me up pretty well and it looked like they intended me to take the fall for whatever dodgy scheme they had worked out. She was right. Now it was too late.

I considered calling The Admiral to tell him my troubles, but I could just imagine the conversation.

"I've been set up by underground bankers who have named me as the mastermind of an eleven-figure fraud, and now I'm going to jail for the foreseeable future."

"Hmm, yes," he'd say. "That *is* a problem, isn't it?"

I'd be better off waiting for the police to arrive and telling them instead. And that's pretty much what it came down to. If I let inertia take control of this situation – and why break the habit of a lifetime? – that meant just sitting here until I heard the inevitable knock at the door.

But what if I chose to be less passive and took decisive action? I had much less experience of this approach but figured it involved two possible routes.

One: I could hand myself in to the authorities. It was likely to take several lifetimes to explain how I became an unwitting patsy for a group of unscrupulous underground bankers and helped them create a bank of ill repute; how I assisted with the formation of a political party that would further their dubious interests and ended up being the one with all the money.

I could plead insanity, but my lawyer would suggest stupidity was a better defence. With leniency I'd probably get fifty years and end up a withered old prune, the oldest living man inside.

Two: I could find my passport, withdraw a large amount of cash and make a frantic dash for the airport, Richard Curtis-style, to catch the next available flight to obscurity. I'd live out my days in a tropical paradise, swim with dolphins by day, and sip rum at a beach bar by night, all without ever having to deal with the whims of lowlife clients.

I went searching for my passport.

By the time I located it, the doorbell rang and the window for weighing up options slammed shut. I stepped to the door, preparing to be handcuffed.

"Are you ready?" said LaFlamme.

"For what?" I said.

"For your close-up," she replied.

I stood with my passport in hand and turned to face the window. A crescent moon hung in the clear afternoon sky, announcing the impending twilight. There was a whole universe out there, by turns terrifying, bewildering, maddening, enlightening and breathtakingly beautiful.

Whatever LaFlamme had in mind was likely to reflect all this and more. I could either be a part of it and risk collapsing under the strain, or watch it happen to somebody else until I eventually decayed and turned to dust. It was a no-brainer.

Postscript:

Sir Frank Godalming was questioned in relation to an alleged fraud involving an eleven-digit sum, but was released without charge. Later he took out an injunction to prevent the media from describing him as a banker, as he had no formal banking qualifications.

Allen Stanthorpe was charged with fraud, but a court ruled that he did not have the mental capacity to assist lawyers and was therefore deemed unfit to stand trial. He is currently at large, and still believes he is at a party.

Brendan 'Matty' Matlock was judged 'guilty as all hell' and returned to Pentonville State to serve the 150 years he had begun previously. An auction of his Manhattan penthouse possessions was organised and a signed photograph of Phil Collins raised an undisclosed sum.

So far, Tony Boaks has not won a Nobel prize.

THE END

STUPID ANIMALS (EXTRACT)

There was an unusual squawking sound coming from within The Admiral's flat. The last time I remember hearing anything similar was when LaFlamme had agreed to give him a haircut, an ill-judged move on The Admiral's part, as LaFlamme kept her shades on and held a glass with a sherry-like substance in it throughout. The results, however devastating, were short-lived, because as everyone knows, a haircut is just for Christmas and not for life.

The squawking continued as I stepped tentatively into his kitchen-office. On the ex-boardroom table where The Admiral conducted his greatest bodges sat a large multicoloured vertebrate. Initially I mistook this for a bouquet of flowers, but as the incongruity of flowers in The Admiral's office sunk in, I realised something was afoot. This was clinched when the bouquet spoke.

"Who are you?" said the bird.

"Tony."

"Hello Tony."

I was somewhat taken aback by this, as it was already more conversation than I would normally expect at The Admiral's.

"I appear to be stuck," said a voice from the other side of the room. The Admiral had most of his upper body crammed into a large wire enclosure on the kitchen floor and for a moment I wondered if there had been a body swap incident, as he is usually the one perched on the table. Unsure whether he was trying to get in or out, I held the back of the cage and let him decide.

"Thank you," he said, removing himself and dusting off flakes of wood shavings from his sleeves. "I'm looking after the little chap and it was time to clean his cage."

"Who does he belong to?" I asked.

"My friend Muriel," said The Admiral. "You know. Journalist. Lots of opinions." He said this in a way which suggested she might be difficult. "He's not generally any trouble, but he's most particular about the materials with which I furnish his lodgings."

"Correct gauge of shavings, or what?" I asked.

"Underneath the shavings," he replied, "is a lining of four or five layers of newspaper and I've been told on no account to use *The Daily Record*."

The parrot piped up. "Utter pish," he said. The animal's use of the Scottish vernacular was striking.

"Why on earth," I asked, "would a parrot object to *The Daily Record*?"

"Utter pish," repeated the parrot.

"Well, parrots are among the most intelligent of birds," said The Admiral. "I can only assume that the quality of journalism within its pages is simply not up to his high standards."

"But he's only going to crap on it," I said.

"Nevertheless," replied The Admiral. "He does not deem it worthy. Apparently it was only a matter of days with said paper before he insisted on crapping on *The Scotsman* instead."

"Bollocks," said the parrot.

"But soon he also became dissatisfied with *The Scotsman*."

"Bollocks," repeated the parrot.

"Several other papers were tried, but eventually only one was considered good enough for the little prince."

"Which was?" I asked.

"*The Linlithgow Gazette*," said The Admiral, waving a copy.

"It'll have to do," said the parrot.

"*The Linlithgow Gazette*?" I said.

"It'll have to do," repeated the parrot.

How peculiar that this most discerning of readers could only find one passable newspaper, and even then it was to defecate on. I can only imagine the foul language had he been raised in Dundee, where he would have to contend with the collective piffle of *The Courier*, *Evening Telegraph* and *Sunday Post*.

"Perhaps there's more to it than journalistic criticism," said The Admiral. "Perhaps he used to write for them." This was suggested without a hint of sarcasm and I therefore concluded that it was a possibility. "In any event, you're perfectly welcome to ask him directly."

I turned towards the parrot. "So, um... *The Daily Record* and *The Scotsman*..."

"Utter pish bollocks," said the parrot.

It wasn't the most eloquent of arguments but then I wasn't the most eloquent of guests and didn't particularly fancy debating the merits of our periodicals much further. Besides, he was starting to win me over with his passionate and forthright take on the subject.

"I think I remember your friend Muriel," I said to The Admiral. "Better get him back in his cage before he starts boffing on about Munros."

He set about returning the polychromatic Polly to his enclosure before pressing 'resume' on a "particularly fascinating" Youtube video, 'Extreme Trams'. It was often best for The Admiral to be glued to his monitor in this manner, as it was preferable to his frequent bouts of boisterousness.

"Don't you have any milk?" I said, trying to find things to combine that might result in a refreshment.

"On the fridge," he said.

"*On* the fridge? You know milk ought to be stored *in* the fridge in order to keep it cold."

"Ordinarily, yes," he replied. "But I was experimenting and now it's behaving like a reverse hotplate." I ran a finger over the fridge's surface and sure enough a layer of frost had developed. The container was practically stuck to it.

I heard a scratching at the front door followed by a thin high-pitched voice, as if a ten-year-old had been compressed within a shoebox. I thought it might be Cyndi Lauper.

"Could you put a little milk in that saucer?" said The Admiral, rising and, without removing his gaze from the monitor, stepping to the front door. For a shoebox, it was large and had long ginger hair. And whilst its skulking demeanour was typical of its species, it had a most unusual cry.

"Noooo," said the cat, in a plaintive monotone.

"Yeeees," said The Admiral.

"Noooo," said the cat.

"Yeeees," said The Admiral.

"Excuse me," I said. It's not that I wasn't bemused by an apparently talking cat, but I felt if this was the level of debate we were going to have, I might as well watch *Question Time*. "Since when do you have a cat?"

"It's not mine," said The Admiral. "I believe he belongs to that chap around the corner."

"What kind of person teaches their cat to speak?"

"I think you'll find," said The Admiral, "that the results of most experiments with verbal communication in felines have tended to be negative. This is not so much a talking cat as one with an unusual pronunciation of the word 'meow'."

"But when you said yes, he said no."

"That's hardly a conversation though, is it? More like a Beatles song. Were I to ask him about Boyle's Law, he's unlikely to explain that, assuming temperature remains unchanged, the absolute pressure and volume of a confined gas are inversely proportional."

"Isn't that just because he didn't study thermodynamics?" I said.

"Admittedly, he may have spent more time on Kinetic Theory. Why don't you try talking to him?"

"Okay. What's his name?"

"I don't know," said The Admiral. "Let's call him Boyle."

I crouched down to welcome the visitor.

"Hello, Boyle," I said, and immediately felt ridiculous.

"Noooo," said the cat.

"Would you like some milk?" I poured a little into the saucer.

"Noooo," said the cat, rushing towards it and eagerly lapping it up.

"You see?" said The Admiral. "His response is not necessarily negative. In fact, we don't even know if he is speaking English. Were he a native Pole, this would actually mean 'yes'. Or were he Japanese it would mean 'of'."

"He's multilingual?" I said.

"I don't think you're quite grasping this," said The Admiral, doing his best to hear an explanation of electrical conduits whilst continuing our discussion. "He's just an eccentric verbaliser, a bit like yourself."

"But he must have been trained to talk like that."

"Actually," said The Admiral, "I believe it may be the other way round. The chap around the corner is quite the curmudgeon and I suspect the cat has trained *him* to take a negative view of life. He may have become so accustomed to hearing the word 'no' that it now plays a huge part in his daily discourse. In which case, Boyle has a lot to answer for, don't you, Boyle?"

"Noooo," said the cat.

It was a very intelligent cat who could not only speak several languages but had trained his master to behave in such a manner. I began to have some sympathy for the man – he may have simply been conditioned. Of course, there are those whose only notion of positivity is to continually repeat that we are positively screwed, but I suspect they're mostly journalists.

"You know, this is exactly the sort of story they might like at *The Daily Record*," I suggested.

"Utter pish," said the parrot.

Use this space to start your own journal!

Basketwork oddity recited.

Also by Greg Moodie

SIX DEGREES OF STUPIDITY

Underemployed graphic designer Tony Boaks creates a coat of arms for Guy LeSnide, a QC ('like a lawyer, but even more so') with monumental delusions of grandeur. Before settling his bill however, LeSnide's delusions turn to madness and he retreats to the fictional English region of Wester – a dense and murky area only accessible by canal. Encounters with a psychotic ventriloquist dummy, a deviant gastrophile and a professional beard-reader are just some of the weirdnesses to expect in Greg Moodie's first delightfully quirky satirical novel.

COOL SCOTS

The Scots pretty much invented the modern world – but you knew that, didn't you? What you might not know is that they did it in style. From Robert Burns to Sean Connery, Flora MacDonald to Annie Lennox, the Scots have a long and colourful history of being ridiculously awesome. The 42 profiles contained in this lavishly illustrated book, by suitably-chilled author and illustrator Greg Moodie, should go some way to explaining why the world would be a much duller place without the cool brilliance of the Scots.

Available from gregmoodie.com